The Demon of Stonewood

Book II of the Stonewood Trilogy

Jeremy Hayes

ISBN: 0991864220
ISBN-13: 978-0991864225

I dedicate this book to all my friends and family who offered such amazing support for my first book, especially Noosh and Lex, (yes, Lex is real and very powerful in person!).

The Stonewood Trilogy

Book I: The Thieves of Stonewood

Book II: The Demon of Stonewood

Book III: The King of Stonewood
Coming Spring 2014

Northlord Publishing

Visit us at: www.northlordpublishing.com for news about upcoming releases or to contact the author.

Copy Editor: Daphne Lavers, M.J.
Cover Art: Mike Kotsopoulos
Cover Design: Robert Przybylo
Website/Logo: Cody Kotsopoulos www.kotsysdesigns.com

PROLOGUE

The sounds of steel on steel rang out from within an apparent abandoned building in the lower west district. Four cloaked figures were engaged in a fierce battle, three men against one. Randar came to the realization that he had been ambushed. The lone man he had been tailing for the last hour just led him into a trap. The Thieves Guild's top enforcer allowed his eagerness to capture this particular individual to cloud his better judgment. Now the odds were stacked against him in a fight he had not expected, but he was not the most feared man in the streets of Stonewood for nothing.

The shorter man to his left lunged in with the hopes of impaling him on the end of his longsword. Randar had barely enough time to parry the attack while dodging the blade of the chunkier man to his right. They were trying to force the Guild thug into a corner of the large storage room. The room was empty save for debris strewn about the floor, making it difficult to navigate properly in the dark.

Sparks flew as the enforcer parried two more attacks then stumbled over the lid of a wooden crate. The third cloaked man, the one Randar had been following, seized advantage of his off-balance pursuer and drew a line of blood across his thigh with a long thin-bladed dagger. Randar grimaced but did not give the man the satisfaction of making a sound, and he hoped that the blade had not been poisoned.

Randar, a short powerfully-built man, ducked under a wild swing then rolled away from another, coming back up to his feet in the center of the room. These men knew how to fight and must have been handpicked for that reason to lie in wait for the deadly Guild enforcer. They should have brought more, Randar mused, as he cut the sword-hand off one of the men. To his credit, the man made not a sound. These Demon Cult members hardly ever did. No matter what Randar had ever done to them, they never expressed any fear of pain. But thankfully, they died the same as any other man.

The shorter of the three Cult members fell back silently, blood spurting from his severed wrist, as the chunkier man stepped up his attacks. Randar was battling strictly defensively, parrying the attacks while trying to avoid the lunging-dagger of the other remaining Cult member. The other man kept just out of reach of Randar's short-bladed sword but would dart in when the opportunity presented itself. The enforcer could not properly counter the dagger strikes while concentrating on the longer sword in front of him. It took all of his fighting prowess, to keep himself positioned so the dagger-wielding Cult member could not get directly behind him.

Overhand-chop, parried. Sideways-slash, parried.

Forward-thrust, parried. Each time Randar wanted to reply with a counter, he was side-stepping a dagger thrust. Frustration was forming on the swordsman's face. The Guild enforcer guessed that this man was a member of the city guard, judging by the blade he held and the style with which he fought.

The demon worshipping Cult had found ways to recruit all kinds of folk in Stonewood. They had blended in so seamlessly, making them nearly impossible to root out, much like the Thieves Guild, only better. For the last six months, the Guild had waged a war with the Demon Cult, if one could call it a war. The Guild had lost more members and had not made much headway at all in eliminating the despicable Cult. Randar had hoped that the man he followed tonight would have led him to a secret hideout, instead, he was led into a trap.

Again the dagger drew blood, this time from the enforcer's elbow. As Randar spun and slashed outwards, the man was already back out of reach. In came the swordsman immediately, putting Randar back on the defensive. A powerful overhand-chop forced the smaller enforcer to one knee as he blocked the head-splitting attack. With his free hand, Randar scooped up a handful of dirt that covered the floor and flung it in the face of the Cult member. The man staggered back momentarily blinded, frantically wiping the dirt from his eyes. It was all the distraction Randar needed. With lightning speed, he ran his sword through the man's stomach and out the other end. A boot to the chest sent him sliding off the sword and onto the floor where he died.

Randar was surprised the dagger-wielding Cult member had not run; he stood in a dark corner, giggling to himself. As the Guild enforcer approached him, Randar heard a faint mumbling from the shadows of the far side of the room, then an explosion of pain filled his head. Randar's body ceased to respond to commands and he fell to his knees paralyzed, drool running down the corner of his mouth. His mind was clear but he could not move.

A dark-robed man emerged from the shadows, a wicked smile visible from within his dark hood. "At last, we have the mighty Randar," the man said, as the other continued to giggle. "It was nice of you to join us here tonight. I am afraid I may have arrived a tad late, but no mind, a small sacrifice to finally rid ourselves of your meddling. With you out of the way perhaps the Thieves Guild will finally realize the futility of it all. You cannot defeat us. We are everywhere. We will summon our lord Lucivenus, and we will take over this city. The Guild should change its mind and join with us. What a powerful allegiance that would make. But I am afraid your time for making choices is at an end."

The Cult priest pulled a curvy-bladed knife from under his cloak and stepped closer to the paralyzed Guild enforcer. But the priest's grin was immediately replaced with a look of horror, his eyes suddenly bulging. He staggered forward, then fell to his face, a dagger lodged in his back. Standing where the priest had stood was a weasely-looking man with a hooked nose.

Gaining control of his body again, Randar stood and growled, "You certainly took your time, Zenod."

"What would you have had me do earlier? I am no warrior," the master thief replied.

"Clearly," the enforcer commented.

Randar stepped over the man who had lost his hand;

he appeared to have gone into shock and passed out. With a growl the Guild enforcer removed the man's head.

"And what of that one?" Zenod asked, motioning to the giggling man standing in the corner. "Should we question him?"

"No," was all Randar said, advancing towards the man, sword in hand.

The Cult member stopped giggling.

CHAPTER 1

High Priest Sarvin sat behind his opulent oak desk pouring over city documents which required his signature. Here in his office, situated inside Castle Stonewood, he was known publicly as the city's Chief Magistrate, Krommel. Sarvin had dark brown hair, with a thin brown beard. There were hints of grey throughout his hair and he appeared to be a man who had seen about fifty winters. In truth, Sarvin was much, much older than that. With the help of an ancient elixir he found in a tomb, he had managed to extend his life long past what would be considered natural, though none save a few knew of that truth. He was a big-boned man, standing six feet tall, strong but not muscular.

Sarvin had risen to a position of much power and respect in Stonewood, but was also secretly the highest ranking priest and leader of the demon-worshipping Cult which made the city their home.

Three hundred years ago, the demon lord Lucivenus had seized control of Stonewood before eventually being defeated. It took the combined might of the first King

Stonewood, The Circle of Three, a group of powerful wizards, and the aid of a demi-god to banish the demon from this world. They had utilized powerful and ancient magic that bound the demon to an extra-planar prison cell. There he was to remain for eternity, but Sarvin meant for that not to be so.

The High Priest had dedicated his life to the study of dark magic and demon gods, and had uncovered a series of rituals and spells which could break the bonds that held the demon and summon him back into this world. Lucivenus promised untold power and riches to those that aided him and Sarvin craved power above all else. When he freed the demon lord, he would be greatly rewarded, as they took back Stonewood and seized control of the surrounding regions. All would kneel down to them in fear, or be crushed liked insects.

There would be no one to stand in their way. The demi-gods were all but memory now and The Circle of Three had long ago become dust in the wind. The current King Stonewood would have no powerful allies coming to the rescue this time. Fezzdin the Fantastic, the King's royal magician, could prove troublesome but he was only one man and would be dealt with soon enough.

Membership in the Cult had been growing. The poor in the city were easily swayed with the promise of a better life and the rich were greedy, their loyalty easily sold for the promise of more wealth. The end was coming, they were told; they could either join and prosper, or die with any who opposed them. A spell cast on new members during their initiation ensured their loyalty, preventing them from revealing any Cult secrets, even under intense torture.

Their members ranged from the poorest of beggars to merchants and nobles, from city guards and officials and of course, right up to the Chief Magistrate himself. During meetings, the High Priest spewed forth lies about the King and his administration, fomenting anger and unrest among the members who now cried for the King's heart. All in good time, Sarvin had promised them.

Without so much as a knock, Sarvin's office door opened and someone entered. Only one person came and went as she pleased, Devi-Lynn. Devi for short, was Chief Magistrate Krommel's assistant but also a high priestess in the Cult. Her cunning and knack for cruelty had allowed her to rise quickly in the order and she was suited to handling affairs that Sarvin did not have time to deal with. She was also a tall, attractive woman in her fortieth year, with long, raven-black hair - another good reason for Sarvin to keep her close by.

"If you are busy, I can come back later," she said, motioning to the pile of parchment spread out all over the desk.

"Nonsense, these are but worthless documents requiring only my signature, none of which will hold any relevance once Lucivenus is freed," he answered. "What news from Brother Jaspar?"

"Nothing good, I am afraid," she replied with a sigh. "Brother Heldon was killed, along with three others."

The High Priest frowned. "The Thieves Guild, I am to assume of course?"

"Yes, it would seem so. Appears to be the work of Randar. Brother Heldon was certain he could trap the cursed thug and remove that thorn from our side. Appears he was wrong."

"We are getting close to our goal now and I do not want us throwing away valued members in street fights with the Guild," Sarvin growled with frustration. "We must use our heads instead if we are to bring them down. We are going to use city resources instead of our own. Now, has Brother Veral made any progress?"

"Very soon, he will report back to me in two days."

Sarvin nodded in approval then pulled out an ancient leather-bound tome from a desk drawer which he placed in front of him on the desk. He carefully turned the brittle yellowed-pages until finding the one he looked for, then motioned the priestess over to view the illustration thereon.

"We have reached the final stages, my dear," he said with a wicked grin. "See here, only five more hearts do we require, but, these are the crucial hearts. They must be hand-picked and our ritual spells are now much more complex. These five will break the last remaining bonds that hold Lord Lucivenus imprisoned. Look, the heart of someone pure will shatter the bonds of his left ankle. The heart of someone brave will shatter the right ankle. The heart of someone corrupt removes the left wrist while the heart of a royal removes the right. Then the last heart, a devoted heart, will shatter the bond around his neck and open the gate allowing him to step through back into our world."

"Then Stonewood will be his again," the priestess finished.

*   *   *   *

"Why would we want to open our gates to all kinds of

bounty hunters?" asked King Stonewood VII.

The King sat at the head of a long table in his council chambers flanked by his two personal guards, Edward and Hurshal, who stood like two statues in gleaming plate armor.

"Because I feel it is the best way for us to combat the Thieves Guild. Their murders are becoming increasingly bolder and why waste valuable men of Stonewood trying to bring them to justice when we can have bounty hunters do the dirty work for us?" answered Chief Magistrate Krommel.

"And how will we justify paying all those wages? The people will not like that waste of coin," inquired Gervas, an elderly advisor to the King.

"The people are tired of being terrorized by these low-life thieves, they will understand. I am certain nobles and merchants alike will not overly complain about a tax-hike if they feel that their businesses and homes will be safe from thieves. And of course, the unsuccessful bounty hunters will cost us nothing," replied Krommel.

"Why do we need to do anything at all at the moment?" asked Prince Orval, the King's eldest son and heir to the throne. "By all accounts, the Guild and the Demon Cult are in an all-out war. Let them kill each other."

The Chief Magistrate scoffed at that notion. "We are not going to get into that debate again are we? The Cult is just a myth, concocted by the Thieves Guild to divert blame from themselves. Someone runs afoul of the Guild, so they cut out the person's heart and spread rumors of an evil cult. We catch thieves all the time, but why is it that we can't seem to find these so-called Cult members? The

Guild has our guards on a wild goose chase and laughing at us all the while."

"What say you, Fezzdin? Is the Cult real or not?" Orval asked, drawing all attention to the royal wizard seated at the table, preoccupied with a scroll which he was reading.

Fezzdin had snow-white hair and a long beard to match. Just like the fairy-tale illustrations from books, the wizard wore a dark blue robe with a dark blue conical hat. His wooden staff leaned against the table, the top end carved into the head of a grinning gargoyle. The wizard always had his face buried in a book or scroll, never appearing to have any interest in the conversations that took place around him.

"Yes, yes, they surely exist," Fezzdin replied, seemingly annoyed and never looked up from his scroll.

That brought an angry glare from Krommel but the wizard seemed not to notice.

"Well, if anyone has any proof at all then please bring it forth. I would love to see that. We know the Guild is very real and they need to be dealt with now. We have let them exist here for far too long," Krommel said angrily.

Prince Orval stood and paced back and forth. The prince was in his thirties and the spitting-image of his father, only much younger. He was tall and muscular, with long dark hair. A fine warrior, who possessed his father's short temper. He commanded Stonewood's army, though had never yet led them in any real battles.

"I say let the Guild and that damn Cult kill each other," he said again.

"Hmmmm," the King grumbled to himself, lost in thought.

He ran his fingers through his short blondish-grey hair. He had seen sixty-five winters and still possessed powerful forearms and wide muscular shoulders. The King looked young for his age, despite the grey that had crept into his hair and neatly-trimmed beard. He was a Warrior-King, who would take to the field with his men instead of ever hiding behind an army. The King hated the Thieves Guild, almost as much as he hated the Cult, which he did believe existed. He knew the stories well, how his ancestor, the first King, had helped defeat the demon Lucivenus. He also knew there were still some that worshipped the evil demon and wished to summon him back. Reports during the last few months had suggested that the Guild and the Cult were at war with each other but he knew that was still not enough.

The King then looked over to Krommel and nodded, "Bring in the bounty hunters."

Chief Magistrate Krommel smiled.

*　　*　　*　　*

The Ogre's Den bustled with activity, nearly every table full. Patrons could hardly hear their own voices over the shouts and singing of the others. Drinking was the favored past-time for those that dwelled in the south district, the poorest part of Stonewood.

Seated at a corner table, were two of the highest ranking members of the Thieves Guild, plus their current leader. It never ceased to amaze Harcourt, who wore the face of the Guild leader Weldrick, just how much his life had changed. It had not been very long ago that he drank in this very same tavern as a homeless, renegade thief, with barely enough coins to feed himself. Now he sat here, a wealthy man, the leader of the city's notorious Thieves Guild, wearing a magical mask. How he would have laughed if someone had told him of this future back in those earlier days.

Harcourt had never believed in magic, it was just parlor tricks performed by conmen, like himself. He believed that, until that fateful night when he ran into the infamous and reputedly dead, One-Handed Bandit, while attempting to flee the city. The bandit Warden had shown tremendous kindness in giving the magical mask to Harcourt as a gift, a gift that changed the thief's life forever. For the good? Harcourt was not convinced of that. Many a night he lay awake in bed pondering the "what if's" of his life. He figured his precious Jalanna might still be alive today if he had never been given the mask. Without the mask though, Harcourt would not have been a part of her life any longer. He would have been imprisoned or killed by the Guild, or forced to live in exile elsewhere. But, Jalanna would have still been alive to continue living her life as she saw fit. For that reason alone, he would always have regrets.

Jalanna was an innocent victim, murdered by the jealous, then-leader of the Thieves Guild, a man Harcourt had known from a young age. That man was now dead but that did not make the hurt Harcourt still felt, disappear. He could have chosen to just waste away in self-loathing, or use his gift to make some sort of difference in this city they had called home. He chose the latter. Using the magical mask he had continued his charade as Weldrick and now tried his best to lead the Guild in a new direction. His primary goal - the complete elimination of the Demon

Cult.

The thief had met with some resistance at first. Some other Guild members thought it bad business to wage a war, they were not an army, after all. But Weldrick had explained to them that the Cult were in every sense criminals, so they were to think of them as a rival guild, looking to take control of the city, their city. The Thieves Guild controlled the underworld and that is the way it should stay.

Harcourt tried to divert all the thugs and assassins of the Guild to concentrate solely on hunting down Cult members and finding out all that they could about the elusive order. There were some very nasty members of the Guild, as one could imagine, and it took much effort on Harcourt's part to tolerate them. It was a necessary evil for the time being he told himself. He did his best to keep these individuals under control, to turn their wicked ways against the Cult and not on the innocent citizens of Stonewood.

Thieving, on the other hand, had remained as it was. It was what filled the Guild's coffers with coins. Harcourt did, however, try to ensure that everyone in the south district was safe from Guild activities and shop owners were no longer "taxed" by the Thieves Guild to remain in business. Shops had their own Merchant's Guild to deal with and from everyone's understanding, they could be just as crooked as the thieves. Trascar, the former leader of the Guild, had introduced that tax, another reason why Harcourt had been determined to put an end to it.

The disguised thief took a sip of his ale and regarded the two associates that sat at his table. Serdic was older than Harcourt, as was evident by the grey that now dominated his dark brown hair and the wrinkles that had begun to form under his eyes. Serdic was a long time member of the Guild and the most business savvy. He owned and operated a very successful inn, The Lonely Traveller, and as well, managed many of the other Guild-front businesses. Serdic was a decent man, as thieves go, and generally saw eye to eye with Weldrick's decisions. The older thief was also the Guild treasurer and valued advisor.

The other man, Zenod, was weasely in appearance with a long hooked nose and shifty eyes. He had the appearance of a man you should not trust, yet oddly, Harcourt did. He had short dark hair with a thin dark moustache but his features were usually hidden within the darkness of his cloak's hood, which he almost always wore around his head. The Guild leader felt more like a kindred spirit to Zenod, than any other member of the Guild. Zenod was a master thief, perhaps second only to Harcourt himself and Zenod did not have the benefit of a magical mask. It was joked that he was like a ghost that could pass through walls. The weasel-like man avoided killing whenever possible, he was not a warrior and Harcourt admired him most for that.

Harcourt trusted these two men but something was missing; they were not true friends, they were just business associates. The thief had no delusions about where he stood in their world. Were he to mess up as Guild leader, he was quite positive either man would not hesitate to cut him loose.

Harcourt had no friends. Jalanna, the only woman he had ever loved, was gone forever. Wulfred, the ex-mercenary from the north who owned the Ogre's Den, believed him dead and Harcourt needed to maintain that charade since his old life was over. Then there was Andil, who Harcourt had believed was his closest friend, a true friend. He missed the skinny thief very much, or rather, he missed who he had thought the skinny thief was. Turned out Andil was an actor and in league with the former Guild leader, involved in a plot to make Harcourt's life miserable over some insane jealousy issues. The fact that Andil seemingly had no hand in the murder of Jalanna, was the only reason the man still lived. He was currently serving a ten year sentence in the castle dungeon. It was exactly what he deserved, Harcourt thought. Almost every day that Harcourt had spent in the dungeon, every time he was separated from Jalanna, had been Andil's fault. The skinny rat had set him up to be caught every time. Harcourt had spent years cursing his bad luck when in truth, his only bad luck was being "friends" with Andil.

The thief felt truly alone. Maybe it was for the best though. Anyone close to him could be in danger now that he was waging a war with the Demon Cult. He would not rest until they were defeated and driven from Stonewood.

"So Randar would have been lost to us, if you had not shown up on time, eh Zenod?" Serdic said.

"It would appear so. Though you can never count out Randar. The man has more lives than a cat," replied Zenod.

"They knew he was onto them. They set a trap for him. All this time and we cannot find one lousy hideout. They have gone into hiding. Have you all noticed, there have been no missing hearts for the last few weeks? Something is up with that," Serdic said.

"The calm before the storm," commented Weldrick. "We have not known the Cult to be cowards. They must be planning something."

The room suddenly quieted as everyone paused to regard two curious strangers that had just entered. First through the door, was a fairly short blonde woman whose body was covered in mismatched pieces of armor. She was rugged-looking, yet still attractive, with her long hair tied back into a ponytail. A crossbow was slung over her back, a curved, thin-bladed sword hung from her hip and various knives and daggers could be seen strapped all over her body.

As interesting as she appeared, it was her companion who entered next, that brought the room to utter silence. The man - was it a man? had to bend over and turn sideways to make it through the doorway. When he finally stood his full height, people stared slack-jawed. He was a giant of a man, standing taller than anyone had ever seen, easily over seven feet and quite wide. Built like a mountain. He had enormous shoulders which sported spiked pauldrons that went all the way down to his elbows. He wore a wide black leather girdle with a skull etched into the front and the rest of his body was also covered with mismatched pieces of leather and plate armor. His head was bald and his skin tone was a shade of grey. An odd pointed tooth protruded upwards outside his mouth from his lower jaw. Slung over his back was a massive warhammer.

"My god," someone was heard saying quietly.

"Yeah, yeah, he's a big one. Get yer starin over with and go back about yer business," shouted the blonde woman to the entire room.

The giant man growled and at once, everyone turned their attention back to what they had been doing previously, or pretended to. They still stared from the corners of their eyes. Gradually though, the volume in the room rose again and the pair sat down at the last empty table. Surprisingly, the chair supported the huge man's weight.

"What is that?" Weldrick said more to himself.

"Bounty hunters," replied Zenod.

"What are they doing here?"

"They are here for us," Zenod said matter-of-factly.

"Huh?" Weldrick said, turning his full attention back to their table.

"They are here for us," the weasely thief repeated. "Though they just don't know it yet. The King has just posted huge bounties on the heads of all Guild members. The higher the ranking of the member, the higher the bounty. There is a small fortune seated at this table."

"I should just turn you both in then," joked Serdic.

Zenod did not find much humor in the comment and continued. "The female there, that's Evonne. She's a former pirate from the western sea. And that monstrosity with her, is Vrawg, a half mountain ogre."

"What did you say? A half what?" Weldrick inquired, shaking his head in disbelief.

"He is half mountain ogre, or so they say," Zenod answered.

"Well then he came to the right tavern wouldn't you both agree?" Serdic said.

Weldrick seemed unconvinced. "What are you going to tell me next, that goblins and trolls are also real?"

"Believe what you want but the ogres' are real. They war with the barbarians in the mountainous regions to the northwest," Zenod replied. "That one there is clearly not a normal human. When have you ever seen a man that size?"

Harcourt had not. Not even remotely close. He recalled that brute of a city guard named Zorfal, the man who had also worked with Trascar and had a part in Jalanna's murder. Even he would have been dwarfed by this Vrawg.

"Are there others in the city now? Bounty hunters, I mean?" asked Weldrick.

"Several others have arrived the last two days. The King is finally playing a different card to get rid of us," the master thief replied.

"We need everyone to lay low," Serdic added. "We need to get the word spread to all members."

"See to it," Weldrick said to the older man.

Serdic nodded.

Zenod glanced over again at the monstrous Vrawg and his female companion. He swallowed hard and said, "Let's get out of here. I have suddenly lost my appetite."

CHAPTER 2

Captain Dornell paced impatiently within a dark south district alley. The captain of the city's Investigation Unit loathed creeping about like a common thief but in this instance, it was necessary to gain invaluable information. The man he was to meet with was late and that annoyed the always-punctual captain.

His city was in peril and he had devoted his life to its protection. The murder rate had risen tenfold in the last several months. By all accounts, the Thieves Guild and the cursed Demon Cult were fighting a war with each other. Dornell could not care any less if members from either were killed, but innocents were caught in the middle and both still forged ahead with their own disgusting activities. He would see them both eliminated, or die trying.

More and more grey had found its way into his brown hair and beard. He had spent over thirty years as a guard in Stonewood. Almost all his time had been spent in the city's south district, a treacherous place on the best of days. He rose to the rank of captain in no time, lacking much competition. Most guards avoided the south district, or were assigned there as punishment. Everyone knew the Thieves Guild were really the ones who controlled things. That never stopped Dornell from trying to change it. There had been many attempts on his life over the years, he had the scars to prove it, but Dornell was a seasoned warrior and still drew breath.

Many months back, he was involved with a plot to discover who the leader of the Guild was and bring them down for good. He partnered with the thief Harcourt who had managed to infiltrate the Guild and discover the identity of the leader. The fool thief went and got himself killed battling a corrupt guard captain, while the Guild leader escaped the city. Dornell had hoped that with the leader gone, there could have been an internal struggle for power that would have weakened the Guild. But alas, rumor was a new leader quickly took over and it was business as usual.

What a waste of a life, Dornell thought each time an image of Harcourt came to mind. The captain had spent most of his life catching the thief and at times having him locked in the dungeon for extended stays. As the pair worked together though, Dornell found he actually liked the thief. He had turned out to be a decent man and made a good partner. He was hoping that after they found the killer of the thief's would-be wife, he could have totally reformed Harcourt and set him on the right path. The gods though seemed to have other plans.

So, Captain Dornell forged on. This night he was to meet with an informant. He had met with this individual on several occasions and the information gained had led to several arrests of some particularly nasty folk. It did not come cheap though. The captain touched a coin purse from under his dark cloak to reassure himself that it was still there.

It was not easy to secure an informant like this. The Thieves Guild dealt in fear. Members tended not to rat on other members and the average citizen was terrified to cross the Guild. Those that did were either found floating in the river, or they were not found at all.

"It's good to see you again, Captain," came a voice from behind Dornell.

The captain did his best not to appear startled, as he usually was by this man's always-sudden appearance.

"You try my patience. You are late," Dornell replied with a low growl.

"All good things are worth waiting for, are they not?" the other man said.

It was difficult to get a good look at the informant. He was always cloaked and hung to the shadows. Every once and a while he shifted into what little light there was and the captain could make out some reddish hair. The man was missing several teeth and spoke with a slight lisp as a result.

"Don't waste any more of my time. What do you have for me?" asked the captain.

"Not so fast," the mysterious man said, holding out his empty palm.

Dornell screwed up his face in visible frustration and dropped the coin purse in the man's hand.

"Much better," he said with his lisp. "The barmaid that was attacked last evening, you will find that man at the Jade Dragon tonight. He will be trying to pawn off the ring that he took from her. Ugly fellow, unkempt blonde hair.

And the man who took the shopkeep's ear the other day can be found hiding out most days behind the Ebony Horse Tavern. Large thug with a black beard."

The man then turned to leave.

"Wait, that's it?" Dornell asked, attempting to grab the man's arm.

"Don't be so greedy, my good captain," the man replied, skipping back out of reach. "That is good enough for tonight."

Dornell was not convinced. "What about Guild locations? I need hideouts, I need senior members."

"All in good time. All in good time," the man said, disappearing back into the shadows.

Ridding the streets of these violent lowlifes was all fine and dandy but the captain really wanted top Guild members. That was his goal. Them or some Cult members, but the Cult was proving to be more difficult to catch.

Noticing some movement to his left, Dornell's hand dropped to his sword hilt. He relaxed when he realized it was just an orange cat sitting on top of an empty crate. Satisfied that nobody else was in the alley to witness the exchange that took place, he departed for the Jade Dragon.

*   *   *   *

Dornell's informant hurried down a dusty street sticking to the shadows whenever possible and looking about nervously. Down in the south district, one had to be careful about who one met with. Not many exchanges could go unnoticed by prying eyes. It was early evening as well, when the district came alive.

Ducking into a familiar alley, the man found a one-legged beggar sound asleep on the ground, his tin cup used for donations empty. He emptied Dornell's coin purse into Kan's cup and then moved the cup under the man's arm to hide it from passerby's. By the time he exited the alley from the opposite end, Harcourt wore the face of Weldrick once again.

As Weldrick, he could walk the dark streets with confidence. Not many people knew him as the leader of Thieves Guild, but they still knew he was a man of importance and not one to be trifled with.

Harcourt had always hated rats, those that ran to the city guards and gave up information about others, but these were different circumstances he had told himself. When he had taken control of the Guild, he immediately set into motion a series of changes. He did not wish to hear that any members had raped or attacked any women. He had made that very clear. There were some still though, who paid him no heed. They were given their chance, Harcourt told himself. If they wanted to continue with despicable behavior, then they had no place in his Guild, or in his district. Those offenders in particular, he had no trouble handing over to Dornell. It was kill them or let the city deal with them, he opted to let the city do the dirty work. And it allowed Dornell to feel as though he was doing his best to clean up the streets.

It made Harcourt laugh when he thought back to how much he had hated the guard captain for most of his life. He could never have imagined himself liking the man, let alone helping him. It took him a very long time to realize Dornell was a good person just trying to do his job. Sometimes he wished he could forgo his deception and let the captain know it was really him, that he still lived. But he knew it best to leave Harcourt buried and end that chapter of his life.

Three rough-looking men stinking of alcohol, suddenly brought the thief out of his contemplations as they stepped in front of him, blocking his path.

"Oy. Where ya think ya goin lad? Dis here is a toll street. You gotta pay a toll to pass here," said the biggest and ugliest of the three.

Harcourt stepped under a lantern that hung from a wooden post and pulled back the hood of his cloak. The man visibly paled.

"Um s-sorry W-Weldrick. Had no idea it was y-you," the thug stammered nervously. "F-forgive us."

Weldrick spat on the ground. "This is not a toll street and you do not steal from people in the south district. You hear me you fool?"

"Of course it w-w-won't happen again," the man replied bowing his head.

"Good," Weldrick said. "Because if I hear that you have continued this, I will personally cut your throat."

With that, the Guild leader continued on his way. It was good to have some power, Harcourt thought. He would be lying if he said he did not enjoy some of the perks his reputation gave him.

He needed to meet with Randar this evening and that was one man he found difficult to control. Randar had been against his taking over the Guild from the beginning but found himself out-voted by several of the senior members. Harcourt had been expecting a fight with the Guild enforcer but it never came. Perhaps Randar still remembered how quickly Weldrick had choked him into unconsciousness and was not sure exactly how another fight would turn out. He did not seem to suspect that some sleep poison had been used to "cheat" during that brief encounter. So, Randar took orders but only to a certain extent.

The man loved to kill and he excelled at it. At first, Harcourt tried to get Randar to deal with situations differently but he wouldn't have any of it. He was just a wild animal on the loose. Thankfully though, the thug was currently caught up hunting Cult members and seemed obsessed with it. So Harcourt let him go and do whatever was necessary.

Feylane, the oh-so beautiful Guild assassin, was also much taken with hunting Cult members. She had made it personal since her run-in some time ago with Lord Mornay. She had met with more success than Randar. Even delusional Cult members were not immune to falling for her stunning looks.

Harcourt was strolling past the orphanage, which was run by his old friend Dahleene, when someone exiting the front door caught his eye. It was a tall, slender woman, in her early twenties, with long brown hair. She wore the simple brown robes of a priestess of the One True God.

The thief recognized her beautiful face immediately. He had not seen Krestina since his "funeral" many months past. Harcourt had meant to seek her out and find out if she had been doing well for herself but in truth his duties as Guild leader and the war with the Cult had taken up all of his time. She looked in good health and still managed to be attractive in the plain brown robe. Harcourt could not resist the urge to approach her.

"Good evening, my lady. 'Tis not a neighborhood you should be strolling through alone at this hour," he said.

She eyed him suspiciously, since she did not know him as Weldrick and she believed Harcourt dead.

"I am quite familiar with this neighborhood but thank you for your concern," she replied.

"And how would a pretty flower such as yourself be familiar with this part of town?" he inquired, though he already knew the answer.

"Because I grew up in this orphanage. This is my neighborhood, I sadly admit. Or, it once was. I return here when I can to see that the children are looked after and provide them with some donations."

"Since when do the greedy priests at the temple hand out charities?"

"I beg your pardon, sir?" she answered, feigning to be offended.

"Oh please, spare me. I know full well how most of the priests operate here. They love to collect coins but they are loathe to give them away. I would be willing to bet your little charity work here goes unnoticed at the temple, eh?" Weldrick said with a sly wink.

Krestina blushed.

"Well......," she started to say but stopped.

Weldrick waved his finger teasingly, "My my, stealing from the temple?"

"I do not steal," she said, this time genuinely offended. "People donate these coins to the temple in the hopes that it goes to some good. I see to it that some of the coins do go where it is needed instead of just filling up some already over-flowing coffers."

"Hey, I don't blame you one bit, my dear. I am guilty of the same. I have known Dahleene for quite some time and I see to it that some of my employer's coins find their way here as well."

She regarded the thief more closely. "I don't think I have seen you around here before. What interest do you have in the orphanage?"

"I have a soft spot for the children," Weldrick replied. "I too grew up on the streets. In another city. My name is Weldrick, may I know yours?"

"I am Sister Krestina. But I must be leaving now. If I am not back at the temple soon, they will begin to worry about me."

"As they should. Growing up around here does not make you immune to the criminal element that is everywhere. Let me walk you back to the temple."

"I am quite safe, I have nothing anyone would want to steal."

"Oh, I would disagree. Many around here have nothing but the rags on their back. That robe of yours would keep someone warm at night. Your sandals there are in one piece. And there are some who would take more from you than just that."

"I have faith in God to look after me and protect me," she said proudly.

"Don't be foolish. Your faith will not save you from a thug's knife at your throat. Now come along, I will accompany you to the temple."

The priestess relented and the pair set off for the west district.

"May I ask what made you turn to the temple?" the thief inquired.

"Well," she paused for a moment. "Where I grew up, a young girl could either become a prostitute, or a priestess. You can see what my decision was."

"You are beautiful, if I may say so. Anyone would have hired you as help."

"Ah, you are kind," she said blushing. "Sure they would hire me and then expect me to act as their own private prostitute. No thanks. I serve the One True God now."

As the pair chatted, they turned a corner and ran into three street thugs, the same three Harcourt had spoken with earlier. Having grown up in the south district, Krestina knew trouble when she saw it and jumped back in fright. Suddenly she was reminded of the constant dangers in the street and wished she had left to go home much earlier.

She was about to plead with the men to leave them alone, when all three nodded in respect to the man she was with and scattered out of their path. It almost seemed as if they wanted to get away from him as quickly as they could.

She eyed Weldrick curiously and they continued to the temple without any further incidents. In fact, on their way, she noted several others who seemed to take to the other side of the street to avoid them.

"Well here we are," she said as they arrived at the temple. "Good night and thank you."

"Wait a moment Krestina, maybe we could get together tomorrow at some point? Grab a bite to eat?" Weldrick asked.

"That might not be such a good idea. But I appreciate you walking me home. Thank you, Weldrick."

"Please Krestina, I would like to see you again," the thief pleaded.

"And I am sure we shall at some point. Good night,

Weldrick," she said and disappeared into the temple.

For the longest time Harcourt stood staring at the temple doors. He had a strange feeling in his stomach, one he had not felt in many years.

*   *   *   *

Fezzdin the Fantastic sat at a desk pouring over some very dusty tomes. He blew dust from the pages each time he turned to a new one. It was the only way to properly read what was written thereon. He could not be certain when the last time anyone had ever opened any of these books.

He was frantically searching for something. The wizard was always reading. He spent most of his time reading. But this was different. He was not just reading, he was searching.

His concentration was broken by a faint scratching at the door to this particular study within his tower.

"Is that you, Lex?" the wizard said aloud.

He snapped his fingers and the door to the study opened. In trotted an orange cat who proceeded directly to the wizard and began rubbing his head against the man's leg.

"Ah my friend, it is you. So, were you a good boy? Did you find him for me?"

CHAPTER 3

High Priest Sarvin stepped outside the altar room into a dimly-lit subterranean tunnel and wiped the sweat from his brow. He had just finished whipping up a room full of Cult members into a frenzy, salivating at the thought of acquiring their next heart. Devi-Lynn slid into the tunnel to join him.

"Do you have a specific target in mind?" she asked the head priest.

"We must choose these next five hearts very carefully. Any mistake during these final stages could prove disastrous. This next heart must be the purest of hearts. A rare find in this city. But it must be tonight. Our brothers and sisters in there are ready for the hunt," Sarvin replied.

"I agree. Finding someone in Stonewood with a pure heart is not a simple task, unless….," Devi rubbed her chin in thought. "Unless it was a child."

Sarvin raised an eyebrow curiously. How devilishly clever Devi was. He had not even been thinking along those lines. She was proving to be an invaluable member of the order.

"If the child was young enough," she continued, "they would not have had the chance yet to let the stink of this city corrupt their innocent little heart. They would not yet know what it is like to hate."

"Will you lead this group tonight, Sister Devi? Can I trust in you to see the task completed?"

"You can always trust in me. I will lead them and you will have your pure heart before this night is through."

The High Priest swelled with pride and nodded.

*   *   *   *

Harcourt, wearing the face of Weldrick, marched down the street with determination. The thief had now grown accustomed to wearing leather armor and was suited up with the best that one could buy in Stonewood. Along with two finely-crafted daggers strapped to the back of his belt, he also now wore a long-bladed sword. For the last six months, Harcourt, under the guise of young nobleman, had been paying a master swordsman to instruct him in the art of sword-use. He was a quick learner. Once satisfied with his own ability to fight with the new weapon, he had a blade custom made from one of Stonewood's best smithies, a dwarf named Wendall.

The Guild leader entered a well-known pawn shop in the lower east district and walked straight past the shopkeep into the back room. He knocked three times on a wall and a door, that was not visible to an untrained eye swung open. Weldrick nodded to a thug posted at the door and entered the downward stairwell beyond.

Weldrick found the room at the bottom of the stairs

occupied by several individuals, one of whom was tied to a chair with a hood over his head. Randar stood next to the man tied to the chair. Zenod, the dark-skinned Jorold and a young Guild member, Norvil, stood off to the side. Jorold approached the Guild leader and pulled him aside.

"Young Norvil here brought us a gift," he said, motioning to the hooded man.

"Who is that?" Weldrick asked.

"That is a Cult member. Our ambitious young friend has been dying to prove his worth to us. He claims he has infiltrated the Cult and brought this one here to us as a gift and proof of his claim," the dark-skinned thief explained.

"This is true then, Norvil?" Weldrick called over to the younger thief. "You have infiltrated the Cult?"

Norvil was in his early twenties, with a smooth face and an average build. He had chestnut brown hair and stood a few inches shorter than six feet. As Jorold had said, Norvil was ambitious. This was the first time Weldrick was meeting this thief but had been informed of some of his recent exploits. Norvil was desperately trying to prove his worth to the Guild and usually took on some very bold jobs. This however was quite impressive. If true, he would be the first Guild member who had managed to fool the Cult priests in order to join their ranks.

"Yes sir, I swear it to you. I have been invited to their next meeting," Norvil answered.

"Excellent. Where is this meeting going to be held?" the Guild leader asked.

"I know not sir. A priest told me that I would be informed the day of. I have no way of contacting them at this point, they said they would find me and tell me."

"I will take ten men with me and we will crash that

meeting, when we find out where it will be," Randar stated.

"No," Weldrick said. "If we do that, then they will just be more cautious in the future. We will only succeed in killing a few members and that's it. Norvil could give us valuable information if he can keep up his charade. We need to find out as much as we can, hopefully, find a way to Krommel himself. He has to leave that castle sometime."

"You can count on me...ummm."

"Weldrick."

"You can count on me sir, or ah, Weldrick. I will not let you down."

"See to it that you don't, Norvil. Good job though. You just earned yourself a promotion."

"Lord Lucivenus is on his way! Tremble in fear you all will in his presence! He shall destroy all who oppose him!" shouted the hooded Cult member.

In one fluid motion, Randar drew his sword and removed the man's head.

*　*　*　*

Evonne leaned against a building wall near the mouth of an alley, cleaning her nails with the tip of a razor sharp knife, one of many that were strapped all over her body. She had spent the better part of the morning sitting across from Tomar's Trinkets on Mud Way. Mud Way was called Mud Way, as it was the muddiest and filthiest street in the south district. The shop owner was a rumored fence for the Thieves Guild and a tip had led her here to wait for two brothers who had broken into a glassware shop two nights previous. She had found that it was not easy gathering information about the Guild in this city; most folk kept their mouths firmly shut.

Her partner Vrawg sat just inside the alley, covered in a thick blanket, doing his best to not stand out so much. He drew stares everywhere that they went. He was trying to appear as any other beggar resting in the alley.

A middle-aged man was approaching their direction at a quick pace, pushing along a young girl, perhaps six years old, in a pretty pink dress.

"Stop dragging your feet. Walk more quickly!" shouted the man in a very gruff tone. "We are running late!"

"My legs are tired daddy," the girl whined.

"My legs are tired daddy," the girl's father mocked and gave her another shove.

The little girl then stumbled and fell into the mud, dirtying her pretty dress. She lay there and began to cry.

"Now look what you have done!" Her father yelled. "You clumsy little brat! Now we have to go back home and get you changed. That was your only clean dress! I can't believe this!"

That just made the girl cry even more. Suddenly, and without warning, the man was shoved roughly into the mud. The wind was knocked out of him as he hit the ground. Vrawg stood over him and rolled him around in the mud so that every inch of the man's body was covered in it.

The man was about to scream in rage until he looked up into the face of the half-ogre which loomed just inches from his, a line of drool hanging from the brute's lower lip. The man paled in fear. Vrawg then picked up the girl and set her down near the mouth of the alley. He ripped a long strip off his blanket and wrapped it around the girl. She just stared in awe, having stopped her crying.

"Ahhhh come along now, sweety. Daddy has to get changed now too. He was also very clumsy," the man said, gently taking his daughter's hand and pulling her along, his eyes never leaving the walking mountain.

Some people chuckled and snickered who had stopped to watch the scene unfold. Evonne just rolled her eyes.

"Way to go," she said. "So much for not drawing attention to ourselves. You keep showing off that soft heart of yours and you'll ruin our reputation. Get back in the alley."

Vrawg just shrugged his massive shoulders and sat back down in the alley, trying to cover himself with the torn blanket.

Not long after, Evonne said, "It's showtime."

Two men had just walked past them and entered the trinket shop who fit the descriptions of Gord and Barlow. Evonne followed them in. One of the men, the heavier of the two, with shoulder length brown hair, was about to say something to the shopkeep, when he turned to regard the woman who entered.

"Deal with her first then we'll talk," he said.

"Hey lass," called the shopkeep, a skinny middle-aged man with shifty eyes. "What can I do for ya?"

"I am just browsing, thanks," Evonne shouted back from a far corner of the shop, pretending to be examining some knick-knacks.

"Look lass," the heavier brother then said. "We have some business to take care of here, so why don't you come back a little later and finish your browsing."

"I will browse right now if you don't mind. I have to leave the city and be on my way later this evening. I need a gift or two before I go. By all means carry on," the former pirate replied.

Gord shook his head in frustration. He was about to take a step towards the stubborn woman when his brother, the thinner of the two with short messy brown hair, spoke up.

"Never mind her. We gotta pay Sorven shortly, so let's just take care of this."

"Well gentlemen, what do you have for me?" asked the shopkeep.

Barlow glanced over at Evonne and when satisfied that she was not paying them any attention, gently placed an object wrapped in a blue cloak on a table. The shopkeep carefully unwrapped the item to reveal a superbly-crafted glass vase, with a solid-gold base and a gold-lined rim.

The shopkeep gave a short little whistle. "Nice, nice. Where did you boys acquire this?"

Gord screwed up his face in anger and shot a look over at Evonne but she appeared uninterested in their conversation. Then he said with a raised voice, "Our Auntie recently passed away and left it to us. As you know, we need the coin before we need a pretty decoration. Auntie is always in our hearts though, bless her soul."

"I can give you sixty pieces of gold for it," the shopkeep said.

"Sixty?" shouted Barlow. "You know how much they were selling that for in the…"

Gord struck his brother in the arm and interrupted.

"What my brother means is, Auntie used to tell us that it was worth a lot more than that."

He tried to motion to Evonne with his eyes. Barlow caught on.

"Yes, yes, I meant to say Auntie told us that she had seen similar vases sell in other shops for at least two hundred gold."

"That's all good and fine but I will only pay sixty for a vase like that," the shopkeep stated.

"Just keep your gold," Evonne then shouted over. "These two will be returning that vase to the owner of the shop they stole it from. And they won't have need of any coins where they are going."

"What did you say, you little trollop?" Gord said turning to face her, his face beet-red.

"I said, you won't be needing any coins where you two are going. There is nothing to spend it on in the dungeon. And that vase is going back to its owner," Evonne said, her hands on her hips.

"That's what I thought you said," Gord growled, drawing his sword and advancing on the brave woman, Barlow drew a long dagger.

In a flash, Evonne had a knife in hand and launched it into Barlow's shoulder. The man fell back with a howl. She drew her thin, curved sword and met Gord head-on. The thief was easily twice the woman's size and then some. His swings were more powerful but much slower than the petite bounty hunter. She chose to duck and dodge rather than to parry. Within moments, Gord bled from several small wounds as the woman smiled.

They had knocked over many displays and several glassware items lay on the floor in ruin, much to the dismay of the shopkeep.

The thief grunted with frustrated rage and swung for her stomach. Evonne leaped backwards. He reversed the attack and swung for her neck. Evonne ducked underneath and rolled to the side. He roared and charged forward, sword aimed to impale the bounty hunter. At the last moment, she side-stepped the attack and brought her own blade down severing Gord's hand at the wrist. His hand and blade fell to the shop floor while he clutched the bloody stump and shrieked.

The shopkeep produced a hatchet from behind his desk and with blinding speed, Evonne grabbed the crossbow that was strapped to her back and fired; the bolt pinned the shopkeep's arm to the wall. His shrieks of pain now mingled with that of Gord's, who had slumped to his knees.

With a look of terror on his face, Barlow sprinted for the back door of the shop. He fumbled to unlock the deadbolt, then dove through the doorway to the alley beyond. The skinnier thief struck something solid and bounced back into the shop, sprawling onto the floor in a daze.

Vrawg bent over to peer down at the fleeing thief and silently shook his head "no."

"I-I-I-I surrender! Just keep that thing away from me," Barlow pleaded.

CHAPTER 4

Krestina lit the fifth candle, then wiped a tear from her cheek and kneeled down in prayer. She knelt in the main chamber of worship in the temple dedicated to the One True God. Priests and priestesses went about their daily business, while other folk sat spread out on benches in their own silent prayers.

It took a few moments before Krestina took notice of a cloaked man, now kneeling beside her. She certainly did not mind sharing the chamber with others but it was a very large room, one did not need to sit so close to her. She was about to comment when the man turned to face her.

"Weldrick? What are you doing here?"

"Isn't this chamber open to the public?" the Guild leader answered.

"Well yes, but I have never seen you here before. What are you doing here now?"

"Just stopped in for a quick prayer," he smiled. "Why were you crying a moment ago?"

"I was offering a prayer for that poor child that was

found this morning," she answered, her eyes tearing up. "I have lit five candles, since she was five years old."

"What girl? What are you talking about?"

"A girl went missing from the orphanage last night. She was found…....," her voice trailed off and did not finish her sentence.

A pained expression crossed Weldrick's face. "The Cult?"

Krestina closed her eyes and nodded. That told the thief all he needed to know without any further gruesome details. Anger boiled up inside of him. Now the Cult was resorting to sacrificing children, this needed to stop. The Guild leader had been so exhausted of late that he actually slept the entire night through and late into the morning. He had dressed and came straight here to the temple so he had not heard the news of the murder. If it were any child it would have pained him but he took personal offence to it that it was a child from the orphanage. By all the gods, did they not have a tough enough life as it is?

"I am sorry, but swords are not permitted in this chamber," Krestina said, changing the subject and looking to the weapon he wore on his belt.

"Yes, I know I was told, but I am afraid I do not surrender my weapons. These are troubling times in Stonewood. I am sure the donation I have brought will help you overlook my breaking of the rules," Weldrick said, producing a small pouch that was filled with gold coins.

"You are donating that to the temple?"

"Sort of," he replied. "I am donating it to you. You can do with it as you see fit. This way you won't have to risk trouble by, umm, diverting temple funds to help those really in need."

"Suddenly you are the charitable type?" she inquired.

"I told you that night, I always have been. But I think you probably know better than me who could use these coins the most. So I will trust in you to put them to the best use."

"That is very kind from someone of your type," she said, accepting the pouch of gold.

"My type?" Weldrick asked curiously.

"Do not take me for a fool, Weldrick. You are clearly a member of the Thieves Guild. And I do not believe they are prone to much charity."

Weldrick put his hand to his heart. "You wound me. A thief?"

"Again, do not take me for a fool. I have grown up in the streets of the south district. That night you walked me here, men, many men, and many rough-looking men, were clearly avoiding us. There is only one type of person that commands that kind of respect in the streets here."

Weldrick gave in. "Guilty as charged. And I did not mean to say you were a fool."

Krestina stood to leave. "I thank you for your donation. But I think you should be going now."

"Look, Krestina," Weldrick said, standing and gently grabbing her arm.

"Sister Krestina," she replied, pulling her arm away from the thief.

"Sorry, Sister Krestina," Weldrick apologized. "I know you must have a terrible opinion of the Guild and its members but it's not what you think. I am not like the others. I am not from this city. I have to co-operate with them in order to keep breathing. Just until I can get on my feet and move out of the south district."

The priestess seemed unimpressed. "Good-bye, Weldrick."

"Sister, please give me a chance to show you I am different. Can we walk later this evening?"

"Good-bye, Weldrick."

The thief's heart sank. She seemed repulsed by him. He wanted to rip off his mask and show her who he really was but he did not wish to risk that. "Has the Guild hurt you in some way?" he dared to ask.

"You mean other than living a life of fear every single time I walked the streets alone? Other than every time a thug tried to put his hands on me and take what he wanted? Other than those things, then yes, there was something the Guild did to hurt me. They stole the only man I ever loved," she replied, anger creeping into her voice.

"I am sorry, Sister. Is that why you became a priestess? Is there no man in your life?"

"There has been only one man in my life who ever showed me any sort of kindness, without ever wanting anything in return. He saved my life on more than one occasion. Even though he may have been too drunk at the time to remember all of them. He was a man like no other. And your Guild ruined him, then had him killed."

A tear ran down her beautiful cheek. Could she be referring to himself, Harcourt thought? He knew she must have thought very highly of him when he had observed her at his own funeral. But, she loved him?

"I don't know what to say, Sister. I am sorry. I would have played no part in what you speak of, nor do I recall anything of that sort. Was this man your husband?"

Weldrick asked.

"No, he was not. He did not even realize I existed most of the time but I loved him all the same. And yes, that is another reason why I joined the temple. He is gone but he still holds my heart. I do not wish to give it to any other," she said, her lips quivering.

Weldrick let out a very deep sigh, then said, "I have a secret I would like to share with you."

"Keep your secrets, I am sure there are many. Good-bye, Weldrick."

And with that, she turned and left.

* * * *

The Ogre's Den was not so busy at this hour of the afternoon, which suited the group of thieves just fine as they sat at a corner table, out of earshot from the other patrons.

"Have they told you when their next meeting is yet?" Weldrick asked, still fuming inside over the news of the orphan girl.

"No, sorry, not yet," answered the young thief Norvil.

The Guild leader slammed his fist into the table and growled. "We need to end this. We need to find a way to get to Krommel. I am positive he is the leader. We need to sever the head of the Cult, now, then worry about the others later."

"That would not be so difficult, if the man ever left the castle," Zenod said. "If we could just find a way to introduce a little Feylane into his life, but alas, I doubt even she could flirt her way into the castle."

"How do you know that Krommel is their leader?" asked Norvil curiously.

Harcourt's blood boiled as he recalled that horrendous night he had stumbled upon one of the Cult's sacrifices. He witnessed Chief Magistrate Krommel, drive a blade into a helpless teen girl in front of an excited group of members. Harcourt had been powerless to save the girl and barely escaped with his own heart. That night had given him many nightmares.

"I had an interesting encounter with the Magistrate once. That's all I will say," Weldrick replied.

"Well, once Norvil here gets the location for the meeting, we will stake it out with our best. Follow those who leave. This is the break we have been waiting for," Zenod said. "I cannot wait for this to be over with and we can go back to the way things were. My skills are getting rusty."

The conversation was interrupted by the tavern's owner, Wulfred, as he brought over three fresh mugs of ale.

"Served by the mighty Wulfred himself," Weldrick joked. "To what do we owe this honor?"

"Couple of the girls are taking a break. I gotta move around sometime instead of just growing old behind the bar," replied the former mercenary.

"Cheer's, big man," Weldrick said, raising his mug as Wulfred went back about his duties.

"He does not look like someone you would want to mess with," Norvil commented.

"No, no, you would not want to tangle with ole Wulfred, that's for damn sure," Weldrick said after downing a mouthful of ale. "He is the bravest man I think

I have ever met. I have watched him single-handedly throw out five men at a time. And then you would be really sorry if he had to grab his axe off the wall. He does not back down from any confrontation. If we only had an army of Wulfred's."

"We are going to need an army soon enough," Zenod commented. "Two more lower ranking members were also picked up by bounty hunters after Gord and Barlow. This is going to be a major problem for us."

A young teen boy then entered the tavern, looked about, then hurried over to the table of thieves. "I thought I might find you here," he said to Weldrick. "Feylane wishes you to join her. All she said was a pair of threes. Said you would know where that was."

The Guild employed several teens to run messages for them around the city. They were boys and girls who had proven themselves to be trustworthy but they were still not privy to any sensitive information. Guild members used code when using a messenger.

Harcourt chuckled to himself at the pair of three's reference. Feylane was at one of their many gambling houses, the location where she had won a large pot of coins, during a card game after bluffing with only a pair of threes in her hand.

"Thank's, son," the Guild leader said, flipping the boy a gold coin, which was a lot for someone of his age but also effectively kept their loyalty.

* * * *

A short time later, the Guild leader entered the gambling room secretly located underneath the Silver Mug tavern, in the lower east district. The room was empty, save for the stunningly-beautiful Feylane, dressed in tight leather clothing, with her jet-black hair worn straight down. She had been pacing back and forth as he walked in.

"I found him," she said, as if the Guild leader should have known exactly who she referred to.

"Who?" Weldrick replied. "Tell me you mean Krommel."

"I wish. I found that renegade thief that has been hitting the merchants in the market lately. He even tried pawning some stuff off to me."

Feylane spoke of a thief who had been robbing merchants blind the last few weeks in the market. The man was not a Guild member, so by Guild rules he had no right to steal a single thing within Stonewood. Harcourt could not have cared any less about the man and what he did, since he himself had been a renegade his whole life and did what he had to do to survive. He never bothered to make it a point to have anyone search for this individual but the man had obviously made a big mistake in crossing Feylane's path.

"Give him a kick in the ass and send him on his way. We have more pressing matters to deal with," Weldrick said, dismissing the issue.

The stunning assassin did not agree. "He broke our rules. Not just once, but several times. People know about what he has done. Let me cut his throat and leave his body in the market for all to see."

"I really don't think that is necessary."

"He needs to be made an example of," she said, drawing a knife she had strapped to the top of her boot. "I will do it."

The assassin then turned and walked towards a door which would have led to the room where she must have left the thief.

"I said, that won't be necessary," the Guild leader repeated as he grabbed her shoulder.

The beautiful assassin turned, anger flashed in her eyes as she raised her knife. Then realizing what she had done, sheathed the blade.

"I am sorry," she apologized.

"Don't be sorry. We all have been under a lot of stress lately. This little war has been taking its toll and I know everyone has been frustrated that we cannot make any real headway. But let's direct all that anger where it helps us the most. These renegade thieves are not our concern right now."

"I am just frustrated. This has dragged on for so long. This is our city, we should be able to eliminate this vile Cult," she said with a sigh.

"Obviously it's their city too, that's what is making this so difficult. They clearly have powerful people in charge which is making them harder to catch. But they are going to slip up soon. Once Norvil attends that meeting, we can get some valuable info. Very soon now."

"Still though, let me cut this thief's throat."

Harcourt could never really get a good gauge on this woman. She could be so sweet and charming one moment and so very vicious the next. He had gotten to experience that first-hand many years back when they had first met at one of Lord Plumberg's parties. He was not sure which side of the woman was her real side. Was she generally a sweet girl trying to play mean and tough? Or was she just simply cruel and played at being nice? The woman was beautiful, flawlessly so. Any number of wealthy nobleman would have done anything to marry a woman like her and show her off as a treasure. Her life could be so easy and yet she lived in the bowels of the city and chose to be a murderess-for-hire.

"Why are you so angry and quick to kill all the time?" Weldrick dared to ask her.

The question seemed to take the assassin aback and she froze expressionless. He continued. "I know a heart beats inside of you somewhere, the Cult hasn't taken that yet. I can't figure you out, Feylane. Which side of you is the real side?"

The assassin turned her back and appeared to be leaving when she stopped and spoke, but did not turn to face the thief.

"I was a country-girl at one time, if you can believe that. I lived on a farm outside of Stonewood. I had a large family but I was the only girl. My mother had died giving birth to one of my younger brothers. We had many goats and chickens, a few cattle. The men in my life were not... kind to me." She paused there for a moment, then continued. "We had a few years in a row of terrible weather and business was not good. My father had racked up some terrible debt and decided that I would make a good payment when the collectors came around. One of them was particularly cruel, always carried a whip. By the time I was fifteen I had had enough. I cut that collector's throat, then the two others that had come with him. My father beat me senseless when he found the bodies. When I became conscious, my brothers beat me too for endangering the family. My father thought to appease the men who would be coming to investigate the disappearance of the others. I would be given away as a gift, to marry, or, whatever. I buried my father, and my brothers, and an uncle too, at the farm then burned it. I came to the city with nothing. My looks got me into trouble with the same kind of men who thought to make me their property. That cycle was not going to repeat itself. I buried many bodies before I even turned nineteen. I was not going to go back to that life. Never again was anyone going to be controlling me. So you see, killing became easy for me. I became quite good at it. But don't go thinking I would take any job I was paid for. I was still selective about my targets. I do not kill anyone that does not deserve it, in my possibly warped opinion of right and wrong. So you will have to excuse me if it seems I lack compassion at times."

Harcourt stood in silence; he did not know what to say. He could not blame her one bit.

"I have never told anyone that before," she said, still with her back to the thief.

Weldrick walked over and put a hand on her shoulder and he could feel her tense up. "We are not all like those men. Go upstairs and get a drink. I will join you shortly, after I deal with this thief. Leave him to me."

Feylane did not say a word and left the room. Harcourt then opened one of the other doors in this room and found a man bound on the floor, wrists and ankles, with a hood over his head. The thief was trembling with fear and for good reason. He would assume that he was about to be tortured or killed, or both. Under Trascar's rule, he most assuredly would have been.

Harcourt nudged the man with the toe of his boot and the captured thief flinched. "You were sloppy, my friend. You sure did choose the wrong woman to try and pawn your goods off to," the Guild leader said. "You are lucky that you still draw breath."

"What would you have me do?" the man replied from under his hood. "I have to do something to support my family. Nobody else will give me a job."

"Oh, I understand that, believe me I do. All too well actually. You were just going about things the wrong way. You did too many jobs in a short period of time. You got our attention. You do not want our attention. You have put me in a difficult situation here. Members want your throat cut and your body dumped in the market."

The thief's body tensed. "Please, I have three children. My wife cannot work. If you kill me, you are slowly killing them as well. They are innocent here."

"Under our old rule, they would have been killed along with you to set an example. But those days are over, luckily for you," Harcourt paused, giving this situation deep thought.

He took several gold coins, one of them a fifty-piece coin from a pouch, then stuffed them inside the man's pocket.

"What was that?" the thief asked, hearing the unmistakable jingle of coins.

"I am buying your life," the Guild leader answered. "In your pocket there is enough coin to last you and your family quite some time, if you do not gamble it away. If I find out that you have, your body will decorate the market. Do not attract the attention of the Guild. We are very busy at the moment dealing with other things. Give it a month or so then go by the Ogre's Den tavern and ask for a man named Weldrick. He will see what he can do about getting you a job."

"I-I don't know what to say," the thief stammered, unable to believe his luck.

"Don't say anything, just don't make me regret this decision."

CHAPTER 5

Krestina's eyes shot open as a wave of panic overtook her. She sat cross-legged in her private room within the temple, she had been meditating and asking for guidance when she received a terrible vision. Without even taking time to find her shoes, she ran with all haste out of her room.

"First Priest Viktor! First Priest Viktor!" she shouted as she navigated the labyrinthine hallways of the temple's living quarters.

Priests and Priestesses stepped aside as they saw her coming, with shocked expressions. First she searched the main hall, then ran to the quiet reflections chambers. "First Priest Viktor!"

"Slow down there, child. I believe you may find the First Priest in the library," suggested Brother Alvo.

"Thank you, Brother," she shouted as she ran towards the library, which housed probably the largest collection of tomes in all of Stonewood.

She arrived at the library quickly enough, but now finding the First Priest amid all of the tall bookshelves was going to be troublesome. She dared not shout for the priest in the library, not wishing to disturb those within. God was with her she thought as she found the First Priest in only the second aisle she searched. The man looked ancient, more-so than any other person she had ever seen. It was said that God had blessed the First Priest with long life, as he had already lived over one hundred years. As frail as he appeared, he was in good health and some believed he would see another hundred.

He was the head priest in the temple. Here they did not believe in titles such as High Priest, insinuating that one person was above others. They were all equal here, having an equal say in matters. The title First Priest only referred to the fact that Viktor was the oldest and most senior member, and the most sought-after for advice. He was a soft-spoken kindly man with only wisps of white hair left on his mostly-bald head. Like all the others, he wore only a simple brown robe. Around his neck though, he wore a chain with a solid silver cross.

"What is it, Sister Krestina? What has you all out-of-breath?" inquired the First Priest.

"First Priest Viktor," she said with a short little bow of respect. "Forgive my intrusion. I was meditating and I received a disturbing vision. I was asking God for guidance with regards to the Demon Cult and all these horrific murders. I saw our temple under attack. I saw Brothers and Sisters murdered. I saw a large monster, the demon himself perhaps. I fear the Cult may move on us soon."

First Priest Viktor patted Sister Krestina on the shoulder and immediately her heart-rate slowed down and she felt her stress levels dropping. He had a warm smile.

"My dear Sister, do not over-worry about this Cult.

They would not dare attack our temple. And to what purpose? We have nothing they would want here. The hearts they seek for their evil rituals are much more easily obtained elsewhere. Do not fear. You are still young, and not long into your studies. It will take you some time to truly master your visions and be able to interpret them accurately. God speaks to us all but you will need more time before you hear him clearly."

First Priest Viktor was wise and his words did make sense. Perhaps she had over-reacted, Krestina thought to herself. This was all still new to her. But the vision had been so vivid and felt so real.

"Now you run along and get back to your studies. How are your spells coming along?" the aged priest asked.

The followers at the temple prayed to God to grant them the ability to perform a variety of spells. Some were simple, some took years and years of study to understand. Krestina never believed in magic, so she had found it difficult to accept their possibility. That may have been her problem in this area of study; she needed more faith in God to grant her these spells.

"Poorly I am afraid First Priest. I have not been able to perform even the simplest yet."

"As I have said, you are young, and not long here at the temple. Keep at your studies and they will come to you, God willing."

"Thank you, First Priest."

Krestina left the old priest and slowly walked back to her room. The First Priest had calmed her down and made her feel a little better, but she could not shake a nagging feeling that danger loomed somewhere on the horizon. Her thoughts then wandered to a particular thief who she had loved with all her heart. She wished that Harcourt was still alive, she was sure that he could have protected her from anything.

*   *   *   *

Chief Magistrate Krommel breathed in the fresh night air from the immense courtyard garden, one of many within the castle grounds. He motioned for his personal guards, who were never far from his side, to remain at the entrance. He strolled through the courtyard, passing several wonderfully-carved marble fountains.

Soon he was out of sight of the gated entrance and found High Priestess Devi-Lynn and Brother Veral quietly conversing near a large pond. The sound of water falling from a nearby fountain made it difficult to hear any of the pairs' conversation, precisely why they had chosen this particular spot.

"Ah Brother Veral, a pleasant surprise," the High Priest said.

"High Priest Sarvin," Veral bowed deeply.

"Brother Veral has done very well, you will be most pleased with his progress," Devi beamed with excitement.

"Do tell," beckoned Sarvin.

"I have names and descriptions of many of the high-ranking Guild members," Veral said with pride. "As well as some secret locations. A weasely man named Zenod seems to be their main source of intelligence, very little that takes place on the streets gets past this one. I have met with Randar of course, and a dark-skinned man named Jorold. But best of all, I believe I know who their leader is. I have met with this Weldrick. Although nobody has addressed him as such, I believe without a doubt that he is their leader."

"I am very pleased indeed," the High Priest smiled from ear to ear. "And they trust you, or, they trust Norvil?"

"Yes, High Priest. Your idea of me bringing them Brother Dann as a prisoner worked like a charm. Unfortunately, Randar beheaded our Brother, but his sacrifice earned me their trust," Veral replied. "There is just one troubling matter."

"Yes?"

"The Guild knows who you are. Somehow, they know that you are the leader of our order. This Weldrick has said so, though he would not elaborate on how he knows this."

The smiled faded from Sarvin's face. "How is that possible? None in our order would betray us. And we have been very careful."

"As I said, your Highness, he would not elaborate. I know not how he knows this. But they are desperately trying to find a way to get to you. They hope you slip up and will leave the safety of the castle. I believe they have assassins constantly on the watch. There is one Feylane, though I have not met her, that they wish to use against you."

Sarvin rubbed his chin in deep concentration. This was troubling news indeed. He had been very careful in keeping his dual identity a secret. The King himself, and his pet wizard Fezzdin, had full trust in the Chief Magistrate. How was it possible that the Guild knew his identity? The elixir that members of their order drank during their initiation ensured they could not divulge sensitive information to outsiders. It magically prevented it.

"We are going to have to speed up our plans sooner than I had expected. We need the Thieves Guild out of our way completely so they can no longer interfere. Sister Devi, I believe it is time to call in Thelvius and his men. Then see to it that you get all the names and descriptions from Brother Veral and pass those along to the bounty hunters," ordered Sarvin. "Brother Veral, you have been a valuable asset to us, I am very pleased with your progress here."

"When will we seek our next heart?" asked Devi.

"Tomorrow. Yes, tomorrow we must find our 'brave' heart for the next ritual," Sarvin replied.

"So the next heart has to come from the bravest of souls does it?" Veral asked curiously. "I believe I know exactly where to find it."

*　　*　　*　　*

Devi-Lynn finished briefing the assembled bounty hunters and then dismissed them, all save one.

"Evonne, a moment more of your time," Devi called to the former pirate before she had left the room.

The bounty hunter turned and raised a curious eyebrow. "Yes?"

"The King and the Chief Magistrate are particularly pleased with the efforts from you and your, ah, partner. They would like to give you a very special assignment, more suited to your abilities."

"Go on," urged Evonne, who suddenly saw the opportunity to earn even more gold.

"We believe we have discovered the identity of the Guild's leader," Devi continued. "This Weldrick will probably prove more difficult to apprehend than the others, which is why we wish to enlist you for the task. Your success-rate thus far has been astounding."

"The Guild leader you say? Hmm. We will want three thousand for his head, not a copper coin less," Evonne demanded.

"Deal," answered Devi. "But not just his head. The Chief Magistrate wants to be absolutely sure this one is alive."

* * * *

"You are late," said the red-haired man with the lisp.

"How dare you comment on tardiness! You think your time is more valuable than mine?" barked Captain Dornell as he turned into the dark alley where he was to meet with his informant.

Two hours ago, a young boy had found Dornell in the lower east district and delivered a message for him to meet three days earlier than they had previously arranged.

"Speak!" the captain demanded.

"You need to investigate deeper into the dealings of the Chief Magistrate, I implore you, good Captain."

"Listen you," Dornell said annoyingly. "We have been over this before. Chief Magistrate Krommel is a fine upstanding citizen. A proud son of Stonewood. Whoever you are getting this information from obviously has some personal issue with the Magistrate. Most likely he was sentenced to spend some time in the dungeon by the man. Some silly plot for revenge to tarnish the good name of

Krommel. The man has done more to clean up the streets of this city than any other who held the position before him."

"And how much headway has he made in ridding the city of the Demon Cult? Eh?" the red-haired man spat. "How many major arrests have there been in that case? I wonder why that is?"

"They are clearly more intelligent and careful than the Thieves Guild," Dornell said.

"They are not!" shouted the man with the lisp as he took a few steps closer to the captain. "They have the backing of high ranking city officials! And Krommel is their leader!"

Captain Dornell took a step back and placed a hand on the hilt of his sword. "Back off and calm down. Is this all you have for me then?"

"Is it not enough? Do not be a fool Captain. Listen to me, I beg you," pleaded the informant.

"Do not waste my time again unless you have something better to tell me."

Dornell stormed out of the alley despite the pleas of the red-headed man. Harcourt growled in frustration and wore Weldrick's face again as he too emerged from the alley onto the same street, watching Dornell fade from sight.

"Hey handsome, how are you?" asked one of two ladies-of-the-night who passed by the Guild leader.

Harcourt ignored them both. Captain Dornell could be so stubborn, he thought. As with Krestina, he had been tempted to rip off his mask and show his old partner who he really was. He was running out of options to get to the Chief Magistrate. Many times he had thought to use his mask to infiltrate the castle and find Krommel's quarters, but he was positive the man was never far from his personal guards. Finding him was one thing, killing him and escaping the castle was another thing entirely. Harcourt was also not an assassin. He had hoped that Dornell would be the help that he desperately needed. Now he would need another plan.

Shaking his head, the Guild leader set off to get some much needed rest. Between running the Guild, dealing with his feelings for Krestina and formulating plans against the Cult he found it very difficult to get any sleep. He was so deep in thought that he did not even notice when Norvil also emerged from the shadows of the same alley and sped off in the opposite direction.

*　　*　　*　　*

Harcourt navigated his way out of the south district without incident. He lived in a small modest home within the lower west district. As a rule, he never took a direct route home and generally changed his face several times before arriving there. Tonight his mind was elsewhere.

The thief had not been completely oblivious to his surroundings though. As he rounded a corner, he was convinced that a cloaked individual had been tailing him for the last several streets. Twice he had attempted to lose this shadow in a crowd, to no avail. As he was now in a predominantly residential area of the city, crowds thinned and the streets became more barren at this hour.

Right down the next street, then left after that, and still the shadow followed. Since he had gone to meet Dornell tonight as the red-headed informant, he was not wearing his armor or carrying his sword. He did thankfully have his two daggers strapped to the back of his belt, and a small knife in his boot.

It was clear that this individual was not going to give up, so it was time to find out who it was and what they wanted. Harcourt kept walking at a casual pace until coming upon a particularly long and narrow alleyway between two buildings of shops. Satisfied that this alley was empty, the Guild leader quickly ducked inside and drew his two daggers. He waited close to the entrance, so he could pounce on the person if they chose to follow.

Tense moments passed by and nothing. The thief dared peek around the corner to find the street he had just vacated empty. Motion to his side caused him to spin around into a fighting stance, a dagger in each hand. He relaxed as an orange street cat nonchalantly washed its face. It then stopped to stare at the thief.

"What are you looking at? Eh?" the Guild leader asked the cat.

Harcourt then spun back into his defensive stance as a voice from the other end of the alley gave him a start. It was his cloaked shadow leaning on an ebony walking stick, with no other weapons visible.

"My friend there thinks he is looking at a ghost. It's not a common sight for the dead to walk the streets of this city," the mysterious man said.

"What madness do you speak? Who are you? You have been following me. Why?"

"Well, when my friend Lex here told me of a dead man walking the streets, I just had to see it with my own eyes," the man said cryptically.

"I don't take kindly to threats," the Guild leader said

as he began to advance. "Or to being followed."

"Now now there is no need for violence, Harcourt, I have only come to talk."

That gave the thief pause. *What did that man just say? Harcourt?*

"I don't know who you think I am, but you have chosen the wrong person to bother tonight. You will remember the name of Weldrick when we are finished."

"As I have said, Harcourt, I only wish to talk," the man said pulling back the hood of his cloak to reveal his snow-white hair and long matching beard.

"Fezzdin?" the thief asked, hardly believing his eyes.

"Aye my boy, tis I," the wizard replied. "You have been very busy I see since your *death*. More clever than I would have ever given you credit for."

"My name is Weldrick"

"Oh please, think about who you are addressing here. I know all about your little magical mask, and how you are currently the leader of the city's Thieves Guild. Clever, very clever."

"But, how do…" the thief attempted to say before being cut off.

"You had first gained my curiosity by merely mentioning the fact that you knew of magical masks many years ago in my tower. Do you recall that meeting? I mean really, how would a south-side thief like yourself, who had never ventured from Stonewood, hear of such a thing? Then it made complete sense to me how you had pulled off that spree of thefts that had the city talking for years. So I decided to keep an eye on you - well, Lex's eyes anyways." The cat meowed. "That was quite the revenge plot that you hatched, then the faking of your own death.

Taking over the Thieves Guild though was a surprise, I did not see that one coming. How you came by this mask is a tale I am most interested in hearing another time."

"So you have come to arrest me then? And take my mask?" Harcourt wondered.

"Not at all, son. I have come to commend you. I will admit at first I was very skeptical of your motives and thought it may be necessary to step in and have you apprehended, but I saw that you made many changes in the Guild's activities. And that you have been directing your resources in the direction of the Demon Cult. In that regard the city and the Guild see eye to eye. So I have allowed you to continue to rule so that you may accomplish this goal of yours. Once the Cult has been destroyed though, we may need to have another talk about this matter. Until then it will be business as usual."

"Who else knows about me and my mask?" Harcourt asked.

"Only me," the wizard answered. "Oh and Lex of course. But I believe that should change. Your Guild has not met with too much success during your little war on your own. Maybe it is about time you let Captain Dornell in on your little secret. You might find the Captain and his unit quite useful. Dornell would probably like to know that you are alive and well, and still willing to help in the city's cause. That would be my advice."

"I had been contemplating that," the thief admitted. "I was hoping to get him to investigate Chief Magistrate Krommel. He is the leader, I believe, of the Cult."

"And how do you know that?"

Harcourt pointed to his face. "While using the mask to appear as someone else, I accidentally stumbled upon a

Cult meeting and sacrifice. Krommel had been the one in charge and murdered a young girl in front of my eyes."

"Of this you are certain?" the wizard asked in a shocked tone.

"Absolutely. I tell no tales here. He appeared to be the one in charge."

There was a long silence while the wizard took in that troubling information. He should have suspected someone on the inside, someone very influential. But in truth the wizard had not really given the matter the attention it deserved, having been caught up in his never-ending studies.

"Troubling indeed. I will look into this but you should consider recruiting Captain Dornell. Also know that Krommel is planning a major move against the Guild, and now has the city surrounded by two thousand mercenary troops lead by Thelvius the Great."

"Who is Thelvius?" Harcourt asked.

"Thelvius is a former gladiator from some southern city whose name escapes me at the moment. A barbaric city where they still have slaves and prisoners-of-war fight to the death in arenas for the amusement of the populace. Thelvius won his freedom by winning every fight he had ever had. Once a free man, what was he going to do? Tend fields on a farm? Run a shop? Fighting and killing was all the man ever knew. So he started his own mercenary company. Men flocked to his banner to serve under the great Thelvius and their services are quite expensive. They have the city surrounded so when the hammer-strike falls on the Guild, they will scoop up anyone attempting to flee."

"I can't thank you enough for the information,

Fezzdin. We just need to get to Krommel somehow. He is the key to ending this."

"I will be in touch," the wizard said. "Oh and for God's sake go and let that priestess know you are alive. The girl was crazy about you."

Fezzdin then disappeared in a puff of smoke.

CHAPTER 6

An exhausted Wulfred waved good-bye to the last three patrons to leave the tavern. They were northmen like himself, who could drink like fish. He thought they would never leave. He had sent his barmaids home hours earlier and so had been doing all the work himself. There was still much to clean up but the former mercenary decided that could wait until he had gotten a few hours of sleep.

Wulfred now lived in the attic of his tavern since all his barmaids had finally moved out on their own. His girls were paid very well and he treated each one as if she was his own daughter. So it was not surprising when the man still shed a secret tear when thinking of Jalanna, one of his former employees. She had apparently gotten herself mixed up with the wrong people and paid for that with her life. Poor girl.

Wulfred walked tiredly towards the tavern's front door to lock it when it burst open. A cloaked man stood at the entrance, his cloak dripping and forming a messy puddle on the floor as it poured rain outside.

"I am sorry, we are closed," Wulfred said to the man. "Two blocks south you'll find the Ever-Flowing Flagon. They never close."

The man said nothing and stepped further into the tavern making room for three other cloaked men who now entered behind. The street lit up with lightning behind the silent men as a loud crack of thunder boomed overhead.

"Maybe you didn't hear me the first time," Wulfred said angrily as the puddle on the floor grew four times in size.

The mysterious men fanned out, making way for a fifth individual, who entered the tavern and shut the door behind him. This man was very tall and gaunt, with skin as pale as a ghost. He had a bald head, protruding cheekbones and sunken eyes. He wore a midnight-black robe.

"Lord Lucivenus needs your help," the tall man said in a surprisingly soft and melodic voice. "You should be honored to have been chosen to aid in this very special ritual. Our Lord will not forget this and he will honor you for your sacrifice."

Before the northman had a chance to react, Brother Jaspar mumbled something under his breath. For a brief moment, his eyes glowed a deep red, then the tavern owner felt as though his head had been struck with a club and he fell to his knees in a daze.

One of the four cloaked men drew a sword and approached. As he got closer, Wulfred was surprised to notice that the man wore the armor of a city guard under his dark cloak. The guard positioned his blade to cut the northman's throat. Not expecting an attack, the man was caught completely off-guard as Wulfred exploded into action. The northman caught the man with a crunching uppercut to the jaw, causing him to bite off the tip of his tongue and drop his sword as he staggered backwards. Wulfred was happy for his northern heritage; it was said the savages of the north were born with thicker skulls than regular folk. So while the mind-blast from the evil priest had hurt, and God did it ever hurt, it had not left him paralyzed as intended.

The former mercenary scooped up the guard's sword and quickly ran for the next closest opponent who now also had a sword in hand. Wulfred wanted to put the man between him and the priest, hoping that would save him from another possible mind-blast spell.

Their swords clashed with a shower of sparks. In his years as a mercenary, Wulfred had learned to fight with almost every weapon imaginable. The guard's sword which he now held though was too small in his hands. It was a sword he would have given his daughter to play with, had he had one. The men of the north preferred much larger and heavier weapons, ones that caused the most damage.

The other two cloaked men now had swords in their hands and attempted to surround the northman. Wulfred parried one attack, then took a slash across his shoulder from another. As he turned to revenge the wound, he took another slash across his back. He growled with fury. Wulfred had seen nearly fifty-two years but had not been involved in actual combat in at least ten. Usually his reputation alone had ended all fights before they even began. He was rusty, very rusty, and much slower than he remembered.

He turned and rushed the man behind him and attacked with tremendous fury. The Cult member attempted to block the attacks but Wulfred's sheer strength knocked his sword from his hand and the northman slashed him across the chest. It was not a mortal wound but served his purpose as the man fell away and gave him an opening to get to his bar. Wulfred threw the sword he was holding at the closest Cult member, then used the distraction to leap over the bar and grab his great battle-axe from the wall. The larger and heavier weapon felt much better in his hands. It had always been his favorite.

He expected another spell from the priest but the tall ghostly man just watched the scene before him with a look of amusement. He walked around the bar and faced the three swordsmen. The man with the chest wound had retrieved his fallen weapon but hung back behind the other two. The fourth stood near the priest holding his mouth which dripped with blood.

"Come on then!" roared the northman. "I will send you to meet your evil gods!"

The first Cult member lunged in with an impaling assault. Wulfred easily stepped aside and struck the man in the face with the butt-end of his axe. His eyes rolled back in a daze, then the northman swung his mighty axe and severed the man's head from his neck. Wulfred felt a sting in his side as the second Cult member managed to slide his blade about an inch into his flesh. He swung his axe backing the swordsman up then took a step back himself.

He panted with exhaustion. He was too old for this, he suddenly thought to himself. Of all the fierce battles he had fought in his life and of all the terrible monsters he had once faced, he was angered that his life might end here at the hands of some novice Cult members. In his prime, these men would not have dared attack him.

The wounded man rushed over to his left side but it was a distraction as the other swordsman slashed him again across a shoulder. Wulfred grunted and swung his axe back at the man but took another slash across his forearm from the wounded fanatic.

Wulfred then bellowed with unbridled fury and went into a berserker's rage, frothing at the mouth like a wild animal gone mad. He rushed forward swinging his axe with wild abandon. The two Cult members were not prepared for such an assault, nor could they have ever prepared for such a thing. They managed to dodge or parry the first few attacks before the already wounded man lost his sword-arm at the elbow. As he fell to his knees, Wulfred came down with his axe onto the man's shoulder, nearly splitting him in half. A second mighty swing cleaved the man in two.

The remaining swordsman scored a nasty gash across the northman's neck. Wulfred kept coming as if he had not felt a thing. A downwards forward chop drove right through the man's defense and right through his armored chest. The axe blade bit so deeply into the man's chest that it took two attempts for Wulfred to pull it free from the now dead man's body. A berserk Wulfred then hacked at the man's body until his head and both arms had been severed in a bloody mess.

Still panting and bleeding from a half-dozen wounds, he turned to face the priest and the guard. Brother Jaspar's look of amusement was now replaced with one of worry. He turned a whiter shade of pale.

Wulfred advanced with a feral growl and the priest mumbled some words under his breath. Black tendrils of mist rose up from the floor of the tavern and wrapped themselves around the legs of the northman like the tentacles of a giant squid. The former mercenary hacked at the mist but his blade passed right through them. He could not believe it since they felt real enough, holding his legs in place with a grip of steel. The tendrils crept their way up the northman's body until his arms were pinned to his sides. He struggled to no avail and roared with fury.

Jaspar looked over to the last Cult member and nodded. "End this, Marven."

The man in the city guard's armor drew a dagger from his belt and approached Wulfred for the second time, this time with more caution. Satisfied the deadly mercenary could not move, he flashed a wicked grin then opened the northman's throat.

Brother Jaspar surveyed the carnage around them. "Well done, my northern friend," he said. "A brave heart indeed."

*   *   *   *

Captain Dornell pushed his way through a gathered crowd to reach the front door to the Ogre's Den tavern. Five city guards had formed a perimeter around the door, keeping the curious crowd at bay. Captain Flannis, of the south district guard unit, stood directly in front of the entrance.

"Good morning, Captain Dornell," he said with a salute to the man who once held his position. "I have kept everyone out until you have had a chance to look at the scene. It's not a pretty one."

Dornell turned to regard two barmaids that wailed

like banshee's as they tried to force their way past two guards. He gave a nod and salute to Captain Flannis and the pair entered the tavern together. Dornell was not prepared for the amount of blood that covered the tavern's floor, walls and ceiling.

"By all the gods," he muttered under his breath.

The large room was awash with blood, but curiously, there was only one body. Dornell carefully approached the man he knew to be Wulfred, the northern-born owner of the tavern. The man had suffered multiple wounds but the one to the throat was the one that mostly likely killed him, the captain thought. The northman was also missing his heart. The damned Cult.

"Another bloody Cult murder," Captain Flannis commented.

"They took their dead," said Dornell.

"Pardon?"

"They took their dead," he repeated. "Look at all this blood. It did not all come from the northman here. And see the blood caked onto the blade of his axe? I would guess that he probably took down two, maybe three people before he fell."

"They dragged out their dead so we would not be able to identify any of them," Flannis reasoned.

"Did you find any evidence or blood trails out in the street?" Dornell asked.

"Nay. It poured all night. Would have washed away any helpful trails left behind."

"I want the cemetery checked. I want to know if any bodies were dropped off there within the last several hours. And I want the river searched for any possible fresh floating bodies," ordered Dornell.

"Aye," Captain Flannis replied.

Dornell was about to leave when something curious caught his eye. He crouched down for a closer inspection. "Umm, Captain?" he said. "Did anyone from your unit investigate this scene at all?"

"Not a one, sir," replied Flannis.

"Are you certain? I need to know for sure," Dornell stressed.

"Positive, sir. One of the barmaids came to open up this morning and stumbled upon the scene first. She ran directly to myself and two of my men who had been patrolling nearby. I peeked inside and after seeing this mess we secured the entrance and called for you."

"None of you stepped inside? Is this correct?"

"I swear to you, Captain, none of us did."

Then why were there bloody footprints left by city-issued guard boots all over the floor, Captain Dornell thought.

*   *   *   *

The sun was fast setting as Harcourt, wearing the face of Weldrick, ran through the streets of the south district as fast as was possible. He had received a message from Zenod that something terrible had happened and to meet with him outside the Ogre's Den with all haste. Harcourt was happy that he managed to sleep most of the day and get a good rest, now that something was set to ruin his mood. He had thrown on his armor, strapped on his sword and left as quickly as he could.

The Guild leader dodged people when he could and shoved them out of the way when he could not. He left a trail of angry faces behind him and was relieved that he had not passed any guards who may have been curious as to where he was going in such a hurry.

As he rounded a corner, he found a large group of people milling about outside the Den. The Guild leader was then intercepted by the master thief, Zenod.

"Stay back here," the weasely man said, pulling Weldrick to the far side of the street. "The Cult has struck again, very early this morning."

The Guild leader was struck with a feeling of panic. "They better not have touched one of those barmaids."

"Not the girls. They got Wulfred," Zenod responded.

"No," Weldrick said softly and was about to run to the tavern's door.

Zenod grabbed him to hold him in place. "Do not go. The guards will not let you pass and we do not need to draw any attention to ourselves."

"Was his…," Weldrick stopped in mid-question.

Zenod nodded. "Yes, his heart was missing."

"How??" Weldrick asked, shocked. "How could those fools have taken down Wulfred?"

"Strength in numbers? Black magic? Or both," Zenod reasoned. "From the reports I have heard, it was a gruesome scene inside. I believe the northman took many down before falling."

Harcourt's head was spinning. He felt awash with despair. His last link to any part of his old life was now gone, ripped away from him. Even though Wulfred had thought him dead, Harcourt still considered him his last friend and had befriended him as Weldrick. While it was true the Ogre's Den was never the same without Jalanna there, and it did bring him many sad feelings, at times

Harcourt could fool himself that things were as they always had been. It was familiar territory for him. It held familiar faces. Now, it was gone.

Harcourt realized Zenod had been talking but he had not caught a word he said. "Randar was supposed to meet us here," was the last thing he heard.

The thief scanned the front of the tavern, wishing to get inside and see Wulfred for himself. He found it unbelievable that the man was dead. Three guards stood watch outside the front door.

Reading the Guild leader's mind, Zenod then said, "And there are another three guards at the back door. So you can forget about getting inside."

It was then Harcourt noticed a curious individual across the street, also scanning the crowd outside the tavern. The Guild leader nudged Zenod and motioned over towards the bounty hunter named Evonne. A quick survey of the street did not reveal her monstrous partner.

Zenod paled. "I think it's time we go separate ways. I will see you later, at the Lonely Traveller."

Harcourt nodded in agreement to the master thief and Zenod vanished into the crowd. The Guild leader left in the opposite direction. Why Wulfred? He could not imagine why they would have targeted the northman. There must have been thousands upon thousands of easier victims in this city if they needed another heart for some sick ritual. Why attack the strong and capable former mercenary? Then it struck the thief. They must have realized Guild members hung out at the Den. This was a message. It told Harcourt that they were watching and this was personal.

Panic then struck the thief again, for if they knew he

was close to Wulfred, did they also know about Krestina? Harcourt quickened his pace.

*   *   *   *

Zenod weaved his way through the streets with the agility of the master thief that he was. He was constantly looking over his shoulder and from side to side. Meeting at the tavern was probably a bad idea, he now thought to himself. It was probably a set up to see who would show their faces and he and Weldrick had walked right into it.

He was sick of this war with the Cult. He was a thief and a damn good one, not some soldier or street thug. They had no hope of getting to Chief Magistrate Krommel, so if he was indeed the leader of the Cult, then the Guild was not in any position to end this. Other Guild members were already beginning to grumble about the futility of it all. The Guild and the Cult had co-existed in the city for so long, neither really bothering the other. Many voices were now saying that they should just leave them be and continue about things the way they always had. Zenod was beginning to think they might be right.

Too deep in thought, the master thief collided with a tall blonde man in chain mail armor, then flinched as something stung his left forearm. He gasped then backed up, inspecting his wound.

"Oh, I am sorry," the armored man said. "Looks like you walked right into my dagger."

The tall man brandished a thin-bladed dagger, which dripped with the thief's blood. Then Zenod realized he had seen this individual once before. A bounty hunter. He turned to run but the man was on top of him immediately, dragging him to the ground. Two women standing nearby began to scream as the scuffle broke out in front of them.

"Fear not, everyone," shouted the bounty hunter. "For I am an agent of the city and this man is under arrest for being a member of the Thieves Guild."

Zenod drew a knife with his left hand and drove it for the man's throat but the bounty hunter caught his wrist in time. The two struggled for a few tense moments before Zenod's wrist was twisted and he was forced to let go of the weapon.

A left hand smashed down into the master thief's face. Then the right. His nose spouted warm blood and his vision was now blurry. He felt the bounty hunter's dagger pressed firmly against his own throat.

"Keep struggling," the blonde man insisted. "I don't have to bring you in alive."

Suddenly, the street went silent. The women had stopped screaming and had left the area entirely. Others now turned their heads and quickly walked away from the scene. Curious, the bounty hunter scanned the street to see what had everyone so spooked. That was when the blade of a short sword came across his face, nearly splitting his head in two. He fell onto his back with a screech of agony. Another slash of the sword silenced him forever.

"Now we are even," Randar said to the bloodied Zenod.

CHAPTER 7

As darkness enveloped the city, Sister Krestina cursed her stupidity for being out so late. She had gone to the orphanage to drop off some more coins and also to console Dahleene who was still very distraught over the murder of one of the young girls. Krestina had ended up staying longer than she had planned. Dahleene offered her a bed but the priestess was eager to get back to the temple and continue with some of her studies before going to sleep. At least, she thought, she was no longer in the south district.

Her feeling of relief was short-lived as a strong hand seized her arm. She yelped in fear.

"Sssh, it's just me," the Guild leader said.

"Weldrick? What are you doing here?" she responded, her heart pounding.

"I was looking for you, actually. I went by the temple first and when you weren't there, I figured you might have gone to the orphanage," he replied.

"Why were you looking for me?"

"I was worried about you. I feared for your safety and wanted to be sure you were ok."

"Why would I be in danger? From who?" she wondered.

"That's not important now. But I would like to ask you to stay inside the temple for the next little while. Please. I will take donations to the orphanage if you want me to. But you try and stay off the streets."

"What? Why? Why would anyone be after me?"

"Look, I am sorry," Weldrick said. "Some bad people want to hurt me and those around me. I fear they may have seen me talking to you. I never meant to drag you into anything like this. Just please try and stay at the temple."

Krestina fumed, "I wanted nothing to do with you and your evil Guild! I did not ask you to come around. I have told you the Guild has already taken someone very dear to me. I just wanted you to stay away. I thought joining the temple would get me away from people like you!"

"I am not who you think I am. Please let me explain. I know this is going to be very hard to understand, but I have a secret I would like to share with you."

"This should be good," Krestina said, folding her arms across her chest.

Harcourt sighed. Alright, this is it he thought. Before speaking the command words to release his magical mask he scanned the street to see who was about. As the words sat on the tip of his tongue, the Guild leader noticed a curious person stick their head around a corner from two blocks away. The person looked to be female, with her hair in a ponytail. Harcourt squinted, then cursed when he realized it was Evonne.

"You have to get back to the temple, now!" he
ordered.

"Excuse me? What happened to your secret?"

"I am sorry, there is no time. Please get back to the
temple right now with all haste. I beg you," Weldrick
pleaded while beginning to gently shove her in the right
direction.

"You are something else," the priestess said
annoyingly. "Do me a favor and do not come by the
temple anymore. I don't think I much care for your
secrets."

"Just go please!" Weldrick insisted and then took off
in the opposite direction.

The thief was hoping that Krestina would not be
mistaken for a Guild member or an associate of his and
wanted to draw the bounty hunter away from her. He
prayed that Evonne would follow him instead. He was the
bigger prize after all, if she had done her homework.

Harcourt jogged at a light pace, trying to let the
blonde woman catch up. Two blocks away from where he
was talking with Krestina, he was rewarded when he
noticed the bounty hunter slinking around a corner. Now
satisfied that she was on his trail, and not Krestina's, he
allowed himself to be seen, then sped off down the street
and around the next corner.

A few twists and turns later and the thief was in the
south district. A glance over his shoulder confirmed that
the bounty hunter was still hot on his trail. At least it was
only the woman he thought to himself, he had yet to spot
her gigantic partner, who would be easily seen. He
contemplated changing his face with the mask but he still

wore the same clothes and guessed the bounty hunter would still attempt to catch him out of curiosity. She would probably try to solve the mystery after he was chained in iron.

Harcourt ducked down a familiar alley and nearly tripped over four men sitting on the ground playing a game of bones. They spat curses at the thief as he skipped his way over-top of them and continued down the alley and out the other end. He turned right and was surprised to find the narrow street blocked off with wagons, and several individuals, probably merchants, arguing with each other. He turned to go in the other direction when he finally spotted him, Vrawg. The massive half-ogre stood in the center of the street about a block away, staring directly at the thief.

Harcourt sprinted down an alley opposite the one with the men playing bones. He hopped over two homeless men sharing a bottle of something and turned left onto the next street. A little ways ahead, he spotted three city guards leaning against the wall of a shop conversing, but not looking in his direction. He reversed his momentum and started off the opposite way when he noticed Evonne emerge from an alley down the street. He sped down a long narrow alley between two warehouses which was his only option. One of the warehouses had its back door wide open. The thief peered into the darkness then continued on his way since he could not be sure who might have been inside.

Before he could reach the end of the alley, the gigantic form of Vrawg appeared to block his path. Harcourt skidded to a stop and ran back the way he had come only to find Evonne waiting at the other end. With no other option available, he ducked into the warehouse shutting the door behind him. The door was missing the bar to lock it with, probably taken by vandals.

The main storage area was a large room that was mostly empty. It was quite dark inside save for a little moonlight trickling through a window near the roof. Harcourt drew his sword and turned to face the doorway that he had entered from. He heard a curious scraping sound from outside, then something bumping against the door. They were blocking the door, he suddenly realized.

The thief ran about the room looking for another way out. All the windows were too high up to reach. There was a second level to the warehouse, more of a large ledge that ringed the entire structure, but the ladder that would have led upwards was missing. He found the front door to the building was blocked by several large crates.

"Nowhere to go, my friend," he heard the female bounty hunter say.

He glanced upwards to find the former pirate perched on the second floor ledge. It then occurred to the thief that he had been led to this exact building. The roadblock, the guards, everything had been strategically placed to lead him here. How had he been so foolish? This was his city, his district. Sensing his thoughts, the bounty hunter laughed.

"Thought you could escape us, eh? We don't get paid wagon-loads of gold for nothing, ya know," she said. A noise behind him caused the thief to spin around. Vrawg had emerged from the darkness, probably through some door that had been hidden from view. The ugly brute grinned and held his gigantic war hammer in both hands. The head of the hammer was larger than Harcourt's own head. One solid strike from that weapon meant game-over, for good.

In that moment, two faces flashed through the Guild leader's mind and he was struck with a pang of sorrow. The situation was grim and he was sad to think that he might never get to see Krestina again, and to finally get his chance to share his secret with her. The face of Jalanna also came to mind and the thief wondered if there was indeed some sort of after-life and if he could be reunited with her again somehow. There were times when he felt guilty for having feelings for Krestina. He would remind himself that Jalanna would always be in his heart, but that she was gone forever and there was nothing he could do about that. Well, he thought, he was not going down without a fight.

Again, sensing what was running through the thief's mind, the bounty hunter said, "Don't worry we are not going to kill you. You are worth more alive to the Chief Magistrate. He wishes to speak with you, Weldrick. However, if you leave us with no choice…"

"Krommel is evil," Harcourt shouted. "The man leads the Demon Cult."

Evonne laughed. People would say anything when backed into a corner. They all did. With lightning speed, she drew her curved sword and cut one of several ropes that had been pinned to the wall next to her. Looking up, Harcourt found a large net falling towards him from the ceiling. The thief sprang forward and rolled just barely out of reach of the net.

As he jumped back to his feet, a crossbow bolt flew past him skinning his left side and tearing a strip off his leather armor. When he looked back up to the blonde bounty hunter, Evonne was dropping the crossbow and grabbing another from the wall. All along the wall hung several loaded crossbows. She had really prepared. She fired again and Harcourt dove to his right, avoiding the deadly bolt.

This time when he stood he had a bigger problem, a much bigger problem. Vrawg charged forward with more speed than Harcourt would have thought possible from the brute. The half-ogre swung his mighty hammer looking to crush the Guild leader's legs. Harcourt narrowly leaped back avoiding the attack, then ducked as another bolt whistled by his shoulder and went straight through the side of a wooden crate.

He dodged another powerful swing of the hammer and managed to get inside the half-ogre's guard. He slashed out with his sword but he was off balance and his blade did not penetrate the bounty hunter's armor. He rolled, putting distance between himself and the brute and avoided another swing. Another crossbow bolt clanged against the hilt of his sword nearly taking it from his hand, which was probably Evonne's goal. Harcourt's mind worked furiously, trying to find a way out of this mess.

Thinking himself absolutely out of his mind, he sheathed his sword and ran full-speed at the monstrous Vrawg. The half-ogre was about to swing his mighty hammer when the foolishness of the unarmed thief gave him pause. A crossbow bolt whistled over Harcourt's head as he dropped to the floor and slid right between the huge bounty hunter's legs. He then jumped to his feet and with the agility of a cat, leaped up grabbing ahold of a large shoulder spike on the half-ogre's armor. The thief pulled himself up onto the stunned brute's shoulder, then leaped off grabbing ahold of the ledge to the second floor landing. Vrawg attempted to grab the rogue's legs but Harcourt quickly scrambled up onto the ledge out of reach.

The Guild leader's left leg stung as another bolt flew past drawing a line of blood across his thigh. He noticed that Evonne only had two more loaded crossbows left hanging on the wall. He drew his sword and sprinted along the ledge towards the blonde bounty hunter who stood on the other side of the building.

Evonne was impressed with how quick this thief was. She was an expert shot and rarely ever missed with a crossbow. He was the Guild leader after all she thought, so it only made sense that he would be the toughest to catch. She grabbed her second last crossbow and took a moment to aim at the charging thief's chest, then fired. Evonne did not know if it was skill, or just plain luck, but the Guild leader batted the bolt aside with his sword. Now with a sense of urgency, she fetched the last crossbow but had little time to aim at the thief who was nearly upon her.

Harcourt dove and rolled in a somersault, narrowly avoiding the bounty hunter's last shot. When he jumped back to his feet, Evonne had her slender curved sword in hand. She advanced with three blindingly-fast jabs of her blade which had Harcourt suddenly backpedaling desperately, doing all that he could to just parry. He was not prepared for how fast the bounty hunter was. He clumsily swung with a counter but met only air. Evonne had stepped back out of reach, then rushed in again with lightning-quickness. As she backed off this time, Harcourt bled from two small wounds on his arms.

The ledge suddenly shook, nearly knocking Harcourt

off his feet. A quick glance back revealed that Vrawg had smashed a section of the ledge with his hammer making it impossible for the thief to retreat the way he had come. A sharp pain from his right hand brought his attention back to the blonde woman who had just scored another hit before dancing back.

Catching motion from the corner of his eye, Harcourt luckily dodged aside placing his back to the wall as Vrawg's hammer came down on the spot where he had just stood. Noticing a glimmer of hope, the Guild leader chopped a piece of rope that was pinned to the wall beside him and a large heavy net dropped from the ceiling to land right onto the half-ogre's head. Vrawg roared with frustration as he dropped his hammer and attempted to free himself from the heavy net.

Evonne drew blood again, this time from Harcourt's elbow. He grunted with anger and launched his own offensive this time. Each swing met with air. The woman dodged every attack, not wanting to match strength with the much bigger thief. The repeated misses were taking their toll on the Guild leader; he was becoming winded and his sword-arm tired. The former pirate feinted a jab with her sword, then reversed her momentum and came across with a slash to Harcourt's already wounded right hand forcing him to lose his grip on his sword. The weapon fell to the warehouse floor below, right beside the still struggling Vrawg.

Thinking her opponent defeated, Evonne rushed in. Harcourt took a slash across his chest which fortunately did not penetrate his leather armor, but in return landed a crunching left-hook to the bounty hunter's jaw. Her sword dropped from her hand as her legs gave out and she dropped to the ledge.

Harcourt drew his daggers. "Let's discuss our options here," he said to the dazed woman.

Evonne then rolled off the edge of the ledge and landed like a cat on the floor below. With the monstrous Vrawg still caught in the net, Harcourt jumped down after her. The former pirate drew two of her many knives and Harcourt now smiled. Now she was playing his game.

Evonne no longer had the reach of her sword; in order to attack, she had to get much closer to the thief. She rushed in with two slashes, only this time, when she backed off, it was her that came away with a wounded forearm. Another two attacks and this time, a wounded shoulder. Her third attempt found Harcourt's boot in her chest which sent her flailing to the floor, gasping for air.

With inhuman strength, the giant half-ogre finally ripped the net to shreds and tossed it aside. As he reached for his hammer, Harcourt knew the end was near. Evonne was back on her feet but before she could rush in again, Harcourt shouted. "Wait! You are making a terrible mistake. I am not who you think I am. I work for the city."

Evonne rolled her eyes. "Vrawg, break his legs."

The Guild leader then whispered the words '*Argon Dol*' and peeled away the face of Weldrick, revealing his own. That spectacle stopped both bounty hunters in their tracks, as they blinked, dumb-founded.

"I am not really Weldrick. My name is Harcourt. I have infiltrated the Guild with the use of magic. I am using Guild resources to battle the Cult of demon worshippers to rid this city of their filth. I spoke the truth, Chief Magistrate Krommel is their leader. That is why he is sparing no expense in having you hunt us down like animals."

"A cornered man will say anything to see himself freed," Evonne answered.

"I am far from cornered," Harcourt bluffed. "This mask is not the only magic trick I have available."

He then reached into his cloak and produced a small pouch which he tossed over to the blonde woman.

"Whatever Krommel is paying you, I will double it and more if you aid me in bringing down his evil Cult. I am sure you have been in Stonewood long enough to have heard what they are capable of."

"They kidnapped and killed that little orphan girl. And killed that tavern owner," Evonne said thoughtfully.

Harcourt nodded. "Yes, they did. And they are just two of many people who have met a grisly end at their hands. If you have been doing your work, then you will have heard whispers that the Guild is at war with them. I am doing my very best to eliminate them."

Evonne opened the pouch to find it filled with precious gemstones. "What is to stop us from killing you right now, and taking these gems and anything else of value you carry?" she asked.

"Because as leader of the Thieves Guild, I am sure you can imagine the wealth I have available to me. Work with me to fight this Cult and as I said, I will see your wages doubled and more," Harcourt replied.

As a show of good faith he laid his weapons on the floor and walked over to the woman, his hand extended.

"Krommel offered us three thousand gold to bring you in," she said.

"Then I offer you six if you will do something for me."

The blonde bounty hunter looked over to her partner who shrugged his giant shoulders. "Do what?" she asked.

"I need you to watch over someone for me. Do you know where the temple to the One True God is?"

CHAPTER 8

High Priest Sarvin returned to the castle through a secret passageway known only to him and Devi-Lynn. Just two hours before, he had performed the ritual involving the "brave" heart which was taken from the northern-born tavern owner. By Brother Jaspar's account, it was a most worthy heart. The ritual went exactly according to plan. The spells involved had taxed the high priest and he felt very weary, but was also very excited. After so many years, they were finally nearing their goal. Only three hearts now remained. Soon, very soon, Lucivenus would walk the streets of Stonewood once again.

The castle hallways were devoid of life. It was well past midnight and everyone slumbered. Sarvin finally turned down the corridor leading to his private quarters and was surprised to find someone seated outside his door. As he got closer he found that he recognized the man.

"Captain Dornell? What a surprise."

"Chief Magistrate," Dornell said with a bow of respect. "May I have a moment of your time?"

"I do not know what could be so important at this late hour. I was hoping to find sleep upon my return," answered Krommel.

"Working late, were you? I thought all you city officials liked to get to bed early," the captain commented.

"Normally, yes. I had trouble sleeping this evening so I decided a walk in the courtyard might help. The night air was very refreshing," Krommel said entering his quarters and lighting two lanterns.

Dornell followed him in. "A lot on your mind, is there?"

"As Chief Magistrate there always is. My work is endless it seems. Now Captain, what is on your mind. I feel very weary."

"As you must be aware, two more people have lost their hearts recently, one was only a child," Dornell said.

"Yes, nasty business that. This Thieves Guild needs to be dealt with and dealt with now. My idea to bring in the bounty hunters has been going well so far," Krommel said, doing his best to shuffle papers about his desk and cover up a certain leather-bound tome.

"These are not crimes committed by the Guild. It's the Cult that removes its victim's hearts," Dornell responded.

Annoyance crept into the magistrate's voice. "Captain, your unit is supposed to be Stonewood's best in investigating our crimes. And you are a highly-decorated Captain. Surely you can see that this Cult was created by the Guild to shift attention from them. This has to be obvious. That tavern owner must have owed them gold."

"And what of the child? That is extremely rare. And when it has happened in the past, it was the child of

92

someone who owed them or crossed them in some way. It was a message. This child was an orphan. There is no motive," Dornell countered.

"The Guild is made up of madmen, killers and rapists, you know this. Who can say what motivates people of that sort? They do not think like you or I," Krommel said.

Dornell stared very intently at the Chief Magistrate. "I am very curious about something. We have arrested a few individuals in the past that were linked to these Cult-like murders. They offered nothing of value at the time but I was looking to speak with them again. They do not seem to be residing in our dungeons anymore. What has happened to them?"

"Probably sent to the mines," Krommel reasoned.

North of the city there was a large iron-ore mine that was worked by prisoners. It was common practice to send political prisoners there or anyone else the city did not want talking to other prisoners and stirring up trouble while still in the city. They were kept at a distance.

"Strange thing about that, though," Dornell said rubbing his chin. "They are not at the mines either. There is no record of them ever being received at the mines."

"This is troubling news indeed," Krommel said. "We cannot have prisoners just disappearing like that. They must be in the dungeons still somewhere. I do not recall there being an order to execute them. Leave this matter to me and I will investigate it fully come morning."

Dornell bowed. "Much appreciated, Chief Magistrate."

As the captain turned to leave, he spotted something curious. "Chief Magistrate, are you hurt?" Dornell asked noticing some seemingly fresh blood stains on the white shirt the magistrate wore underneath his formal robes.

Krommel quickly closed his robe tying his belt tight around his waist. "I am fine yes, Captain. I was so tired I tripped in the courtyard and skinned my hand. It's nothing at all but I am in dire need of rest so if you don't mind."

Captain Dornell nodded then excused himself from the magistrate's quarters thinking it strange that the man's hands had not appeared injured.

Krommel locked the door after the captain left, then stashed his tome back into his top drawer securing it with a lock. That was an unexpected meeting and the captain was behaving very oddly. He cursed himself for being so sloppy to have exposed his blood-stained shirt. *What is he up to?* the magistrate thought. *What has made him so curious all of a sudden?*

* * * *

Captain Dornell turned the corner of a hallway and nearly knocked Devi-Lynn to the floor.

"Apologies," he said. "I was not expecting anyone to still be up and about at this hour."

The Chief Magistrate's assistant picked up an envelope that she had just dropped. "That is quite alright Captain, I should have also been watching where I was going."

"Working a little late, are you?" he asked.

"Yes, an important document has just arrived that requires the Chief Magistrate's immediate attention. I am always on-call with this job."

Dornell lowered his voice. "Tell me Devi-Lynn, have

you noticed anything unusual about the Chief Magistrate? You have been his assistant for many years now. Is he normally up and about at all hours of the night?"

Devi narrowed her eyes. *What does he know?* she thought to herself. "No Captain, I have seen nothing out of the ordinary. He has had trouble sleeping of late so keeps strange hours. He is so dedicated to his duties, so much so that I fear he never gets enough sleep. Work is always on his mind."

"Yes, well, please keep me informed if you notice anything strange going on, will you?"

"But of course, Captain. I will keep my eyes open for such things. Good-night to you."

Dornell wished the woman a good-night and stared at her back as she walked away. He was wondering who left the bloodied fingerprint on the envelope that the assistant carried.

*　　*　　*　　*

Not long after her encounter in the hallway, Devi-Lynn stood across from High Priest Sarvin in his private quarters.

"He suspects something for sure. But how?" the High Priest asked in disbelief.

"He did not seem to bear me any mistrust," the female priestess said. "But yes, he definitely thinks there is something going on with you. How this has started I know not."

Sarvin paced back and forth in deep thought. Then Devi-Lynn remembered the message she carried. "This was sent to me from Brother Veral. He said it was urgent.

I brought it here in great haste."

Sarvin snatched the envelope from her hand and tore it open. As he poured over its contents, a worried look crossed his face. "One mystery solved, another one deepens."

"What does he say?"

"He says that he has witnessed a secret meeting between our good Captain Dornell and that Weldrick, the Thieves Guild leader. He says that this Weldrick appears to be some master of disguise, and that he overheard the pair discussing me. Now we know where Dornell's suspicions have come from, but I still cannot fathom how this Weldrick knows anything about me," Sarvin said, taking a seat behind his oak desk.

"What would Dornell be doing meeting with the Guild leader?" Devi wondered.

"If I had to guess," Sarvin replied, "I would suggest that the Captain did not fully know with whom he spoke. But now, he endangers our plans. We must deal with Dornell now. And what about this Weldrick? What news from the bounty hunters?"

"Strangely, I have heard nothing from Evonne. I am positive if they had found Weldrick, they would be at the castle immediately demanding their payment," the priestess reasoned.

"We cannot rely on them. I have an idea. Summon Brother Veral in the morning."

*   *   *   *

Krestina bolted upright, letting out a cry. Her body was covered in a cold sweat. Was she just dreaming? Or was she meditating? She was not sure if the vision she just had was only a nightmare. As she oriented herself in her surroundings, she found that she was laying on her bed, a book on her chest. A candle nearby burned low and was nearly spent. *I must have been just dreaming,* she thought. She had been up late studying her spells which she was still finding very difficult to learn, and must have fallen asleep while reading.

She had dreamt that Harcourt was in trouble. So there, Harcourt is dead, so it must have been just a dream. The funny thing about the dream was that Harcourt looked like Weldrick. He was Weldrick in appearance, but somehow in the dream, she had known it was Harcourt. He had made some powerful enemies and they were moving against him.

The young priestess let out a sigh and rested her head back down on her pillow. Why was she dreaming about Weldrick? She hated the Thieves Guild in Stonewood and was disgusted by the thought of anyone being involved with that lot. And yet he popped into her head almost on a daily basis. There was something different about him though that she could not deny, something different from the other thugs who roamed the south side of the city. Krestina was fairly street-wise and would get a certain feeling or warning when around others that were dangerous. She never got those same feelings when Weldrick was near. In fact, she almost did feel safe when he had been about.

She shook her head. He was still a thief, and a Guild member. Best to get him out of her thoughts. And besides, she was a priestess now, she was dedicated to serving God and doing good within the city, the exact opposite of what the thieves did.

Krestina picked up her book thinking to resume her reading, then placed it back down on the bed. She felt that she needed some fresh air. She slid into a pair of slippers and quietly made her way to the third floor of the temple. Up there was a large window from which to view the city and the river that cut it in half. She propped her elbows on the ledge, rested her chin in her palms and gazed out at the city at night.

There was a nice cool breeze from up here, but not uncomfortable. It was just perfect. At night, the city looked so peaceful and so beautiful. She knew looks could be deceiving. For at this hour, she knew what sorts of things were going on right now on the streets and alleyways below.

Her thoughts once again drifted back to Weldrick, and she wondered what he was up to this night. She wondered if Weldrick was more like Harcourt, a thief by necessity, and not just a mean thug or criminal. She scolded herself again and tried to clear her thoughts of the thief. Both of them actually. Harcourt was gone so it did not do her any good to still be pining over him.

Her attention was drawn to the street below where one lone person was walking quite casually. She leaned over the ledge and squinted her eyes, trying to make out the person in the gloom of the night. It appeared to be a woman, with blonde hair tied back into a ponytail. As the woman leaned against a wall across the street from the temple, it struck the priestess that she had seen this woman before. She had seen her twice actually in the last day, once in the market when she had been picking up some fruit, and once again as she was returning to the temple. Why was a woman strolling about these streets by herself at night? The blonde woman did wear a sword and had a crossbow slung over her back but still, she was alone. Or was she? Krestina thought she spotted a hulking form moving about in the shadows of a nearby alleyway. Had she seen it? Or was it a trick of the eyes at night? She must have been seeing things - no man could be that big.

Suddenly, the woman on the street looked up and appeared to be staring directly at the priestess. Krestina ducked back behind the ledge. She remembered Weldrick mentioning that bad people were looking for him and he feared for her safety. The priestess was struck with a feeling of panic; maybe this woman had been following her. She ran back to her room and locked her door.

*   *   *   *

"It sure looked like her up there," Evonne said out loud, seemingly to herself since nobody else was about. "Ok yeah, we are getting paid more for this than any other previous job, but I am bored. Since when did we become babysitters? I feel like getting drunk. Are you with me?"

When no response came, the bounty hunter rolled her eyes. "Suit yourself then. You get night watch alone. I am going to find somewhere to drink."

CHAPTER 9

Beads of sweat dripped off Fezzdin the Fantastic's forehead to the table below. His bony hands were cupped around a crystal ball as he stared intensely at the swirling mists within. For the better part of an hour, the wizard had been attempting to locate Chief Magistrate Krommel, to no avail. With the right amount of concentration and effort, Fezzdin could usually get an image of anyone he so chose, until now. Something clouded the ball's mystical vision. All he saw was a dark swirling mist.

Finally accepting defeat, the old wizard collapsed back into his chair exhausted. There was only one sure way to block the vision of the crystal ball and that was magic. So there was more to the Chief Magistrate than met the eye. Fezzdin had been a little skeptical of Harcourt's claims at first, but now there was something definitely worth investigating here. If Krommel was the leader of the Cult that would explain a lot. The man held a very high position in Stonewood and Fezzdin wondered just how difficult might it be to remove him from power. Krommel had his fair share of loyal supporters, the King being one of them. By all appearances, he was a good and noble man but in Stonewood appearances could be deceiving. Harcourt was a perfect example of that.

Weary and needing rest, Fezzdin rose and wrapped the crystal ball in an ebony cloth and returned it to its drawer. He navigated his way through the extremely cluttered workshop located at the highest point of his tower, thinking to first extinguish the three candles that burned before retiring to his bed.

Fezzdin bent over to blow out the first of the three, but instead of winking out of existence, the flame flared even brighter. The wizard jumped back and watched as the flame grew in size. In fact the flames of all three candles grew until they reached the size of the wizard himself and took on a humanoid shape. Flame Devils, the wizard finally realized. They were creatures not of this world, but could be summoned with magic and controlled by someone who was strong of will.

The closest creature screeched and extended a fiery-arm sending forth a fist-sized ball of fire. Fezzdin managed to duck behind a cluttered workbench and the fireball exploded against a wall, luckily just missing one of the many bookcases that lined the workshop. Two stone gargoyles perched atop bookcases suddenly sprang to life, sensing their master was in danger. They swooped down upon stony wings to engage the other two devils. The creatures swatted and struck at the gargoyles with fiery-fists leaving scorch marks behind with every successful attack. While it appeared the devils could not harm the stony beasts, the gargoyle's claws and teeth seemed to pass right through the flames without any effect at all. But at least they kept them occupied.

Another screech and another fireball flew past Fezzdin and struck a table, igniting several scrolls that lay upon it. The wizard raised a hand reaching for his staff that rested against a wall several feet away. He whispered a few words of a spell and the staff flew straight into his grasp. He pointed his staff and a bolt of lightning arced out from the tip and passed harmlessly through the chest of the closest flame devil. He did not think that would work but he figured he would try. All it did was enrage the creature as it hurled another fireball. Fezzdin dodged it but just barely, his blue robe catching fire. He dropped his staff to use both hands to frantically put out the flames. He then dove to the floor to avoid another fireball which ignited a bookcase behind him.

Fezzdin got to his knees as the closest flame devil approached with the intent to wrap him in a fiery-embrace. Thinking of an idea, he whispered the words of another spell and a small ice cube appeared in his palm. He raised the cube to his lips and blew upon it. The wizard's breath became a blast of frosty, frigid air which shot forth to strike the flame devil. Fezzdin continued to blow his frost breath until the flame devil stood frozen in place, no longer a creature of fire, but a sculpture of ice. A whistle from the wizard brought the closest gargoyle swooping straight down and flying right through the frozen devil. Its body shattered into thousands of shards of ice.

Fezzdin stood and repeated the same spell with the second flame devil. A moment later the same gargoyle shattered the frozen devil. The wizard was now unable to use that particular spell again, and his mind raced to think of another option as the two gargoyles did their best to hold the attention of the remaining flame devil.

Needing to take care of another urgent matter, Fezzdin scooped up his staff and a white foamy substance shot from the tip to coat his burning bookcase and workbench, effectively extinguishing the flames before they could spread and cause further damage. He did not believe the foam would be enough to destroy the last devil and he wracked his brain for a solution.

Remembering a spell that he had written on scroll, Fezzdin frantically searched through piles and piles of parchment spread out over another nearby workbench. Scrolls scattered everywhere as he tried to recall exactly where he had left it. It was an old spell and one he had never committed to memory. The flame devil screeched in anger, swatting at the two gargoyles and slowly began making its way closer to the wizard. The creature left charred black footprints on the floor with each step.

"Ah ha!" the wizard said as he picked up the scroll containing a spell that should drop a wave of water onto the head of the flame devil.

Fezzdin began to read the spell aloud then was thrown back to land on a table as a fireball exploded in front of him incinerating the scroll. Glass beakers broke beneath the old wizard as he landed atop them. Jagged shards of glass penetrated his skin.

Luck was with him though as a particular ancient scroll, one that he had even forgotten he had, floated down amid a swirl of flying parchment to land on his chest. Fezzdin whistled for the gargoyles to back away from the creature that reached out to grab him, then he began reading the spell. It was written in a forgotten tongue from a long-ago age but luckily he had studied the language enough to read through the scroll without slipping up on any of the words.

As the flaming-hand was a few inches from his blackened robe, there was a sudden "wooshing" sound as a near-invisible bubble appeared and enveloped the creature, effectively trapping it inside. The devil pounded its flaming-fists against the side of the bubble which was as solid as stone and screeched inhumanly in rage. Fire needed air to breathe and survive and the magical bubble was air-tight. Fezzdin allowed himself to relax as he watched the creature slowly fade and eventually wink out of existence.

Perhaps he needed to pay a personal visit to the Chief Magistrate.

*　　*　　*　　*

Elsewhere at that moment, seated on the floor within a ring of candles in his private quarters, High Priest Sarvin let out a long sigh. His mental link to the flame devils was suddenly severed which told him that the meddlesome Fezzdin must have found a way to defeat them. That particular spell of summoning was taxing and his body felt extremely exhausted and weakened.

"Is it done then?" a nearby Devi-Lynn asked, excitement in her voice.

"No," Sarvin replied. "I fear the wizard yet lives. He is more resourceful than I gave him credit. We must not underestimate him again."

"It is only a matter of time then," the priestess purred. "And our foes will still be dealt a mighty blow before this night is through. All the pieces are now in place."

*   *   *   *

"Krommel? I find that hard to believe," said Captain Flannis.

"Well, I have no solid proof yet, but yes, I have strong suspicions," answered Captain Dornell.

The two guard captains sat in a corner of the Boiled Frog tavern in the south district. Dornell was nearing the end of his shift and Flannis was just beginning his. The men were long-time friends and tried to meet at least twice a week to share information and catch up on rumors.

Captain Flannis was the captain for the south district guard unit. He replaced Captain Dornell when the older man was promoted to the Investigations Unit. Flannis was tall, nearly six-foot-four with a strong muscular frame. He was born in Stonewood but his long blonde hair and blonde beard bespoke of some northern heritage. The man was only in his late twenties, very young for a captain of the guard, but then not many people sought the position of captain in the south district. He was head-strong and quick to join in a fight. His reputation of being skilled in battle had helped him avoid many confrontations.

"By all the gods, if this is true who can we trust?" the younger captain asked.

"Nobody at the moment," Dornell replied in a whispered voice. "I have told only you about this. I need a little time to gather some solid evidence. This is not going to be easy."

"What can I do to help? Just name it."

"As strange as this might sound, try and leave known Guild members alone for a bit. Right now, the Guild is also attempting to destroy the Cult. So, for once we are actually working towards the same goal. Let them keep each other occupied while I do my best to sort out what I can," Dornell said.

Captain Flannis laughed. "I never thought I would live to hear you say leave the Thieves Guild alone. But your logic is sound, makes perfect sense."

A young boy wearing torn and dirty rags entered the tavern then and approached the two men. "Are you Captain Dornell?" he asked.

Dornell nodded, not recognizing the boy at all.

"A message for you, sir," the boy said, handing the captain an envelope then quickly leaving.

Dornell quietly read over the message. "I need to excuse myself, my friend."

"Is everything alright?" Flannis asked, concerned.

"Yes, I just need to tend to something."

Captain Dornell slapped his friend on the back and left the tavern. It seemed that his weasely red-headed informant had some urgent information and needed to meet immediately. Dornell was glad the man wanted to meet as he was most curious now about what made the man suspect Krommel as the Cult leader.

It was dark and the streets of the south district bustled with activity. Dornell did not wear the hood of his cloak. His face was very recognizable down here and usually helped clear a path on the street. He made his way through the winding labyrinth of streets seeking the address he was given in the message. This time the snitch did not request to meet in their usual alley. So Dornell would have to proceed with the utmost caution.

He found the address soon enough and it appeared to

be an abandoned warehouse with boarded up windows. Nothing remained abandoned for long in the south district. He figured it was probably occupied by a few homeless people at the very least. With his right, he gripped the hilt of his sword tightly, then entered the gloomy building.

The dirty bottom-floor room appeared empty, save for a lone man leaning against the back wall. Captain Dornell drew his sword when he realized it was not the red-headed informant whom he expected. The man against the wall was about six foot with a shaved head and a thin goatee wearing leather armor with a black cloak.

"Who are you? Speak quickly," the captain demanded.

"My name is Weldrick."

"I am looking for a red-headed rat of a man with a lisp," Dornell said.

"Yes, he is known to me. I am here in his place."

"Where is he? Tell me now. And what are you doing here?"

"His services are no longer needed," Weldrick said. "You will deal with me directly from now on."

"What have you done to him?" Dornell said, pointing his sword menacingly at Weldrick.

"He is safe. I have done nothing to him. He works for me. He has been feeding you information at my request."

"And just who are you exactly?"

"I, good Captain, am the leader of the Thieves Guild."

Dornell stood there blinking, unable to formulate a response.

Weldrick continued, "And I believe you and I have an understanding with regards to the Demon Cult."

"You lie," said Dornell accusingly. "The Guild leader would never be fool enough to stand here and tell me that he was the leader."

"But I am, I assure you. And I don't think you are going to arrest me because we have a common goal in mind. Let us pool our resources and work together in ridding this city of the Cult. Then you can decide what to do with me later."

"There is no way that you were sending that other man to deal with me. No leader would be ratting out his own members," the captain reasoned.

"I am not the evil man you take me for," Weldrick said and Dornell laughed. "I am not the wicked man the previous leader was. Those names my associate turned over to you were evil men. They had no place working for me."

Weldrick then proceeded to give many of the names to prove that he had indeed provided the information. Dornell was now presented with a dilemma. What to do with the man standing before him? By all rights, the man needed to be arrested and thrown into the dungeon for life, if not hung from the castle wall. But at the moment, the captain could not deny the usefulness the man might provide.

"I need to know why you believe that Chief Magistrate Krommel is the leader of the Cult?"

"Ahhhhh," Weldrick smiled. "You have finally come to your senses. Are you finally ready to explore the possibilities that we are right? Is that why you set up this little meeting tonight?"

Harcourt was pleased. It seemed he had finally made some headway with the overly-stubborn Captain Dornell. He had taken a big gamble coming here and revealing himself but he trusted in his instinct that Dornell could be reasoned with. Especially since they both held about the same level of hatred towards the Cult.

"I am willing to explore the possibility, yes," Dornell said. "If you are willing to provide me with some evidence to back up your claim. And it was your red-headed friend who set up this meeting, not me."

What did he just say? Harcourt thought to himself. *My red-headed friend set up this meeting?* Warning bells went off in the thief's head and he drew his sword, causing Dornell to take a cautious step backwards.

"What are you about?" the captain asked suspiciously.

Both suddenly heard the sound of many booted feet and the jingle of armor from outside the building.

"I think we are in trouble," Weldrick said as a feeling of panic washed over him.

There was a shout from outside. "Captain Dornell! We are soldiers of Stonewood. We have the building surrounded. You and your friend Weldrick need to lay down your weapons and come out peacefully."

Dornell shot the Guild leader a nasty look. "What trickery is this?"

"I was about to ask you the same thing," Weldrick replied, making his way to the stairs leading to the second floor. "We need to find a way out of here."

"We? I have done nothing wrong. I am the Investigations Unit captain." Dornell laid his sword on the floor then did the same with a dagger. "You have nowhere to go, thief. You might as well join me and we shall see what this is about."

Harcourt peeked out of a hole through a boarded up window facing the back of the building. Soldiers lined the streets with crossbows, and he even noticed some archers on rooftops. He ran over to the front door and it was the same there. This building did not have a basement so there really was no where for him to go. He had been a fool. He had let his guard down and now he would pay for it. He found it funny that, in this moment of panic, when thinking of all the possible outcomes presented here, it was Krestina that came to his mind and a feeling of sadness that he would never see her again.

"Let's go," Dornell urged.

Defeated, Weldrick tossed his sword to the floor. Then his two daggers from the back of his belt. And a knife from his boot. Then a smaller knife from his left wrist. The pair exited the building slowly and a rush of heavily-armored soldiers surrounded them.

Before Dornell could speak, a large guard with a bald head and a grey beard approached. "Captain Dornell, you are under arrest for treason. How long did you think you could conspire with the Thieves Guild and get away with it?"

"Are you mad?" the captain shouted.

Dornell scanned the faces of the nearby guards looking for anyone familiar but there were none. This unit was dispatched by the castle and he did not have any usual dealings with them. Two guards shoved Dornell roughly to the ground, chaining his wrists behind his back.

"You are making a terrible mistake," he growled. "Take me to the King."

"You are in no position to make demands, traitor,"

the grey-bearded guard said. Then he turned his attention to Weldrick. "And this is the leader of the Thieves Guild, is it? Caught like a rat in a trap. Chain him."

Another two guards approached and one doubled the thief over with a punch to the gut with a gauntleted fist. He was shackled roughly, his wrists behind his back. Harcourt was doomed. He had been working so hard of late to actually aid the city and now, in the blink of an eye, it was all over. He could understand that he would be arrested, after all he was the leader of the Guild. But why Dornell? Someone had wanted to set up the both of them. But who?

CHAPTER 10

High Priest Sarvin stood in front of a mirror within his bedchamber as he donned the robes of the Chief Magistrate. Today was a big day. He would be sentencing Captain Dornell and the leader of the Thieves Guild in the same hearing. This was a crippling strike against his enemies. Sarvin was hoping the Guild would collapse with in-fighting or at the very least back off until the arrival of Lucivenus. The nosey Captain Dornell needed to be taken care of swiftly before his snooping uncovered too much. Brother Veral had done a fantastic job of getting the two men together in a place and time of his choosing. There was, however, still the matter of Fezzdin. Once he was dealt with, none could oppose them.

The High Priest heard the door to his office open. Since the door was always kept locked, it could be only one person.

"Devi, do you know where my…," Sarvin's question was cut off as he walked into his office and found someone other than his assistant standing there. "Why

Fezzdin, what an unexpected surprise."

"Good morning, Chief Magistrate," the old wizard said, with a slight bow.

Fezzdin would have liked more time to properly prepare for a face-to-face meeting with Chief Magistrate Krommel following his encounter with the flame devils from the other night. But he was not afforded that luxury after hearing news of the arrests of Dornell and the man he knew to be Harcourt. Something needed to be done now.

"What right do you have holding Captain Dornell in the dungeons? He is a highly-decorated and respected officer," Fezzdin inquired, leaning on his staff.

"The man was working together with the Thieves Guild. He is a traitor to Stonewood. I am just as shocked and disappointed by this news as you are I assure you," Krommel replied, observing silently that some spots of the wizard's blue robe had been burnt. "What has happened to you?"

Fezzdin wore his burnt robe purposely to gauge the reaction it got from Krommel. "Oh, this? It was nothing. A little experiment gone awry. You should be careful when lighting candles though, they can prove to be quite dangerous to some."

Krommel shrugged, feigning indifference to the wizards verbal jab. Fezzdin continued, "What proof do you have against Dornell?"

"Much," Krommel replied. "We have agents that have witnessed him meet in secret with Guild members, even paying them coins from the city treasury. He was caught in one such meeting with the Guild leader himself. If you want all the details, by all means attend the hearing today."

"What does the King say about this? Or Prince Orval?"

"Actually, I am on my way to council the King at this very moment. So if you will excuse me," Krommel said, annoyance creeping into his voice.

"Perhaps I will join you," the wizard said.

"Perhaps not, you are not invited to this meeting."

"I do not recall asking for your permission," Fezzdin locked stares with the Chief Magistrate.

"And I do not take orders from the likes of you, old man," Krommel growled.

Tension levels in the room rose. The office door opened startling both men. In walked Devi-Lynn. An expression of shock crossed her face but she quickly regained her composure.

"Oh, I am sorry, I don't mean to interrupt. I didn't realize you were in a meeting," she said.

"No worries my dear. Fezzdin here was on his way out."

"No, I was not," Fezzdin said keeping his eyes locked on Krommel's. "For your safety, get behind me girl. I believe your boss has some explaining to do. Now Krommel, why don't you...." Fezzdin never finished his sentence as the floor suddenly rushed upwards to meet his face.

The Chief Magistrate stood speechless, then gave a great booming laugh as he regarded the wizard laying on the floor, his head bloodied with broken shards of a vase strewn about. Devi stood holding what was left of a gift the King had given Krommel years ago.

"Sorry about your vase."

Krommel just laughed even more. "Three flame devils could not take the wizard down. And now here is the mighty Fezzdin, laid low by a cheap vase."

His laughter echoed out into the hallway.

*   *   *   *

Harcourt lay in the corner of a dark cell within the castle's dungeons. He was certainly no stranger to these cells but never thought he would have to visit them again. He risked removing his magical mask for a brief moment to splash some cold water onto his face, his real face. Very shortly he and Captain Dornell would learn their fate. Life in the dungeon or hung until dead were most likely their only two options. The thief had been feverishly trying to think of a way out of this, with the aid of his mask. Five guards stood outside his cell so there was no chance of fooling one of them into opening the door for him this time. He truly did not know what he could do.

*   *   *   *

Krestina pushed her way through the gathered crowd who were watching two prison wagons roll down the street towards the western gate leading out of Stonewood. As soon as she heard the buzz on the street, she ran with all haste to see for herself if it was true. For some reason, her heart sank at the sight of Weldrick, wearing filthy rags, chained in a prison wagon with two others. People hurled rotten fruit and vegetables at the wagon and cheered as pieces showered the prisoners.

The priestess had heard rumors that the notorious

leader of the Thieves Guild had finally been arrested, and that his name was Weldrick, a former thug from the city of Hartlan now living in the south district. She could not believe her ears. Weldrick was the leader? It certainly made sense when she remembered the level of respect he seemed to command when they walked together on the streets. It would take a terrible man to lead that pack of criminals and killers. Perhaps she had been wrong about him from the start. Deep down, he must have been like all the rest. He had fooled her.

Now she had to wonder if Weldrick had really played any part in what happened to Harcourt. At the time of Harcourt's death, though, there were rumors that the Guild leader was a man named Trascar, and he had fled the city. Weldrick must have seized control shortly thereafter, she reasoned. Regardless, he was still the leader of a band of ruthless killers. But why did it still bother her to see him locked up?

Weldrick had been sentenced to hard labor in the mines north of the city. He was to work in the mines until his body could no longer handle it, then he would be brought back to Stonewood and hung. One of the other prisoners in the back of the second wagon was a disgraced former guard captain. His sentence was the same. It was said that the traitorous captain conspired with the Guild and gave them gold from the city treasury. Krestina recognized the man as Captain Dornell. She always thought he had been a decent and noble man. She figured gold and power could corrupt just about anyone, it seemed.

"Oh, look at the great Captain Dornell now! See how you like sitting in a cage!" shouted a filthy man standing to

Krestina's right as he tossed a rotten tomato at the wagon.

The priestess scanned the crowd, feeling sick inside at how the people jeered and enjoyed the spectacle. They were like animals whipped up into a frenzy. She felt that if they could break open the bars of the wagon and rip the prisoners to shreds they would have, with smiles upon their faces.

While gazing at the frenzied crowd, one familiar face came into view and a feeling of panic overtook the priestess. Krestina noticed the blonde woman with the ponytail about a block away. She too was facing the prisoner wagons and hopefully had not spotted the priestess. Krestina turned and ran with all speed back to the temple.

*   *   *   *

Evonne let out a long sigh as she stared at Weldrick, her now former employer, chained in the back of the prison wagon. It was just her luck, she thought. She and Vrawg had just landed the juiciest contract of their lives and now it was gone. The pair had already collected three of the six thousand gold piece payment from the Guild leader, but there had been promise of much more. She wondered if the man was right about the Chief Magistrate, but this was not her city and it was not her concern.

From the corner of her eye, she noticed the priestess Krestina run from the crowd and head back in the direction of the temple. She thought to follow but then figured, what was the point? Her employer was gone.

*   *   *   *

"This presents us with a major problem," Serdic said, as he watched the prison wagons roll up to the western gate.

"Indeed," replied Zenod who did his best to hide his still-bruised eyes and cheekbone with the darkness of his hood.

"I did not see that coming. I do not believe we are prepared with a contingency plan. I fear there is going to be a power struggle," Serdic reasoned. "I think Randar is going to make a move for leadership. He is a dim-witted thug. That would not be in our best interest."

"You have enough men in your employ," the weasely Zenod said. "You could take the seat and hold onto it."

"I do not wish to be leader," the older thief stated.

"So you would rather have Randar instead? I believe with Weldrick gone, our quest to rid the city of the Cult should end. But Randar will seek to continue it. He is bent on vengeance."

Serdic mulled that over in his mind. "I still do not want the position. During my father's early years in the Guild, he told me of a time when there was no one leader, the Guild was run by a council. Perhaps that is our solution."

"A fine idea," Zenod answered. "But you tell Randar that when he declares himself leader."

Serdic did not look forward to the days ahead. He was actually very content with how Weldrick had been running the Guild. It was welcomed after years of Trascar's rule. Ah well, such was the life of thieves he thought. Things could change in the blink of an eye. Now, of course, there was the danger of Weldrick talking under torture. How much did the city now know about the rest of them?

*   *   *   *

The prison wagons rolled out of the city and the western gate locked behind them. They passed through the ring of mercenary warriors that still surrounded the city under the leadership of Thelvius the Great. Weldrick rubbed his face against one of the iron bars trying to remove bits of rotten fruit since his wrists were chained behind his back. Dornell did nothing but stare at him. The captain had not said one thing since their sentencing. His silence was aided partially by the fact that the pair had been muzzled in the courtroom, probably for fear of the accusations they might hurl. Harcourt had been watching for Fezzdin, hoping the wizard would step up and come to their aid, but he never even showed up. Forgetting about himself was understandable, he was just a thief. But it did not make sense letting Dornell take a fall like this. It was so obvious he had been set up. Dornell was the most law-abiding citizen in Stonewood, the thief thought. He wondered what the captain might have done to cross Krommel.

"Now I know why your name sounds so familiar," Dornell finally said as he broke the silence.

"Eh?" was all Weldrick said.

"The name Weldrick. I knew I had heard that name before. You were picked up by my unit months ago. A fleeing thief from Hartlan. I was told you had been executed."

"I suppose you might have gotten the wrong

information then," the thief replied. "I am very much alive at the moment, though I fear soon enough I may wish that I wasn't."

"You sitting before me then is just more proof of the corruption that is so rampant in this city," Dornell said with a defeated tone.

"You are one to talk," laughed the third prisoner chained inside their wagon. A chunky bald man with bad teeth. "A traitorous guard should not be one pointing fingers at others."

"I am no traitor!" spat Dornell. "I was set up!"

"Sure, sure. We are all innocent, didn't you know?"

"Shut up."

The bald man just laughed more. "You have no more power over anyone, *Captain*. In fact you are lucky we are chained. I think I am going to deal out some revenge for all my brothers and sisters rotting in a dungeon cell when we reach the mines."

Weldrick cut in. "You are the lucky one that we are chained, my mouthy friend. You touch this man and I will make you wish you hadn't."

The man stared hard at Weldrick. "I know they say you are the leader of the Thieves Guild. But we are not on the streets anymore. I have many friends that have been sent to the mines. I can make your stay there more miserable than it will be anyways."

"Well then, it might be a good thing that we are not going to the mines," Dornell said.

"What do you mean?" the bald man asked.

"If we were going to the mines, we would have turned onto the road leading north. Only we are continuing west. So that tells me that they have somewhere else in mind for us."

Weldrick and the bald man looked about at their surroundings and noted that the road leading north was now far behind them.

"Where are they taking us?" the bald man inquired, panic creeping into his voice.

"I know not," Dornell replied. "But it's not the mines, of that I am certain. I do not know who you are, but Weldrick here, and I, are special prisoners, so it would seem that we might have a special punishment awaiting us."

It was then that Dornell noticed the mounted guard riding to the right of their wagon was a man that served under him when he was the captain of the south district.

"Norbert?" Dornell called over to the guard.

"Aye, it's me," the guard replied.

"Norbert, you know I am no traitor. How many years have you served under me? I have been set up. You need to help me escape and get back to Captain Flannis. He can explain everything," the former captain pleaded.

"There will be no escape for you. I serve Lord Lucivenus. Soon he will reclaim Stonewood and Captain Flannis will join us or die," the guard replied.

Dornell's heart sank. Stonewood's corruption ran deeper than he ever imagined. And now his fears were given merit. They were not going to the mines. The Cult had something else in mind.

"Where are you taking us?" he then asked.

"You shall see," was all the guard said, then urged his mount on so he rode further away from the wagon.

The two prison wagons and their escorts traveled on well into the night before they stopped for a few hours rest. They continued on before dawn's first light and did not stop until mid-way through the second day. A large mountainous region could be seen in the distance. That told Dornell that they now turned in a northerly direction. If he had his bearings correct, it was the Black Peaks he could see in the distance. As far as he knew, it was a virtually uninhabited region and also impassable. Yet they seemed to be heading straight for the mountains.

Harcourt was totally lost. This was the farthest he had ever been outside of Stonewood. He did not even know which direction they were going in. Without Fezzdin's tower he did not know north from south. He had drifted in and out of sleep for most of this day so he had not noticed if the wagons had changed their directions at all. Wherever they were going was not going to be good. It seemed the Cult had special designs for them. He was hoping when they reached their destination he would be given a private cell where he could possibly use his mask to formulate an escape.

His mind drifted to Jalanna. He thought at least she had not been alive to witness him being taken out of the city in the wagon. That would have torn her up inside. She had been around for most of his failures but this would have been the worst for her. God, he missed her. And now he found he also missed Krestina even though he barely knew her. There was something about her. He had been willing to share his secret with her but fate intervened and now it was too late.

The sound of Dornell's voice brought the thief out of his quiet reflections.

"Where are you taking us?" he shouted at the guards. "Those mountains are impassable. We could never make it to the other side."

"Who says we are going to the other side?" answered one of the guards.

Four guards unfolded two very large dark sheets and threw them over the prison wagons. Now, the prisoners were blinded to their surroundings. Shortly thereafter, they began moving again.

CHAPTER 11

Another half-day passed and the sheets were then pulled from the wagons. The prisoners noticed they were now in what appeared to be a gloomy cavern, lit only with torches lining the walls. Dornell guessed they must have been taken inside one of the Black Peak mountains. More armed and armored cultists surrounded the wagons within the cavern. The wagon doors were opened and the six prisoners in total, their legs stiff, were led out.

The first thing Dornell noted was that the cavern floor was smooth; someone had been at work here, this was not in its natural state. The former captain had never heard of anyone aside from the odd nomad living in the Black Peaks. And nomads generally were not ones to smooth out cavern floors to make them more livable.

"Where are we?" Weldrick whispered to Dornell.

Dornell ignored the Guild leader, not really wishing to converse further with the criminal that had led him into this mess. The former captain had hoped that somebody would have fought for his release, realizing that he had been set up. But help never came. Never in a thousand years could he ever have imagined his city turning on him, not after the lifetime of service and loyalty that he had given. Krommel held more power than he could ever have believed. And it seemed that everyone was oblivious to his dual identity. The only ones who knew were now standing here in this cavern so far from Stonewood. Well, Dornell had told Captain Flannis but he would be helpless to do anything without any allies to lend him aid. If Flannis poked his nose into the Chief Magistrate's affairs, he would likely be joining Dornell here, wherever here was.

Harcourt did not like the feel of this place. It was cool, damp and gloomy. He felt as though he was underground, or possibly inside one of the mountains he had seen the previous day. He figured this was a secret hideout for the Demon Cult and his suspicions were confirmed when three men in dark robes entered the cavern from one of many side passageways. The thief immediately recognized the tall, gaunt priest in the middle with the sunken eyes. What was his name again? Jaspar?

"Greetings," said Brother Jaspar in his gentle melodic voice. "Welcome to my humble abode. Now if you gentlemen will all follow me, I will show you to your quarters."

Armored cultists shoved the prisoners along in single-file behind the tall bald priest, their wrists still shackled behind their backs. They wove their way through winding tunnels that were all smoothed over. The sounds of hammers on steel could now be heard, echoing down the tunnels. A wave of heat hit the group as they entered another cavern, much larger than the first one they had seen. This cavern housed several large forges where it appeared that weapons and armor were being crafted. But the most curious sight here, were the ones doing the crafting. All the prisoners stared slack-jawed, Harcourt the most bewildered.

"Wraggoth," Dornell whispered under his breath.

Dornell had heard of wraggoths but had never seen one of the subterranean creatures with his own eyes. They were spindly, albino humanoids, the same size as the average man. They had hairless bodies and white eyes with no pupils which could see quite well, but were more adapted to the dark. The tips of their fingers ended in razor-sharp claws and their teeth were similarly as sharp, preferring meat as their main diet. Wraggoth were said to possess minor intelligence and lived in clans with an established hierarchy. Attacks on humans were known to happen but were rare, as the creatures preferred to remain underground. The former captain had never heard of the creatures crafting weapons. And what were they doing here with the cultists?

Harcourt could only shake his head in disbelief. He wondered if he would wake from this dream, where strange creatures populated the cavern working the forges. One turned to glare at him hungrily and hissed. Stonewood was full of tales of bizarre monsters that walked the wide world, though the thief had never chosen to believe them. Fairy tales, he had always thought, stories concocted to frighten little children. And yet here he was, walking through a cavern of albino monsters. The thief never believed in magic either, but he now wore a magical mask. So, he figured, he was wrong again. He longed to be back in Stonewood, even the dungeons. Anywhere was better than here, especially since he imagined they might have been brought here to be food for these odd-looking creatures.

"These are your friends you spoke of?" Weldrick jested to the bald prisoner who had ridden in the same wagon.

The other prisoner ignored the comment, his face pale with obvious fright. The group was led from this cavern through another series of narrow, winding tunnels which opened up again into another large cavern. This time, they walked along a ledge that looked down upon the cavern floor. The prisoners stared at the hundreds upon hundreds of armored wraggoth that stood in formation below. A dark robed cultist shouted instructions that they could not make out. It would appear the Demon Cult had an army. But for what purpose, the thief and former captain both wondered at the same time.

"Now that we have seen all of this, we will not be leaving here alive," Weldrick commented while standing next to Dornell.

Not long after, they arrived at a long tunnel where cell doors lined both sides of the walls for as far as the eye could see. About mid-way down, each of the prisoners was pushed into their own cell, the doors locked behind them.

"Gentlemen," the pale priest could be heard saying from the tunnel, "enjoy your stay."

The priest and the other cultists left; there was an unnerving silence in the tunnel.

*　　*　　*　　*

Dornell lay on the floor of his dark stone cell. A half-day must have passed before the door to his cell swung up and two armored cultists dragged him to his feet. He was shoved along two passageways before he was pulled into a larger room and chained to the wall in a standing position, his hands above his head. The cultists left him alone for what felt like an hour before the tall pale priest entered and stood before him.

"Well, well, well, the great Captain Dornell," the priest said in his soft voice. "I hope your accommodations here are not so bad."

"What the hell is going on here? Why have you outfitted an army of monsters?" the former captain shouted.

"The way it normally works here is, that I ask the questions," Brother Jaspar said. "But as you are no ordinary guest, I suppose it would do no harm to enlighten you. After all, you shall never be leaving here. We know you had your suspicions about the Chief Magistrate and you were correct in those. We will get back to what led you to that line of thinking shortly. Krommel is indeed the leader of our order and has been for quite a long time. He was right under your nose all these years. King Stonewood is a fool and will pay dearly for his foolishness. You see, good captain, we are very near to our goal now. Only three hearts remain before we summon forth our Demon Lord back to this realm. We will usher in a new era on the King's birthday. And the army of wraggoth that you have seen will be marching on Stonewood very soon."

"Putting armor on those beasts and swords in their hands does not make them warriors. They are beasts. They will be no match for Stonewood's soldiers," Dornell said with confidence.

"Your faith in your beloved city really is

commendable. Over the last few years, the Chief Magistrate's agents have been promoting members of our order to positions of power within the city's army. And their guards," the priest winked with that last comment. "They will be moving the bulk of the army far from Stonewood on training maneuvers. There will not be much resistance left when our wraggoth arrive. Our hired mercenaries already have the city surrounded. Thelvius the Great does not come cheap, but he follows the trail of gold no matter where it leads. When Lord Lucivenus arrives he will personally deal with your precious King and take back his throne. Everyone else in the city can fall in line or be destroyed. It will be their choice."

Dornell had wanted to say something along the lines of "you will never get away with this," but for some reason, he believed they just might. He was unsure about the whole demon business. There were stories that this demon lord had once taken over Stonewood, hundreds of years ago, but the former captain did not know how much of that story was real. It could have just been some evil sorcerer posing as a demon. All that aside though, the city was in trouble. Deep trouble. And nobody knew it was coming.

"What? No more shouts of defiance?" Jaspar said with a smile.

"Why don't you return to whatever dark pit you crawled forth from," Dornell spat.

The evil priest only laughed and then produced a red-bladed dagger from within his dark robe. "Now, how about you tell me where you got your information about the Chief Magistrate. Just tell me everything. You do not want to play the hero here, Captain. Trust me."

*   *   *   *

Harcourt was thrown roughly against the cold stone wall and his wrists chained above his head. The two Cult members then left him alone in the dank room. The room was featureless but the thief took note of some blood on the floor underneath him and it looked fairly fresh. Someone had occupied this very same spot not long ago. He wondered if it had been Captain Dornell.

Harcourt felt very badly that Dornell was wrapped up in all of this mess. He blamed himself for that. If he had not been meeting with the captain, he would not have been set up the way he was and disgraced in front of his peers. Of course, the thief had no way of foreseeing this outcome, but it weighed heavily on his heart all the same. Again, he found those thoughts mildly amusing since he had spent his entire life hating the guard captain.

But it was time to focus on the situation at hand. Not one opportunity had presented itself for an escape and he figured it was likely that his heart would be pulled from his chest in this very room. This was not the end that Harcourt had ever imagined. Rotting in a dungeon, surely was quite possible. Sacrificed by a cult, surely not.

The Guild leader was torn from his inner thoughts by the arrival of the tall pale priest. Brother Jaspar did not waste any time.

"You have been quite the thorn in our side, Weldrick. For many years, our two groups co-existed in Stonewood, one never bothering the other. Then you came along. You made this personal for some reason. You wanted us obliterated. So now it has come to this. Here you are, chained before me for your efforts. To your credit, you were not an easy one to catch. But thanks to Brother Veral, or you would know him as Norvil, we finally got you."

Harcourt cursed inwardly. He had never suspected anything out of the ordinary with the young thief Norvil. Their eagerness to find the Cult's hideouts led to their trusting the thief far too much. Now if Norvil really was a Cult member, that meant the rest of the Guild was in danger of sharing the same fate as himself.

"Now," the priest continued. "I am most interested in knowing just how you and Dornell knew that the Chief Magistrate was our leader? Was it you that told the captain? Or did the captain tell you? The good Captain Dornell was not very cooperative with me. And I thought I was being very persuasive. So, how about you tell me."

There was only silence from the thief.

"No? You are going to make this difficult on yourself?" Jaspar asked.

The ghostly-pale priest closed his eyes and began chanting in some language unfamiliar to the Guild leader. Harcourt gasped out loud as his eyes felt as though they were on fire. He closed them, tightly, and the searing-pain only got worse. His eyes felt as if they were about to explode. Despite his best efforts, he cried out in pain. Then it stopped.

"I could melt your eyeballs right inside your head," the priest said with an evil grin. "Or, I have other methods."

Jaspar produced his red-bladed dagger and teasingly ran the tip of the blade across the thief's bare chest. Harcourt almost thought he could hear a humming sound emanating from the evil-looking blade. Jaspar then pressed harder and the blade bit into Harcourt's skin, drawing blood. The small cut seemed to sting a lot more than it should have and then, to the thief's horror, it appeared that his blood was being drawn into the blade. The dagger blade pulsed and seemed to "drink" his blood, becoming a brighter shade of red.

"So? Is there anything you would like to say before I continue?"

Harcourt had no delusions that talking would in any way save his life. He knew they were never letting him leave here alive. The thief was a stubborn man, always had been. He surely did not relish the idea of being tortured to death but his pride would not allow him to give into any of the priest's demands. He gritted his teeth, clenched his fists and stayed defiantly silent.

Jaspar only shook his head in disappointment. But it was then that his face took on a totally different expression. Shock? His jaw hung open for several tense moments. He appeared dumb-founded. Harcourt had no clue what had come over the evil priest. Jaspar then leaned in closer to the thief's face, his expression turning to one of curiosity.

"What do we have here?" the pale priest said, lifting Harcourt's mask from his face.

CHAPTER 12

High Priest Sarvin marched through the underground tunnel with a feeling of supreme confidence. All of his schemes had been working out to perfection. The troublesome leader of the Thieves Guild and the meddlesome Captain Dornell were now out of his hair and in the capable hands of Brother Jaspar. If anyone were to extract information from that pair, it would be him. Their fates had been sealed, information or no. And with Fezzdin out of the way, nobody could stop their order from succeeding now.

The High Priest nodded to two fellow members as he passed them by and entered a large altar room hidden beneath Castle Stonewood. A black obsidian altar stood prominently displayed on a raised dais at the far end of the room. A mural of the Demon Lord Lucivenus dominated the entire wall behind the altar, painted with the blood of his victims. This was the largest of the orders' secret meeting places and reserved for special occasions. Tonight was a special occasion indeed.

The altar room was teeming with activity. It was filled to capacity with Cult members, the most ever assembled in one place. They were abuzz with discussions until the arrival of the High Priest. Conversations came to an abrupt halt and all members turned and bowed in respect. Sarvin nodded to the assembled host and they parted, providing him a path to the altar where the lovely and terrible Devi-Lynn stood waiting. She held out a soft hand and guided the High Priest to his desired position on the dais, then he turned to address the order.

"Brothers and Sisters, welcome. I thank you all for taking time out of your busy schedules to gather this evening for a special occasion. Soon, very soon, Lord Lucivenus will rule Stonewood, and we, his loyal subjects, will be waiting to serve and rule this city beside him. As you know, we are down to the final few hearts that are required to release our lord from his bondage. Recently, we acquired our most difficult heart yet, the brave heart. The donor most assuredly had lived up to his reputation. So tonight we gather to honor one of our fellow members who played a key role in obtaining this crucial heart. He is one of our newer members but has earned his place within our order. I would like to call on Brother Marven to step forward and join me upon the dais."

Marven, who was a city guard stationed in the upper west district, was beside himself with joy at the mention of his name. He had only been told that tonight they would be honoring a special member of their order; he never imagined it would be himself. A month earlier, he had been approached by Syrena, a minor sorceress in charge of recruiting new members into the order. She was a tall dark-haired beauty, with olive-colored skin from lands far to the south. She would tell potential candidates about the myriad number of ways their lives could be better within the order. Changes were coming, she would tell them, and woe to those that stood against them. She would weave subtle spells into her speech. That combined with her looks and ample chest, was usually enough to convince anyone to listen intently to whatever it was that she had to say to them.

Marven, however, did not require the use of any spells, nor was it her feminine charms that seduced him. The veteran guard had been passed over several times for promotions; the man was bitter. He was unhappy with his station in life, but did not know what he could do about it. Then he met Syrena. The order made him feel valued, important. He was a brother to them all. He was hand-picked to be a part of the group that went to the northman's tavern to obtain his most important heart. Marven had been the only member left standing, aside from Brother Jaspar, and had delivered the killing strike to the immobile northman. He had proven his worth and now he was fully accepted into the order. And being honored by High Priest Sarvin no less!

Marven could not contain his smile. He practically glowed as he joined the High Priest on the dais and turned to face the crowd of his fellow brothers and sisters.

High Priest Sarvin welcomed the man and put an arm around his shoulder. "Brother Marven, you have come a long way in a short time. Your value to us is beyond reckoning. Your bravery in the face of that very dangerous northman is commendable. Only you and Brother Jaspar survived that encounter, proving that we had made the right decision in accepting you to join with us."

Marven was in his glory. "I was merely doing my duty, High Priest."

"Merely doing his duty, he says," chuckled Sarvin. "Brother Marven, you were chosen by Lord Lucivenus. He requires your aid. You now serve a higher purpose."

It took a moment before Marven even realized that a dagger was now buried hilt deep in his chest. He had first regarded the shocked expressions from the gathered host, wondering what had happened. Then he noticed it. Sarvin had driven a red-bladed dagger into his chest, the sister-blade to the one that Brother Jaspar also carried. He felt a strange sensation. The blade pulsed and felt as though it was drinking his insides, devouring his very life-force. He staggered back to lean against the altar and a moment later he was dead.

Shortly after his death, Marven's body lay across the altar and High Priest Sarvin held his heart aloft. "Brother Marven was indeed chosen by our Lord. His was the third heart required. Now only two remain!" he shouted.

The gathered members cheered in unison, having recovered from their initial shock at the unexpected spectacle they had just witnessed. They took up chanting the Demon Lord's name.

Sarvin drank it all in. Brother Marven's sacrifice had been a last-minute decision. But indeed, it was the right one. The third heart they needed had to be a corrupt heart. And who better than a city guard, sworn to protect and uphold justice, who had turned willingly to their order. Syrena had informed Sarvin that her spells were not even necessary in tempting the guard. He was the perfect candidate.

Nearby, the cruel and loyal Devi-Lynn smiled at the

High Priest, and led the others in chanting.

*   *   *   *

Evonne finished her morning feast in the crowded tavern and tossed a silver coin tip to the serving girl before leaving. With her belly full, she was ready to start the day. She and Vrawg could live comfortably off Weldrick's payment for quite some time, but she hated being idle. The bounty hunter got bored quickly. She needed to find them a new client and considered going back to see the Chief Magistrate's assistant. There were still a lot of thieves in this city and they were paid well to catch them. She considered the claim that Krommel was the leader of this vile Cult but found it hard to believe. How could a man with that position hide his true self from everyone else? It might have been possible, but Evonne did not think it likely.

The petite blonde glared dangerously at a group of teen boys who were whistling and giving her cat-calls as she passed them by. It was enough to silence them. Her reputation was quickly spreading throughout Stonewood. Now she needed to go have a talk with her partner, lest his soft heart ruin their reputation.

Evonne found Vrawg sitting in his usual spot, wrapped in a thick blanket, sitting on the ground in an alley across the street from the temple of the One True God. From this vantage point, the half-ogre bounty hunter could keep an eye on the temple's front entrance and watch for the Priestess Krestina.

Evonne kicked her partner who seemed not to notice her arrival, so intent he was on watching the temple. "Oy, you plan on eating anytime soon? You remember what food is? I am going to have to find a new partner if I am to eat all my meals alone now. Actually, wait, it is good to finally eat some meals in peace without the whole of the tavern staring at us 'cuz of you."

Vrawg just shrugged his massive shoulders.

"You stubborn oaf! Here then!" she tossed her partner two fresh bread rolls that she took with her from the tavern, then sat down next to him to regard the temple. "Vrawg, our employer is gone. Weldrick is never coming back. He will work in those mines until they deem it time to bring him back here to hang. We have no more obligation to watch that temple tart anymore. This was the easiest coin we have ever earned. But let's move on now. I will get us some more business. Let's go hunt us some more criminals. This babysitting is beneath us."

Still silence from her huge partner.

"How long do you plan on watching her?" Evonne shouted then. "You think because we were paid so much gold we have an obligation still? We have to put in the proper amount of time? Weldrick is dead to the world. That terminates our contract. We owe him nothing."

Vrawg turned to his partner and frowned.

"Oh lord. I thought you always said not to let things become personal? Remember? You used to say letting a job become personal was the downfall of a bounty hunter. That it was of the utmost importance to view everything as only business."

Vrawg pointed to a dark-robed figure leaning against a shop wall about a block's distance away. The person was also watching the temple.

"So. Big deal," the blonde bounty hunter said, not

understanding. "Looks like another priest. Maybe he came out for some fresh air from that stuffy temple."

Vrawg shook his head.

"Well, this city is full of folk leaning against walls. Look, I am going to find us some more work. Are you coming?"

Vrawg sat silently.

"Fine!" yelled Evonne in total frustration. "You know where you can find me," and she stormed off, muttering to herself about the stubbornness of her partner.

*   *   *   *

Krestina tossed her book onto her bed and sighed. She found it difficult to concentrate on her spells; her visions, or dreams as they may have been, kept creeping into her thoughts and distracting her. She got up from the floor and went over to the mirror and started brushing her long brown hair. Priestesses at the temple were not supposed to fuss over their appearances anymore. Looking beautiful was not supposed to matter, since God saw beauty in all his children. It came from inside. But Krestina still cared, more for herself than for anyone else. Looking good made her feel good, even though she had nobody else to look good for.

Her thoughts went back to Harcourt, and strangely, as well to Weldrick. For some reason, her mind linked the two men together, even though the priestess had seen them as opposites. Despite Weldrick being the leader of the Guild, she found herself feeling sorrow for the fate the man had been given. She had dreamt of the two thieves again the previous night. Danger always surrounded them both. But they were both gone, she thought. So what was the purpose of these dreams?

The beautiful priestess longed to go for a walk and clear her mind. But she had been too fearful these last few days to leave the temple. She had not even dared to venture to the orphanage which she usually did on a daily basis. That strange blonde woman was always about, and there was something else, something large, that lurked nearby the temple. It was just out of sight, but Krestina knew it was there. She remembered her vision of the temple under attack by the Cult and again wondered if the demon they worshipped was skulking about, watching their movements. First Priest Viktor, though, had told her not to worry, that an attack on the temple was highly unlikely. And it did make sense. There was nothing here in the temple that the Cult could not get much more easily elsewhere.

With nothing much else to do, Krestina walked over and laid down on her bed, picking up her book to continue her studies.

*   *   *   *

Captain Flannis returned to the south district guardhouse after doing a patrol. He was one of the few guards who could get away with walking the streets of the district alone. He was a large and fierce warrior with a quick temper. The captain did not make a habit of solo patrols but he had a lot on his mind and needed the time to himself. Captain Dornell had been his friend and mentor. It was too much of a coincidence that shortly after the man had told Flannis about his suspicions concerning the Chief Magistrate that he was set up and arrested. For set up he was. Flannis knew there was not a traitorous bone in Dornell's body. He was a model citizen and loved Stonewood.

Captain Flannis did not want to believe that Krommel was involved with the Demon Cult, but if Dornell believed it, then the claim must have merit. Flannis wondered what he could do about this. Dornell apparently rocked the boat and look where that got him. Someone should pay for what they did to the former captain, but Flannis was at a loss as to what he could do.

The guard captain found four of his men playing cards in their lunchroom.

"Anything exciting going on out there?" asked Willam, a bushy-bearded guard.

"Nothing at all," replied Flannis. "There has been an eerie calm in the south district of late. I don't like this."

"Well, I certainly like this," said Donny. "I don't need any excitement, thank you very much. I just hope severing the head of the Thieves Guild keeps things nice and quiet until I can put in for my transfer out of this district. No offence, Captain Flannis."

"None taken. I have no delusions that you all enjoy your assignments at this post. Nobody desires to stay down here for long. But I think things could become worse. The last few months, the Guild was focusing on a war with the Cult. Oddly, that was working in our favor. With their leader gone, there is going to be a power struggle within the Guild to see who takes over next. Things could get ugly in the streets. We all need to be prepared," Flannis warned.

"A power struggle can only benefit us," Willam said.

"Hopefully, the thieves will kill each other, make our jobs easier. And I suggest whoever takes over as their new leader, we don't befriend them like that traitor Dornell did."

Without even thinking about it, Captain Flannis struck Willam, breaking his nose and sending the guard sprawling to the floor. "Dornell is no traitor!" he shouted. "I will not have any of you speak of him as such. Ever! Or suffer my wrath!"

The three other guards stared up at their captain with astonishment. None dared say a word. Willam held his bloodied-nose and also said nothing.

Flannis walked back outside to calm himself down. He wondered how many of his own men he could even trust now.

CHAPTER 13

Harcourt punched the cell wall in anger. It hurt tremendously but he seemed not to notice. His only way of escape was now lost to him. The vile priest was now in possession of his treasured magical mask. The thief had lost track of time, being imprisoned as he was in the Cults' secret fortress.

On that night that Warden, the One-Handed Bandit, had given him the mask, he was told not to wear it for more than three days straight. Warden had not known why, only that he was told that. It seemed that the mask lost its magical ability after three full days and reverted back to its featureless self. It chose the least opportune time to cease working. Harcourt was not sure if that meant the mask would never work again, or perhaps it needed time to "rest." Either way, it was of no more use to him. The thief shuddered to think of what that priest could do if he managed to figure out how the mask worked.

Harcourt leaned against the back wall and slumped to the floor. The only positive to losing his mask was that he

escaped his torture session, for now anyway. So taken with
the mask, the evil priest left with all haste to examine it
and Harcourt was dragged back to his cell. He knew it was
only a matter of time though before he was brought back
again for questioning. He did not look forward to the feel
of that unholy blade again.

Now, Harcourt, for the first time, wondered if the
Cult could actually summon this demon of theirs. He had
always thought it some silly fairy tale. The idea of real
demons actually living in some abyss was laughable. But
now he was trapped in some mountain home by some
monsters he had heard Dornell refer to as wraggoth. The
Cult priest even used some magical spell that nearly melted
the thief's eyeballs.

So many things he believed were untrue turned out to
be true. If the demon was real, what did that mean for
Stonewood? Or more importantly to him, what did that
mean for Krestina? Was Fezzdin powerful enough to save
the city if it came to that? He hoped that the beautiful
priestess could find some way to escape. And if Jalanna
was still alive, he would have been worried sick about her
safety.

The thief rested his forehead on his knees and
succumbed to feelings of ultimate despair.

*　　*　　*　　*

Harcourt was dreaming of Krestina. Again he was
about to pull off his mask and tell her who he truly was.
Then his eyes flew open. He was back in his gloomy cell
and someone was fumbling with the lock on the door.
Perhaps it was time to resume his torture session, or have

his heart removed.

The door creaked open, but not all the way. In crawled someone wearing a very thick and dark cloak, the hood pulled over their head. Harcourt was about to ask who it was when the person held up a finger indicating for him to remain silent. The person pulled back the hood just enough to reveal their face. It was Captain Dornell!

"Keep quiet," the former captain whispered. "There are no guards presently in this hallway but they cannot be too far away."

Astonished, Harcourt scrambled over closer and whispered, "How did you escape?"

"I feigned an illness. The guard came in and I strangled him. Luckily, I did it silently enough. We have to find the man named Weldrick and get out of here. He must be in one of these other cells."

Harcourt suddenly remembered he no longer wore the mask, but Dornell did not recognize him for who he truly was. The man did believe him dead though, and the cell was dark.

"Weldrick is gone from this world. His life was taken by the pale priest," Harcourt replied.

"Pity," Dornell said. "Then the two of us must make our escape. I am a criminal now in Stonewood. We must find a way to get to the secret Guild headquarters. Only they can help us now. Are you a Guild member? Can you guide us?"

"Yes, I can, if we can find our way out of this maze of tunnels alive."

"I memorized our route in. I can retrace our steps back. We must be stealthy. Now, follow me."

Dornell crawled out of the cell and remained stooped

over as he made his way silently down the hallway.

"What about the other prisoners? We have to free them," Harcourt risked saying.

"No time for them, they are not our concern. Come, let's go."

Harcourt did not like the idea of leaving anyone behind to be tortured and killed by the Cult. Besides, if they needed to fight their way out, the more the merrier. The thief paused in front of one cell and peeked through the small barred window. He stood there curiously for a long moment until Dornell urged him again to follow and leave the prisoners behind.

"We can send help back here for them once we escape," Dornell said.

Harcourt silently caught up to Dornell and the pair crept further down the hall. Then, without warning, the thief leaped upon Dornell's back and slammed his head into the tunnel wall. Dornell grunted in pain and dropped to his knees, momentarily dazed. Harcourt slid his right arm around the captain's throat and held him tight in a choke-hold. He said the words "Argon Dol" aloud and Dornell's face shimmered and became featureless. The thief pulled off the mask and threw it aside revealing the tall pale priest.

Brother Jaspar gasped for air, then managed to pull out his red-bladed dagger and slice a deep gash in the thief's forearm. Harcourt let go and recoiled from the bite of the blade which had immediately began to "drink" the blood from his wound. Jaspar struggled to his feet and the thief kicked him out of reach.

The pale priest spun back to face the thief and whispered the words of a spell. An invisible force slammed into Harcourt's head, stunning him but he did not fall. Jaspar rushed in, attempting to bury the hungry dagger into his opponent's chest. Harcourt's legs were unsteady but his head cleared quickly. He side-stepped the attack and grabbed the priest's wrist. A simple twist and Jaspar dropped the weapon with a gasp, then the thief threw him hard against the wall. As Jaspar turned, Harcourt launched a crushing left-hook to the priest's jaw. Blood, and possibly a tooth, flew from the man's mouth. A follow-up right hand bloodied the priest's nose.

"Please! Free me!" shouted the prisoner that had shared the wagon-ride with Dornell and Weldrick.

The man had heard the commotion and now had his face pressed against the bars of his cell door window.

"Oh thank the gods, free me too!" shouted a second prisoner.

"Shut up all of you. If any guards come, none of us are leaving," Harcourt said just loud enough for them to hear but not too loud.

That gave Brother Jaspar enough of a distraction to shake the stars from his eyes and mumble the words to another spell. A blast of wind hit the thief, sending him flying several feet down the hall and landing hard on stone floor.

At that moment, an armored cultist turned into the hallway at the sounds of the struggle. He drew his sword and charged forward. Jaspar quickly scooped up the magical mask and ran in the direction of the other cultist. The unarmed thief spied the red-bladed dagger on the floor and sprinted with all possible speed for the weapon.

Jaspar passed the cultist and now had a buffer between himself and the thief. He kept running. More prisoners were now shouting and kicking the doors to their cells. *Curse them all,* Harcourt thought to himself. He dove for the dagger just as the cultist reached the same spot and swung his sword. Harcourt grabbed the dagger and rolled under and past the sword-strike to stand up behind the guard.

Harcourt missed the opportunity to strike at the guard's flank as a wave of emotion washed over him giving him a moment's pause. He was suddenly awash with a deep, burning hatred. He desired nothing else at that moment but to bury the red-bladed weapon into the body of the cultist. The urge to kill was overwhelming and the dagger seemed to hum within his grasp, hungering for the blood of the man before him.

The sword blade travelling towards his neck snapped him out of his trance. Harcourt ducked under and skipped back out of reach. Instinct told him to stay away from the swordsman, to wait for the proper opening. But before he even realized what he was doing the thief charged straight in. Luckily for him, that caught the cultist off-guard as he was not expecting the sudden and ferocious attack. Harcourt slipped past his guard and since the man wore a steel breast-plate he elected to aim for the throat. The blade slid right in with ease, like a hot knife through butter.

The cultist dropped his sword and grabbed the thief with both hands, choking on his own blood. Harcourt felt ecstatic, the dagger hummed and pulsed with a life of its own. It drank in the blood, the life-force of the cultist who died only moments later. Not a drop of blood found its way onto the thief, the blade absorbed it all.

Harcourt pulled the dagger free and admired the bright-red glow of the blade. Prisoners continued to shout

at him to open their cells, but instead Harcourt scanned
the hallway hoping for another enemy to kill. The ghostly-
pale priest was nowhere to be found, but he was rewarded
with the sight of two more Cult members turning into the
hallway, obviously alerted by the priest. These two carried
spears, the preferred tool for prodding prisoners around at
a distance. Harcourt charged.

"Pick up the sword, you fool!" shouted the chunky
bald prisoner.

The thief had no desire to pick up the dead Cult
member's sword. He craved the exhilarating feel of driving
his new dagger into flesh. The man on the left hurled his
spear at the charging thief. Harcourt dove into a
somersault, the spear passing harmlessly overhead. He was
up on his feet a moment later, continuing to close the
distance. The cultist on the right, still holding onto his
spear, confronted the thief with a worried look upon his
face. He was not expecting to find a crazed madman
running straight at him with Brother Jaspar's dagger.

He nervously thrust his spear at the thief's chest.
Harcourt knocked the weapon aside, but not before taking
a minor hit to the shoulder. The thief ignored the wound
and drove the dagger right through the cultist's chest plate
as if it was made of parchment. The man's eyes went wide
with horror as the blade "drank." And while it drank,
Harcourt felt his shoulder tingling, almost as if his wound
was healing. The lifeless body fell to the floor with the
dagger still lodged, taking it from the thief's hand.

Harcourt stood blinking, as though he had just
awakened from a dream. The remaining Cult member
turned and fled. He looked down at the dead man and
wondered what had come over himself. He needed to

escape, but he had never killed anyone before. The prisoners renewed their shouting which brought the thief out of his silent contemplations. He shook his head, ran over to the dead cultist and removed a ring of keys which hung from his belt. Time was not on his side. They needed to find a way out before every Cult member in this place was on top of them.

Harcourt fumbled with the first lock, then managed to release the loudest of the prisoners, the bald man who had shared their wagon. When the cell door swung open, the man shoved the thief aside and ran for the sword lying on the ground.

"There is no time for the others, we must run now!" he said.

Harcourt did not even comment as he moved to the next occupied cell. As the door swung open, the thief was greeted with a curious sight. Out walked a black-skinned man, taller than the thief and powerfully built. The curious thing about him was that he was still wearing a steel breast plate, his chest and back covered in armor. He also wore a steel mask that covered his face from his nose up. His black hair hung in braids to his shoulders. Why would he have been allowed to wear armor as a prisoner?

"I thank you," the strange man said with an accent Harcourt had not heard before. "We must be quick - the other man was right, we do not have much time."

The armored man grabbed the spear that had missed Harcourt and stood watch as the thief released three more prisoners. The thief finally found the cell he was searching for and peered in to find Dornell lying on the floor near the back of the cell. It was this sight that confirmed for him that the Dornell who had rescued him was not the real captain. He quickly unlocked the door and ran to kneel next to the guard captain.

"Captain Dornell, come on get up. We have to go."

Dornell opened his eyes and his face paled, taking on a look of utter despair. "Oh god, I am dead and I have gone to the Abyss."

"You are not dead. Not yet anyways. Come on get up," Harcourt said, trying to lift the captain up to his feet.

"Well, you are dead. So if I am seeing you, that makes me dead as well. I spent my entire life doing good and now I must spend my afterlife in the company of criminals. The gods hate me."

"I am very much alive but there is no time to discuss this now. We must get out of here," Harcourt urged as he managed to get the man to his feet.

Dornell shook his head in disbelief. "I always imagined the afterlife to be much different and I still feel much pain. This must be a punishment."

"We are being punished alright, I won't argue with you there. But I swear to you that we are both still in the land of the living. I would like to keep it that way so if you wouldn't mind," the thief said, shoving Dornell out the door. He turned to the bald prisoner, "Give Dornell that sword, he is three times the warrior you are."

"Over my dead body," the man replied.

Harcourt was about to answer him when Dornell held up his hands. He had been cut between each of his fingers. "I cannot hold a sword. And what do we have to fear if we are already dead?"

Harcourt ran to the last occupied cell and released a very tall man with long blonde hair, a northman. "My thanks," he said.

Shouts and booted feet could now be heard around the bend at the far end of the hallway where Jaspar and the last Cult member had fled. The group of escaped prisoners ran in the opposite direction, their only option. Harcourt took up the rear after retrieving the red-bladed dagger. The moment his hand gripped the hilt, his blood-lust returned. This time though, common sense prevailed and he followed the rest. As the thief turned the corner into the next hallway, shouts of alarm erupted from the one he left behind.

The prisoners made many twists and turns having no idea which direction they were heading. Harcourt heard a grunt of pain from up ahead, then passed a dead cultist who appeared to have been run through with a sword. A few moments later another dead body. Luck was with them thus far, having avoided encountering a large group. They were poorly armed and like Dornell, not all were fit to fight.

As they passed a side-passage that branched off from the main one, a cultist stepped out behind the thief, a spear in hand. Harcourt whirled around as he spotted the movement from the corner of his eye. As he raised his dagger, a spear whistled by his head to impale the Cult member, forcing him to the ground. The black-skinned man gave him a nod, then retrieved the spear before catching up with the others.

Harcourt found the group stopped and arguing as they came to a split in the passage. One tunnel led upwards and the other downwards.

"We are inside a mountain, we need to go down to get to ground-level," argued the mouthy bald man.

"We do not know how deep we are into this

mountain. We might already be underground," reasoned the blonde northman.

Harcourt turned to Dornell, knowing the man to be wise and would value his opinion. The former captain just shrugged his shoulders. "We are all in the abyss, there can be no escape."

Harcourt would reason with him later. Right now was not the time. "I go up," he said.

Harcourt had never been inside a mountain before so everything felt like it was underground. Going upwards seemed like the logical choice. Their time for discussion though was now at an end, as one of the unarmed prisoners fell to his knees, choking from a crossbow bolt now lodged in his throat. A large group of screaming cultists had just rounded a corner and whooped with excitement at the sight of the escaped prisoners.

"RUN!" Harcourt shouted, sprinting through the passage leading upwards.

The northman and the strange armored warrior followed quickly behind, as did Dornell even though he did not quite understand why they should run if they were already dead. He had witnessed Harcourt's death at the hands of that traitorous guard Zorfal. He had not imagined that. He even attended the thief's funeral. So he reasoned that he himself must have been killed by the tall pale priest. But why he was being punished in this hell, he could not fathom. He had led a clean life always. Why would the gods have forsaken him? Or was this possibly a dream and he was still lying on the floor of his cell? Whichever it was, he still ran and kept up with the others.

The two unarmed prisoners, both pale and skeletal, ran downwards thinking that the best choice. In a split-second decision, the chunky bald prisoner with the sword opted to follow the others upwards, preferring his chances with those who appeared to be capable warriors.

On they ran, twisting and turning through dimly-lit tunnels which were beginning to grow tighter. Sounds of pursuit could still be heard from behind. They reached another fork in the tunnel. To their left was a narrow and very dark passage, no longer smoothed over; it was left in its natural state. Ahead, the tunnel opened up into a very large cavern. Harcourt and the northman crept up to the opening to cautiously peer into the cavern and found that they were elevated about forty-feet from the cavern floor. There, a narrow ledge led downwards to the floor but the cavern was occupied by what appeared to be thousands of armored wraggoth, an army of the albino creatures.

"Looks as though our decision is made for us. It's the dark tunnel then," the blonde northman whispered.

Harcourt nodded and sprinted back to the others. He felt an urge to descend into the cavern and allow his newly-acquired dagger to drink the blood of the beasts, but better judgment won over. Considering the dagger though had given him an idea. The blade still glowed with a red radiance from its recent kills. He held the blade before him and it did somewhat illuminate the dark passage, enough anyway to see where he was going. In he went.

"I don't like this idea," the bald man with the sword commented. "That passage is too narrow - we cannot fight. We do not know where it goes. If we get trapped in there, it is over for us."

Ignoring him, the others disappeared into the darkness. The sound of booted feet drawing nearer helped him make up his mind and he followed reluctantly. The tunnel grew extremely narrow at points, causing them to turn sideways; to squeeze their way through. They reached another point where they were forced to hang-drop from a ledge, to another tunnel ten feet below. These passageways would have been in pitch darkness were it not for the glow from the thief's dagger. They stopped for a brief moment to catch their breath, until the voices of the pursuing cultists spurred them on once again. It would not have been difficult to figure out which way the escaped prisoners had gone.

Several more twists and tight-squeezes led them to a larger cave. They were hit with a heavenly blast of fresh air but their hearts sank as they realized the cave had no apparent exit. It was a dead-end. Or was it?

"Look there," the black-skinned warrior shouted as he spotted an opening roughly ten feet up the cave wall.

All eyes followed his outstretched arm to the opening. It did indeed lead somewhere outside the mountain but it was night-time, which made the exit hard to notice at first. It, too, looked like a tight-squeeze but not impossible; reaching it was the most pressing matter. Harcourt ran over beneath the opening, scanning for a way up, but the angle of the wall would not allow him to climb it.

Thinking quickly, the northman positioned himself under the opening. "On my shoulders, we can reach it."

"What of you then?" Harcourt asked, concerned.

"Last man pulls me up," he answered.

The thief nodded and patted the man on his broad muscular back. Harcourt scrambled up to stand on the tall man's shoulders and could now reach the lip of the opening. With all his strength, he hauled himself up and through the opening. He found himself looking downwards from the side of this particular mountain. Wind howled all about him and the moon just barely peeked through the dark clouds of the night. He would have to slide several feet down a steep slope to the next closest ledge from which to stand on. It looked like a long and dangerous trek to the bottom, but not impossible if they took care.

"Hurry, we can do this. I believe we can get down from here," he shouted below, trying to hear himself over the rushing wind.

Dornell was up next, requiring Harcourt's help because of his wounded hands. As the thief pulled up the former guard captain, Dornell appeared confused.

"This wind feels real enough," Dornell commented. "This cannot be a dream. The wind, the pain, all too vivid."

"You are not dreaming, my old friend, I swear it. I have much to tell you but let's get down the mountain first," Harcourt replied.

Dornell and Harcourt slid down the rocky slope to the next safe ledge to make room for the black-skinned warrior to haul himself up through the opening. He then slid down to make room for the chunky bald prisoner, who struggled the most to pull himself up, an effort that left him thoroughly winded.

"Lean over and lower your hand. Have them hold your legs, I can jump," the northman shouted up, desperately glancing behind at the sounds of cultists drawering nearer.

The bald man leaned over and extended his arm, but then quickly retracted it. Their escape through the tunnels and his little climb here had been exhausting. He figured he needed all the strength he had left to get down the side of the mountain. Pulling the northman up would just be too taxing.

"What are you doing??" shouted the northman.

The other man just shrugged.

"You coward! Throw me the sword then, so that I can make a proper stand," the tall warrior pleaded.

The bald prisoner thought on that, but only for the briefest of moments. They were not out of danger yet and figured he would need this sword still. "Nah, I think I will hang onto this."

He slid down the slope to join the others and despite the howling wind, he thought he could hear the northman bellowing curses. In fact, he was sure of it.

"What of the northman? Where is he?" Harcourt asked over the sound of the wind.

The bald man shook his head and feigned a very distressed look. "The cave flooded with men. Alas, he was overwhelmed."

Harcourt was saddened by the news. He fought back the urge to climb to the opening to see for himself; he knew there was nothing left he could do. The man had sacrificed himself to save the others so they should not let that sacrifice go to waste. The thief turned his attention to the rocky slope looking for the best way to get down. This was not going to be easy.

CHAPTER 14

Harcourt tossed some more wood into the fire and took a seat as near as he could to ward off the chill night air. The going had been slow. The four escaped prisoners had spent an entire day working their way down the side of the mountain and it was now well into the following night when they reached the bottom. They were in desperate need of rest and warmth, for the wind carried a chilling bite in this mountainous region.

Small trees sparsely dotted the base of the mountain and the men determined that it would be safe enough to risk a fire. There were no visible trails or cave entrances to be found and there had been no sounds of pursuit.

"We do not even know the name of the northman, who gave his life so that we could escape," the black-skinned warrior said, breaking the silence. "For I would like to whisper it to my gods and ask that he has safe passage to the underworld."

"And what is your name, my friend? I am Harcourt,"

asked the thief.

"My name is Na'Jala. And I thank you, Harcourt, for freeing me from my cell. I had prayed to my gods for so long but I thought them ignoring me. I truly believed this was the end of my life's journey," the man said in reply.

"It would appear we have some more journeying still left to us. My silent friend over here is Captain Dornell," the thief said, motioning to the former captain who had remained silent and stared intensely at the thief. Harcourt turned to the bald man, "And you are?"

"Garth," was all he said in return.

"Tell me, Na'Jala, why were you allowed to keep your armor while in your cell, when we have all been stripped of our belongings?" Harcourt inquired.

"Mine cannot be removed," he answered. All three men turned to regard the mysterious man with quizzical expressions, so he continued. "I was a gladiator in the great southern port city of Gladenfar. My owner sought an advantage for his gladiators over others. Many men thrown into the arena were unfamiliar with different forms of armor. It weighed them down, made them clumsy in battle. My owner came up with the idea to graft armor to the skin of men, so that it would become like skin. If you survived the process, and many did not, in time the armor became part of your body. You would not even know it was there. It seemed to work. We did become much faster than our opponents."

"That must have hurt," Garth commented.

"Beyond imagining," Na'Jala said with a distant look, as if remembering that nightmarish day.

"You must have been a great warrior then, where you are from," Harcourt said.

That brought forth a chuckle from Na'Jala. "We had no need for warriors on my island, for we did not make war. I was a fisherman, like my father before me, and one of my people's best."

"An island savage," Garth said quietly, but loud enough for all to hear.

Na'Jala did not appear angry but turned to the man. "It is funny how my people are referred to as savages, and yet we do not take slaves and throw them into an arena to fight to the death like the so-called civilized people of the world. My people are peaceful. I was fishing one morning when I was taken by pirates. Taken from my wife and two children. I was sold to a man in Gladenfar who made me a gladiator. He gave me my armor-skin and mask, and made me kill men to entertain crowds of civilized people. I became a warrior to survive, to one day return to my family on my island. After eight years in Gladenfar, I was sent by my owner to guard a shipment of goods to another city in the north when our caravan was attacked and overwhelmed. I was brought to this mountain and spent the last two months forced to help with the forging of weapons and armor for that monstrous army. I suppose I have been spared the ritualistic death by that Cult because my heart is not accessible," he said tapping his armored chest. "Other prisoners have not been so lucky."

Harcourt felt saddened by the man's tale. He knew the feeling of losing your loved ones, never to see them again. "We should get some rest, we probably should not linger long near this mountain," he suggested.

Dornell stood then and approached the thief. "We should have a word first. Privately."

His tone told the thief that this was not open for

debate, so Harcourt followed Dornell away from their makeshift camp, out of earshot of the others. When satisfied they were far enough away, Dornell whirled on the thief. "I watched you die, killed by Zorfal in that warehouse."

"No, you only thought that is what you saw," the thief responded.

"It is not what I think, it is what I know. I watched the two of you kill each other from that damned crate you locked me in. I attended your bloody funeral! If you are no ghost, and we are not both dead, then explain how it is that you stand before me," Dornell demanded.

Harcourt let out a very long sigh. This was not going to be simple. "You only thought that was me battling Zorfal in that warehouse. But it was....an illusion. It was someone else made to appear as me." Dornell shook his head and was about to reply when Harcourt cut him off and continued. "It was really Trascar, the leader of the Thieves Guild, that you watched fight Zorfal. Remember that elixir that Fezzdin gave me to alter my appearance? Well, I had come across a magical mask, one that did pretty much the same thing, only better. I became Weldrick with that mask. That is how I truly infiltrated the Guild. When I discovered that Trascar and Zorfal were the ones behind Jalanna's death, I manipulated them both into battling each other, after giving you the confession you needed to hear. I had to be sure that my name got cleared before having them kill each other. A deserved end to both."

Dornell stood silent for a moment, digesting the tale. "You are going to tell me you have a magical mask? Really? You expect me to believe that?"

"I had a magical mask, I have it no longer. That cursed priest took it from me. And yes, I expect you to believe it. How do you think it is that Weldrick accompanied you here as a prisoner, and yet it is me that is here with you now? I have been Weldrick all along, since my death."

The thief then described all the alleyway meetings the two of them shared while he posed as the red-headed man with a lisp. "I was using the Guild to battle the Cult. I wanted to be rid of that Cult. And I was giving you the names of the worst criminals inside the Guild, the ones who could not change their wicked ways. I was working on your side."

Dornell found it difficult to argue the thief's claims. There must have indeed been a magical mask. He knew magic existed in the world, Fezzdin was proof of that. But one thing left him puzzled. "Why did you not just tell me this before? I thought we had become friends?"

"We were friends. But once Trascar and Zorfal were dead, that part of my life was over. I did not have Jalanna so I did not have a life to return to. I decided to start anew. My plan was to leave Stonewood and start fresh someplace else. But then an interesting twist of fate led me to the position of Guild leader. So I decided to lead the Guild against the Cult and eliminate them."

"Well, Krommel fixed us both," Dornell said.

"Not yet, he hasn't," Harcourt answered. "We yet still draw breath. Perhaps we can make it back to Stonewood and still do something about him. We have to try at least."

Dornell silently nodded. Harcourt put his arm around his shoulder, "Come, Captain Dornell. Let us get some rest so that we might return to Stonewood."

"I am a captain no longer, I am just Dornell now."

"Nonsense," Harcourt replied. "You will always be Captain Dornell. Krommel can never strip that from you."

*　　*　　*　　*

Harcourt sat with his back against an uncomfortable rock, close enough to the fire to still keep the chill night air at bay. He had volunteered to keep first watch while the others tried their best to shut their eyes and get some rest. As the flames burned low, the thief found himself repeatedly touching and admiring the red-bladed dagger.

He considered all the many times in his life that he had been in fights and never once had he ever killed anyone. He had always been proud of that fact. He considered himself a thief, not a thug or assassin. Strangely, though, he found he enjoyed the feeling. Surely those Cult members deserved no less and what a thrill it was to end their miserable lives. He found himself oddly disappointed that there appeared to be no further pursuit. Secretly he had been hoping for more cultists to try and stand in their way.

He marveled at the craftsmanship of the weapon. The red glow had faded but how he wished to see its radiance yet again. The blade was sharper than any he had owned before; he recalled how it sliced through the man's armor as though it had been nothing but paper. It felt perfect within his grasp, as if it had been tailor-made just for him.

Harcourt almost thought he could hear the dagger whisper to him. Was it a whisper? He shook the silly notion from his head and tried to turn his thoughts back to Stonewood, and to Krestina. He hoped that she was safe and that the bounty hunters he had paid would still watch over her.

*   *   *   *

As the first rays of sunlight began to peek over the mountain range, the four men considered their options.

"I can only assume that these are the Black Peak mountains," Dornell said, scanning their surroundings. "Before our lovely hosts covered the wagons I noticed we were headed in this direction. But by the look of things we are now on the opposite side of those mountains, and as far as I know, this region is impassable."

Harcourt turned to regard Na'Jala and Garth, but both shrugged, neither familiar with this part of the world. "So what are you saying? We will have to go back through the same mountain? Is that the only way? Can we not go around? Surely they do not stretch on to the edge of the world," Harcourt inquired.

"No," Dornell answered. "They do not stretch on forever but it would be many days for us to go around and many more days again to get back to the road. We have no food and no water."

"Back to what road? Where is it that you plan to go?" asked Garth.

"Stonewood, of course," Harcourt said matter-of-factly.

"Stonewood??" Garth could not believe what he was hearing. "We are fugitives there! We will be arrested on sight and hung this time so we cannot escape! You both are mad. We need to head south and away from the long reach of Stonewood."

"Go where you like, we make for Stonewood," Harcourt responded.

"Madness!" Garth continued. "Utter madness! We cannot split up. We have to stay together to survive. We need to go south!" He then turned to Na'Jala. "Your family is in the south! You are free now. Do you not wish to get home?"

Na'Jala thought on that, then answered. "For me to get home I need passage on a ship. To get passage on a ship, I need coin. Coins I do not have. For now, I follow Harcourt and Dornell, until such time as I am able to get home."

Harcourt nodded. "If you come to Stonewood with us and help us right some wrongs, you will have those coins."

Garth opened his mouth in protest then stormed off to go sit on a rock. Harcourt was hoping the man would press the matter further as he was beginning to get a strong urge to silence him with his new dagger.

"We are going to have a problem, of course, if we can reach the city," Dornell surmised. "I am a fugitive and you are no longer Weldrick, the leader of the Thieves Guild. You are a man believed dead. Krommel knows your face well and it could be safe to assume that his agents also know your face. We can also assume that the priest here has already sent word of our escape. They will be looking for us and possibly even waiting for us to attempt a return. We will never get through the city's gates."

"If you can get us back to the city I can get us into the city," the thief promised.

"How?"

"Let's just get there first. That seems to be our

biggest problem right now. Are there no trails at all between these mountains?"

"Well….," Dornell's face took on a troubled expression. "There is a fortress that blocks off a valley in this region, Morgaldrun. It was manned a very long time ago by Stonewood troops to keep barbarian hordes away. They abandoned it long ago."

"That's perfect then," Harcourt said, feeling a little better. "We can find this fortress and cut through the mountains."

Dornell did not share his enthusiasm. "It was abandoned by Stonewood, but it is said that it does not lie empty. The Lich Lord of Morgaldrun is said to occupy the fortress now."

Harcourt looked puzzled. "Lich Lord? What is a lich? It sounds like some kind of bug."

"It is no bug. A lich is said to be an undead wizard of terrible power, wizards so powerful they have managed to find a way to exist long after death," Dornell replied in a serious tone.

Harcourt was about to laugh at that but then remembered that much had changed about the world he lived in. There was magic. There were monsters in the form of these wraggoth. So too then might there be some undead wizard. It was a little far-fetched, but then so was everything else. "Well, we could bargain with him to let us through. Surely he could be reasoned with."

"I am not so sure about that. His name is spoken in fear and nobody in their right mind ventures anywhere near the haunted fortress. I cannot say for sure if he truly exists but many times, rumors have some foundation. It is my opinion that we take our chances going around the mountains and hope that we can find a water source and some food. I just hope that we are not too late. That priest told me this army of wraggoth will be moving on Stonewood shortly. It would be best if we could beat them there and give warning," Dornell said.

"Then our minds are made for us," Harcourt replied. "We cannot waste time. We need to find this fortress and take our chances with this shortcut. Na'Jala?"

Na'Jala nodded. "I am with you both wherever that path follows. You have been nothing but good luck for me so far."

Harcourt wanted to mention that good luck was not something he was overly familiar with, but remained silent. He was happy that the former gladiator intended to follow them. He was definitely handy in a fight and Harcourt foresaw many to come before this was all over. Garth could follow them or not, Harcourt did not care which.

"Do you have any idea where this fortress might be?" the thief asked.

Dornell looked up at the position of the sun, then around at the mountains that surrounded them. "That way would be my guess," he pointed in the direction he believed to be correct, though he was not sure if he wanted to be right.

CHAPTER 15

King Stonewood jolted awake as his two sons entered his private chambers. The King had been sitting in his favorite armchair, enjoying the view of his city from a window when he had drifted off to sleep. Prince Orval and his younger brother, Prince Denniz, marched over to stand before their father, expressions of worry upon their faces.

"Speak, my sons," the King said. "What troubles you so and makes your faces long?"

Orval, the eldest brother, spoke up. "Nobody has seen or heard from Fezzdin in about a week."

"He is a wizard and not the most social of people on the best of days," the King said matter-of-factly.

"I have knocked upon his door almost every day and there has been no answer at all," Denniz added.

"Perhaps he is away from the city. Fezzdin often combs the countryside for rare ingredients for his wizardly projects. Or perhaps he is working on something and does not wish to be disturbed," the King reasoned.

"If he simply did not wish to be disturbed, we would

know. Fezzdin, I feel, thoroughly enjoys berating people who bother him at inopportune times," replied Denniz.

Of all the members of the inner court, Prince Denniz had the most dealings with the royal magician. The younger prince was eighteen years old and not very big, or very strong. He stood four inches shorter than six-foot and was rather skinny. The dirty-blonde haired prince had never been good at fighting, so was groomed for a more scholarly career where his brains would be put to better use. He studied to be a magistrate and it was thought that he would one day replace Chief Magistrate Krommel when he eventually retired.

Secretly though, the young prince longed to be a wizard. Ever since he was a child, he marveled over the wondrous things that Fezzdin could do and wished he could one day do those same things. He made it a point to visit the wizard on a weekly basis and hound the old man to teach him some magic. His constant badgering had paid off and slowly, very slowly, Fezzdin had begun to teach the young prince a few minor things. Denniz had felt that Fezzdin might have actually enjoyed his visits; as his father had stated, the wizard was generally not a very social individual. So the sudden disappearance of the royal magician troubled the prince.

Sensing how distraught his youngest son was, King Stonewood stood up and stretched his weary limbs. "Alright then, I will have the castle staff alerted to this and find out where our mysterious friend has gone."

*　*　*　*

High Priest Sarvin was enjoying a rare moment of relaxation. He was stretched out in his bed with an ancient tome resting on his chest, but he was doing more daydreaming than reading. Between his public work as the Chief Magistrate and being the secret leader of the Cult, it was not often he found some quiet time to himself. He did not realize how tired he felt until he lay down. Perhaps it was time for another sip of his elixir, which would reverse his aging process by a few years and give him some renewed and much-needed energy, energy he would be needing in the weeks to come. He had to be careful not to drink too much at a time; he did not want a much-younger appearance to draw the curiosity of others.

A shuffling sound from down the hall told him his quiet time had ended. He donned his black robe and joined his faithful assistant in his office.

"Have you considered our next move? We require the heart of a royal, someone from the King's bloodline," asked Devi-Lynn.

"I have given it much thought," Sarvin replied. "I believe Prince Orval to be the best target."

"Orval? But he is the most capable and dangerous of the family, aside from the King himself."

"Precisely why we should eliminate him before the King's birthday ceremony," the High Priest explained.

Devi could not understand the rationale. "Surely a cousin would be much less missed and more easily acquired. Royal blood is all that matters. The heir to the throne is too ambitious a goal, I feel. An unnecessary risk."

"On the contrary, I feel it is a necessary risk," Sarvin said. "When we take our last heart during the King's birthday, we will have a lot to deal with already. The elder prince is a capable warrior by all accounts so I would prefer not to have to deal with him along with the rest of the King's guard that evening. We have already removed Fezzdin from the equation, now I would have Prince Orval also removed. As well, his heart would be the best to use for our ritual."

"The grief will be too much for the King, he may just cancel the celebration and ruin our plans," reasoned the priestess.

"I do not believe that will happen. The King's birthday celebration is more of a party for the people than it is for the King himself. People spend the entire year since the last one, preparing for this evening. The King will be grieving, but the party will go on."

"And who will you trust with this task? Brother Jaspar is still overseeing our army of wraggoth and interrogating our prisoners," Devi wondered.

"I will deal with the upstart prince myself," Sarvin declared confidently.

"You? We cannot risk that. Let me deal with the prince instead. If anything were to happen to you…."

"You think that young pup is any threat to me?" the High Priest said with a raised voice.

"No, no, not at all. My apologies. I only meant there is a risk of witnesses. The prince is almost never alone. His personal guards shadow him everywhere. There is also his annoying younger brother."

"Leave it to me."

The High Priest was about to dismiss his assistant when there came a knock at his office door. "Chief Magistrate? Are you around? It's Prince Denniz. I would like a moment of your time."

Sarvin and Devi exchanged quizzical glances, then the High Priest motioned for her to answer the door while he went to change robes.

"Why, Prince Denniz, what brings you here?" the priestess asked, using her sweetest voice as she opened the door.

The young prince was flanked by two personal guards. "I only wish to speak briefly with the Chief Magistrate about some troubling news. Is he about?"

"Yes, he is. He was about to retire for the evening. Come in, he will be here shortly."

Prince Denniz instructed his guards to remain in the hallway and then entered the office; Devi-Lynn closed the door behind him and watched the prince curiously.

"Troubling news, you say?" she asked.

"Yes. Concerning Fezzdin," he answered.

"What has my old friend done now?" Sarvin said, returning to the office and now wore the robes of the Chief Magistrate. "Has he burned down another laboratory? Accidently turned someone into a frog?"

Denniz gave a short bow of respect. "Chief Magistrate Krommel. No it is nothing like that. Fezzdin has gone missing."

"Missing? That's absurd. How could that man go missing? Locked in his tower, no doubt. Working on some secret project," Krommel replied, waving off the silly notion.

"That's what most believe, only I have been to his tower for several days straight. There is nobody home. I meet with Fezzdin at least once a week for some studies. It is not like him not to at least allow me in."

"Well, what brings you here, young man?" asked Krommel, who was genuinely interested in the answer.

"I have been inquiring all over the castle. Fezzdin was

last seen on this floor, apparently coming to speak with you. Did you speak with him? Perhaps he may have given you some clue to his whereabouts."

The Chief Magistrate relaxed. It appeared the prince was sincere in his questioning and suspected nothing out of the ordinary. Krommel rubbed his chin in thought, as if trying to recall a conversation with the wizard.

"Hmmm. Well, yes, Fezzdin did mention he was going over to Fort Barron," Krommel lied, referring to the ruins of an old outpost about four hours south of the city. The old fortress was rumored to be haunted and generally avoided. "Said he was looking for something. Some old records, I believe."

Prince Denniz looked distressed. "Something must have happened to him there."

"Nonsense. What could have happened to a wizard as powerful as Fezzdin?" Krommel flashed his assistant a knowing smile. "More likely, he is still there. The tunnels of that old fortress extend far underground. He is probably camped there while he continues his search for whatever it was he was looking for. You know Fezzdin, always lost in his own little world."

The prince nodded his agreement to that last statement. "I shall go there and look for him."

"Your father would never allow that. Those haunted ruins are no place for a young prince. And the area is full of wolves."

"Well, I would not tell him then. I do not fear any spook or wolf. I will take two of my men with me."

"Three men leaving the city, one prince and two guards, would draw attention and your father would be alerted. Also you forget, the city is surrounded still by

Thelvius's mercenary army. They are charged with catching those fleeing the city."

"Are you not in command of that army?" Denniz asked. "I could go alone then. You could get me passage through without questions asked."

"Alone? As I said, those ruins are no place for a young prince. It is too dangerous."

"I have been there before and I am not afraid. Besides, I would leave first thing in the morning and be back long before nightfall."

Krommel sighed. "It seems I cannot dissuade you from this course." Denniz stood, arms crossed in defiance. "Alright, I will aid you. Fezzdin is an old friend and I would like to know he is safe. But you must promise me you will not tell anyone of this plan. I would not want your father angry at me for helping."

"Not a word. This is between us three here," the prince replied.

"Good. Leave at first light, and be well disguised. Thelvius's men will allow you through. But promise me one other thing. Leave a note behind in case anyone is looking for you. Maybe mention a last-minute decision to visit Bluebarrow. Best not to mention the ruins to alarm anyone."

"A fine idea. Thank you, Chief Magistrate, for your help. It is greatly appreciated," said Denniz, and with that, the young prince left.

After the door closed behind him and the footsteps grew faint, Krommel turned to Devi and smiled. "We have a change of plans."

*   *   *   *

Zenod casually strolled through the crowded taproom of the Lonely Traveller Inn and nodded to a flat-nosed thug standing next to the door leading to the cellar. The thug opened the door and allowed the master thief entry as he had a hundred times before. Zenod required no escort and showed himself down the stairs. He nodded to one more large thug whose name he had forgotten and then joined Serdic in the older thief's private office.

"Randar is gathering his goons around," the master thief said, sitting himself down in a chair opposite Serdic. "He means to take over the Guild."

Serdic looked up from the inn's ledgers. "And you still think I should be the one to oppose him?"

"Yes! You said yourself he was a dim-witted thug. I fear for the future of the Guild with him as the lead. You are the only member with men enough to stand against him."

Serdic sat in silence for a moment before speaking again. "The Guild's future is already in jeopardy. How did the city know that Weldrick was our leader? And now that he is in custody, what information have they gotten out of him?"

"I do not believe that Weldrick would talk," Zenod reasoned.

"Torture can turn the hardest man into a bubbling mess. If they knew Weldrick was our leader, what do they know about the rest of us? And if he was right, and Krommel is the leader of the Cult, then we cannot win this battle against them. We have the Cult and the city bent on our absolute destruction."

"So? What are you saying?"

Serdic let out a long sigh. "Perhaps my friend, it is time we leave the Guild. Let Randar have it if he wants. I feel it will not be long before it collapses anyway. I have the most successful inn and tavern in the city. I am more than happy to just focus on my own legit business. And you, Zenod, you must have a small fortune stashed away. Disappear into the night, retire and enjoy your wealth."

"You would so easily walk away from the organization we have dedicated our lives to? I do not wish to retire yet. I enjoy being a thief."

"Then go south. Find a new city to terrorize with your master thievery. Or stay here and stay out of sight."

Zenod shook his head in disbelief. "And you think Randar will just let us walk away like that? Or continue to operate in what he will deem *his* city?"

"I am not looking for Randar's permission to do anything. As you said, I have enough men to oppose him. So he should see it as a wise decision to leave me be. Work here with me then, if you like, you will be under my protection," the older thief offered.

"Doing what? Pouring drinks? Guarding a door? Come on, you know that is not for me."

"Then take my advice and go south. The weather is much nicer there. I am sure there are guilds operating in the southern cities, they would be most pleased to have a member of your skill. Or stay here and take orders from a thug."

"What about the idea of a ruling council you mentioned before? I think most members would prefer that over Randar," the weasely thief asked.

"Well, as your news suggests, it does not look as though Randar is preparing for a civilized debate. He will probably announce his leadership and dare anyone to oppose him."

The pair sat in silence again when a knock at the door disturbed their contemplations. Serdic bade the man enter.

"Pardon the intrusion sir, but this message just arrived for you," said the tall man in the chain mail vest as he handed Serdic a sealed envelope.

The older thief opened the envelope and read over the message contained within, then looked up at the master thief seated across from him. "Randar is calling a meeting, in two days' time."

CHAPTER 16

Garth trudged along the rocky slope, bringing up the rear of their group. He was not guarding their rear out of any sense of duty, he was just finding it hard to keep up. Na'Jala was scouting so far ahead Garth could no longer see the man. The former gladiator was not familiar with mountainous terrain but was the only real hunter of the group, with sharp eyes and a keen sense of hearing. The rogue Harcourt was almost out of view and Dornell was somewhere in between.

They had thought it best to travel by day. It made them easy targets for searching eyes but the footing here was treacherous and they chose not to take that risk. They believed they were heading in the direction of the old fortress of Morgaldrun, though Dornell had never actually seen the place. Garth did not believe in the tale of an undead wizard, so he was looking forward to finding shelter in this fortress and then to better assess their future options.

The sound of falling rock had Garth whirling around

with sword raised. He scanned the mountainside for any clues of what loosened the rocks but saw none. Crevices and caves littered these mountains, making for many hiding places.

"What was it?" asked Dornell, who now stood beside Garth also scanning for trouble.

"Nothing I can see. A mountain goat, most likely."

"Mountain goats do not lose their footing or make noise," deduced the former captain.

Just as they turned to continue their journey, an inhuman shriek caused both to spin back around. In the distance, three wraggoth had appeared and howled with delight at the sight of the two men. These wraggoth were neither armed nor armored like those within the cultists' base, but that did not make them any less dangerous. They still possessed razor-sharp claws and teeth, and Garth was the only man with a sword. Dornell still could not even hold a weapon in his damaged hands.

Panic overtook Garth. He thought the gods cruel to allow him to escape his mountain prison only to be eaten by these savage beasts. So he did the only thing he thought would help him escape; he tripped Dornell. The former captain crashed to the hard ground and Garth took off running. He hoped that Dornell would be enough of a meal that the wraggoth would not give chase.

"Coward! You have the sword," Dornell shouted, but Garth kept running.

Dornell found his feet and managed to pick up a fist-sized rock. Ignoring the pain in his hand, he hurled it with all his strength at the nearest wraggoth. It struck the beast in the face and it stumbled back with a howl. The second of the three leaped with great agility and tackled Dornell back to the ground.

Momentarily winded, Dornell still found the strength to hold the wraggoth's snapping jaws at arm's length. The former captain was unaccustomed to fighting without armor and he was rudely reminded of that fact as claws dug deep into his side.

"Mannnnnnnn flesssssh," hissed the wraggoth as drool dropped from his lower lip onto the face of his pinned victim.

Dornell grabbed a handful of the rag this beast wore as a shirt and attempted to yank him off but his wounded hands would not allow him a grip strong enough. The former captain howled as another of the wraggoth sunk its teeth into his left shin. Of all the manner of deaths he could have met in his life, being eaten alive by wraggoth had never been one that Dornell thought he would meet.

The wraggoth that Dornell had injured with the rock now loomed over his head with a wicked grin. But as quickly as he appeared, he fell away as a spear suddenly protruded from his chest. He fell back and died without a sound. The albino creature perched upon Dornell's chest howled with rage and rose to his feet. He moved quickly, thinking to take down the large but now unarmed black-skinned warrior, but was intercepted by Harcourt who slammed him hard with his shoulder and followed the wraggoth to the ground.

Harcourt recovered first and rolled on top of the creature, burying his thirsty dagger into the wraggoth's gut. The blade pulsed and even hummed softly as the wraggoth's pupiless eyes went wide with horror. Harcourt felt ecstatic as the weapon drank the life from the beast. The thief hungrily glanced to the third wraggoth with the hopes of also stealing its life, but the fight had left the last of the three and it turned and fled with all haste. Harcourt thought to give chase but the wraggoth moved too quickly on the rocky terrain.

Dornell rose, shakily, as he bled from two fresh wounds. "My thanks," he said to his two saviors. "That would have been the end of me."

Na'Jala nodded, then frowned when his spear snapped in half as he attempted to remove it from the dead wraggoth. "Cheap weapons," he commented.

"Coward!" Dornell roared as Garth appeared, having decided it was now safe to do so. He advanced on the bald man. "You tripped me and left me to die!"

Garth raised his sword in defense. "Nonsense! I merely tripped over you in my haste. We could not stand and fight, three on two and you were unable to fight."

"You had the only sword and you just left me to be eaten!"

"I could not fight all three myself and I am sorry if this upsets you, but I am not dying for you," Garth stated.

"Give Na'Jala the sword," Harcourt demanded of the man.

"Oh, I think not," Garth replied. "I am not wandering this region unarmed. I took this sword, it's mine."

"It is useless in your hands. Na'Jala's weapon is broken so I would see that sword in his capable hands since Captain Dornell cannot yet wield it."

"No," was Garth's answer.

"I was hoping you would say that," Harcourt said advancing, his hungry dagger blade glowing red.

Garth backed up in a defensive stance but then

regarded that glowing blade. He remembered well the feel of its bite in the hands of that evil pale priest during his questioning session. Garth was one of those men who was brave in numbers, but never alone. Knowing what this man was capable of and not wishing to feel that blade again, he wisely threw the sword to the ground.

"Take it, then," he spat with disgust and walked away.

Na'Jala scooped up the sword. Having spent so many years as a gladiator, he was well versed in nearly every weapon known. He was best with the sword. The quality of this particular blade was not great, but he did feel more comfortable having it in his hands. He looked over and noticed a disappointed expression on Harcourt's face. He appeared upset that the other man gave up the weapon without a fight. Then he too regarded the strange red blade that the thief now owned.

"It is an evil weapon," he said to the thief before leaving to continue scouting ahead. "Personally, I would not touch it."

Harcourt found he felt extremely annoyed by the gladiator's comment. Who was he to tell him not to touch the weapon? Maybe he was jealous of it? Yes, he thought, that must have been it. The black warrior knew well the power of the dagger and wished it for himself. He would have to watch him closely.

The thief then shook his head, as if confused by his own thoughts. He looked down at the weapon in his hands, then shrugged, following Dornell back the way they were headed.

*   *   *   *

Later that day, as the sun was beginning to disappear behind the mountain peaks, the group was thirsty, hungry and tired. Na'Jala had again vanished from sight and Dornell had caught up and kept pace with Harcourt. The thief was getting very anxious to find this fortress and escape the mountain range. Out here, he felt very vulnerable and very uncomfortable. He longed to feel the safety of the confined streets of a city.

The pair walked side by side in silence until Dornell spoke. "So that pale priest has your magical mask?"

"Yes. I was told long ago that it should not be worn for more than three days straight. I lost track of the time and the mask ceased to work while Jaspar was interrogating me. Poor timing. He has the mask now and that is a very troubling thought. I shudder to think of the evils he could accomplish with it. Things just got much worse," Harcourt replied.

Dornell sensed the sorrow in the thief's voice. "It is not your fault. You could not have known that he would discover it."

"Never-the-less, he is the new owner and appears to know how to use it. He will probably run straight to Krommel with it when he also tells the tale of our escape," the thief supposed.

"All the more reason for us to make more haste. When we reach Stonewood, what then? Do you have a plan in mind?" Dornell asked.

"Regrettably, no," the thief replied with a sigh. "Our first stop should be the Temple of the One True God. I have a….friend there. Maybe we can get your hands healed. As for getting to Krommel, I still do not know. Even as Weldrick, with all the Guild resources at my command, we still could not reach him within the castle. We will need to seek out Fezzdin. He will aid us and hopefully guide us."

"After your stunt in the warehouse, I feel you are pretty good at plotting revenge," Dornell said with a sincere smile.

Harcourt allowed himself a chuckle. "I really am sorry for deceiving you that day. And every day since. I have never been one to make the right decisions in life. Call it a bad habit."

"Well, it takes a mature man to admit to his mistakes. You have come a long way from that ten-year-old pickpocket I first met in the market square." Now it was Dornell's turn to chuckle. "To think, if someone had told me then that one day I would be walking side-by-side with you through the Black Peak mountains plotting the downfall of Chief Magistrate Krommel, well, I would have called them mad!"

"When we get your hands healed," Harcourt said, "there is no other person I would rather have by my side in this confrontation to come."

Harcourt knew that Dornell was a seasoned warrior and highly-skilled with a sword. He imagined that getting to Krommel was not going to be easy, not by any stretch of the imagination. Having the captain's sword would prove invaluable. But most of all, having someone he could fully trust was of the most value of all. With the deaths of Jalanna and Wulfred, and the betrayal of Andil, Harcourt had kept telling himself that his previous life was over, that all his friends were gone. That was not true at all; he had just not realized it. Dornell was a friend, and a good friend. He had dragged Dornell down with him and for that he was deeply sorry. But he would do his best to right this wrong and see his friend restored to his previous glory. He would die trying if need be.

A sharp whistle from up ahead drew the two mens' attention. Na'Jala appeared from around a rocky slope and motioned them over. The pair joined the gladiator and stopped in their tracks. A small valley lay before them and the ebony walls of the fortress of Morgaldrun stood dominating their view. So Dornell's instincts proved true. The opposite side of this fortress held their escape from the mountains and would set them on the path back to Stonewood.

"So what now?" asked a winded Garth as he finally caught up to the others. "It would seem the gates were not left open for us to just stroll on through."

The man had a point. The fortress stood much as it had in its glory days. A twenty-five foot tall, black stone wall, stretched from one side of the valley to the other, connecting the two mountains that it was nestled between. A large gate in the center stood firmly shut, barring any entrance. Beyond the wall loomed the fortress itself, built with the same black stones, its battlements devoid of life. An eerie whistling wind blew through the valley and all four men felt the hairs on the back of their necks raise.

The sun had now completely vanished, leaving only the bright full moon to illuminate the dark walls of Morgaldrun. "Well," Harcourt said, "it would appear nobody is home."

"And what makes you say that?" Dornell asked, unconvinced.

"I can see no light sources. And it's pretty quiet."

"The dead require no light," Dornell commented.

"And they make no sound unless they wish it."

"I am not buying the undead wizard tale," Harcourt said, approaching the fortress wall and running his hands over the surface. He was feeling for crevices, hand and footholds. "I guess I am going over this wall and I will open the gate for you three from the other side."

"How will you accomplish this feat?" Na'Jala inquired. "We have no rope or anything that can stretch that high up."

Without another word, Harcourt began to climb the side of the wall like a spider. His hands and feet found the smallest of indents in the stone surface. Impressed, Na'Jala turned to Dornell with an expression that bespoke of a need for an explanation.

"What can I say? He is a master thief," was all Dornell said.

A few moments later, Harcourt hauled himself up to sit on the ledge of the wall, then dropped out of sight to the other side.

*   *   *   *

Prince Denniz had pressed his horse hard for the last few hours but was just about to reach his destination. The Chief Magistrate was right, it really was not safe for him to be out this far from the city, especially without an escort. But there had still been not a sign from Fezzdin. The wizard had mentioned Fort Barron to Krommel so he must still be out here. Luckily for the young prince, he had not encountered any wolves which tended to dominate the hills and woods surrounding the old Fort. His bigger worry was bandits, but they tended to emerge at night. He planned to be back in Stonewood long before nightfall.

The dusty road he travelled wound around one particularly large hill then led him straight to the ruins of Fort Barron. It had been a walled keep long ago, but now lay in ruin, destroyed by siege weapons in some long forgotten battle.

Prince Denniz dismounted and tethered his horse to a pillar that jutted from the ground on an odd angle. His horse was exhausted and needed the rest. The prince fed him one of his favorite apples before climbing up a pile of rubble to survey the ruins before him. He had come here years ago with a group of friends but did not remember much of the layout. He wondered how structurally sound the main keep was and how safe it would be to enter. It was said that many tunnels lay beneath the ruins but how to enter them, he had not the slightest clue.

"Fezzdin?" he risked shouting, his voice echoing off the crumbling walls. "Fezzdin, are you here?"

He carefully navigated his way closer to the entrance of the main keep. The prince figured Fezzdin must have gone underground during his search. Perhaps there was a stairwell or a trapdoor somewhere within the keep.

Motion startled the young prince and he looked up to notice the figure of a stunning woman now standing in the doorway to the keep, roughly twenty feet away. Her hair was long and dark, similar to the robes that hugged her body. Bronze-colored skin bespoke of a southern heritage.

Once the prince was able to find his voice he called over to the woman. "Hello, my lady. Ummm, are my eyes deceiving me? A beautiful woman here in these ruins? They say this place is haunted. Are you some specter then, some former princess that lived in this place long ago?"

The woman smiled. "No, my young prince, I am very real. Though you are going to wish that I was not."

Syrena the sorceress began chanting the words of a spell as five cloaked cultists leaped from behind piles of rubble to rush the unfortunate prince.

CHAPTER 17

The courtyard of the fortress was enveloped in darkness; the only source of light came from the moon. Harcourt sat crouched in the shadows next to the wall, motionless and practically invisible. He was skeptical about the undead wizard but that did not mean that bandits could not have taken up residence in the abandoned compound. It would have made the perfect base.

The thief scanned every window and every battlement for signs of movement. He was certainly no ranger, but he also examined the ground of the courtyard, searching for possible footprints, and found none. The idea seemed strange to him that bandits would not have taken over this place. Perhaps rumors of the undead did keep everyone away. But since this was their only option to cut through the mountains, then undead or not, they were going through.

Once satisfied that there appeared to be no spying eyes, Harcourt crept over to the front gate and searched for the mechanism which would open it. He found a rusted lever that looked as though it had not been used in a hundred years, which could have possibly been the case. His first attempt at using it failed; it did not budge. With a grunt, he used his full weight the second time and was rewarded as the gates slowly, and unfortunately quite loudly, began to open outwards.

Harcourt gritted his teeth and screwed up his face as if his expression alone would help quiet the sound of the opening gates. The creaking chains and pulleys echoed off the mountains. When the gates finally stopped moving, Harcourt's three companions stood there motionless.

"Well," Dornell finally said. "Everyone in these mountains, and fortress, now knows these gates are open. Great idea."

"You could have followed me up the wall then to avoid this. If I was alone, I would have passed through here as silently as a ghost," Harcourt countered.

"Let us not speak of ghosts right now," said Na'Jala, looking about nervously.

"Trust me. We would be better off coming across ghosts instead of the Lich Lord," Dornell said, motioning for them all to enter.

They decided the damage was already done, that opening the gates had made so much noise that closing them could hardly make things worse. But they found the lever stuck in place and were unable to shut the massive doors. Giving up, they proceeded across the courtyard to attempt the front doors of the fortress. As Harcourt cautiously reached for the door handles, the four men jumped at the sound of the gates slamming shut behind them. Their hearts raced and their neck-hairs again stood on end.

"Well….that was interesting," Harcourt whispered.

"At least that will keep others out," Garth said.

"Or was it meant to keep others in?" Dornell wondered.

Harcourt did not want to dwell too much on Dornell's musing, so he wasted no further time checking to see if the fortress doors were unlocked, and luckily they were. He was also thankful that they did not make the same racket as they swung open. There was a chill to the fortress air that hit the four companions immediately. It was cooler inside than it was outside, and even darker. Some moonlight did spill into the fortress from its few windows, but was not much at all. The thief was used to creeping about in dark places but his companions were not.

"Can't you use that dagger to give us a little light at least?" asked Garth.

Harcourt regarded the red blade which had gone dull since its last kill. "I believe it needs fresh blood in order to glow. Care to contribute?" the thief said with a wicked grin.

Garth positioned himself so that Na'Jala stood between them and did not bother answering. Dornell looked at his friend curiously. Something had changed in the thief. He did not remember there ever being a cruel streak in the man. And there was a time when Harcourt preferred not take a life. Now it appeared that he reveled in it. The former guard captain wondered if spending all that time with the Thieves Guild had changed him, being surrounded by all those cold-hearted killers. He would need to talk to his old friend, but right now they had more pressing matters.

The group moved cautiously through the hallways of the dark fortress. Harcourt took the lead and did move as silently as a ghost, his feet making not a sound. The rest followed behind but were not as graceful with their steps. So far the fortress was devoid of decorations or furniture of any kind. Whether there was none to begin with, or it was all pillaged long ago, none of them could say. Dirt and dust littered the stone floors and as far as they could tell, there was no signs of recent traffic.

They travelled through a long hallway which appeared to head in the direction they wished to go. Harcourt checked each door they passed but curiously found all to be locked. He was not in possession of any lockpicks, and did not feel it a good idea to try and force any of the doors and make any further noise.

The main hallway ended in a set of locked doors but a stairwell led upwards to their right. Having no other options, the thief silently led the others up to the second floor of the fortress. The décor, or lack of, was consistent with the lower level. They found two more locked doors but three more hallways with which to choose from. The thief picked one and they continued on.

A shuffling noise from up ahead and around a corner, froze the thief in his tracks. He motioned for the others to stop and be silent, and now they heard it too. It definitely sounded like someone walking, but with a possible injury. The movements sounded slow and the feet shuffled on the floor. Harcourt crouched low and pressed his back to the hallway wall. He knew that he was invisible in the shadows but his companions were not.

As the shuffling sound grew closer, Harcourt spied a door across from him that appeared to be ajar.

Investigating further, the door was indeed open and led to another hallway beyond. He signaled to the others to follow quickly and just as the shuffling sound was about to round the corner he quietly closed the door behind them. He was curious to see what was making the noise, but not that curious.

They passed another series of locked doors which eventually led them to another stairwell leading back down to the ground level. At the base of these stairs, they found three doors, two locked and one wide open. They entered a small room, again devoid of anything save dust and rubble, which led them to another hallway. The pattern continued, several locked doors then an open one. The thief was getting the feeling that they were being led somewhere, purposely, but did not voice that to the others.

They were forced to take another stairwell which led them beneath the fortress. Here they discovered a very long hallway that was lined with suits of armor against both sides of the walls. There were ten suits of armor per side, then there was an intersection with two more halls branching off, then another ten sets of armor with an opened door at the very end. Strangely, there appeared to be a glow from some unseen light source within that room.

So, Harcourt thought to himself, *we are led to our destination*. Then Dornell gave voice to those thoughts. "I think we were meant to find this room."

"Do we go?" Na'Jala whispered.

"We have no choice," Harcourt answered and started to make his way carefully down the hall.

He stopped briefly to inspect one of the suits of

armor. They were all sets of ebony plate armor, helms and all. The visors on the helms were down and if the thief did not know better, one would think that real people stood there standing guard. Each set wore a sword and daggers strapped to a belt. Harcourt was about to lift one of the visors when he decided against touching it and moved on.

As they passed the branching hallways, shuffling sounds emanating from each urged them to quicken their pace toward the illuminated room. The four companions entered and fanned out so as not to be a single target. The room was quite large, perhaps a hall that was once used for greeting guests. Rotted tapestries hung from the walls and it was impossible to guess what they once depicted. A rotted red carpet led from the doorway they had entered, straight to the back of the room where there was a raised dais, on which stood an ebony throne.

Upon the throne sat a motionless figure. Four burning torches along the walls between the tapestries illuminated this room, and as the men approached the throne, they realized it was a skeletal form seated there, dressed in a shimmering, long black robe. Bony hands clutched the arms of the throne and two tiny pinpoints of crimson light burned in each of skeleton's empty black eye sockets.

Harcourt thought it strange that the carpet and tapestries were rotted, and yet the skeleton's robe was immaculately clean; it even seemed to have a pattern that shimmered and shifted making it difficult to focus on the garment. The thief wondered just how long the skeleton had been sitting there. No cobwebs were visible. It appeared dead enough, save for those red pinpoints of light where eyes would have been in life. The thief found them unnerving. Also unnerving was that the chill in the air, which permeated the entire fortress, seemed to get stronger the closer they got to the throne. Harcourt found himself shivering as he now stood about ten feet from the throne and its apparently ancient occupant.

And then it spoke, if speaking was what one could call it. It was a terrible raspy voice that raised goose bumps, like fingers on a chalkboard. The skeleton's jaw did not move and yet they all knew where the voice originated from; it was as if the voice was right inside their head.

"A thief, a guard captain, a fisherman, and a rapist. This is an odd quartet that now stands before me," the voice rasped.

The mention of the fourth title caused the other three men to turn and regard Garth who had turned very pale, but then their attention was brought back to the figure on the throne. Each man felt his heart racing as a feeling of dread washed over them.

"What brings you to Morgaldrun? This is my home, and I do not suffer intruders," it rasped again.

So the rumors were true, Dornell thought to himself. Here sat the Lich Lord of Morgaldrun, an undead wizard of untold power. The former captain found his knees shaking, hoping it was due to the chill air. But he was the first to speak up.

"My lord, we only seek a way through these mountains. We did not mean to intrude on your home. We did not know that anyone still dwelled here."

"I have dwelled here for over a century," the lich said. "I do not receive visitors."

Dornell swallowed hard, and his voice revealed his nervousness. "Do not consider us visitors. We wish to be gone from here and bother you no more."

"But what brings you here? From who do you flee?"

"We were held captive in one of the mountains. We managed to make an escape and wish only to return to Stonewood," Dornell replied.

"Fleeing from who? The wraggoth do not generally take prisoners."

Harcourt then spoke up. "There is a vile cult that has a base within these mountains. They wish to summon their demon lord back to this world and have gathered together an army of wraggoth."

"Ahhhh," the raspy voice said. "The followers of Lucivenus are still active then."

"Yes, very much so. And they apparently draw nearer to their goal of summoning this demon. We need to get back to Stonewood and warn them," Harcourt said.

The lich made a sound that could have been laughing, but came across as someone wheezing for breath. "A near-impossible task to release that demon from his magical prison. They will not succeed."

"And what makes you so sure of that?" the thief dared to ask.

"Because I am one of the ones who imprisoned him," the lich lord replied.

"You are a member of the Circle of Three?" Dornell inquired.

"Was," the lich replied. "The Circle of Three is no more."

"But that was three hundred years ago."

"And? Do I not look a few centuries old?"

Harcourt began scanning the room for any potential hiding spots. He was beginning to wonder if the Lich Lord was merely a prop, and nearby hid someone who could throw their voice. Then the undead wizard addressed him.

"What is that you carry, thief? I wish a closer look."

The lich raised a bony hand and then some invisible force pulled the red-bladed dagger from Harcourt's grasp. The weapon flew straight into the awaiting wizard's hand. The moment it left the thief's possession, he was hit with a wave of emotions. Guilt. Sadness. Confusion. The full weight of the lives he had taken fell upon him suddenly. It was as if someone else had been in control of his actions, but they were now gone.

"An interesting weapon for a common thief," the lich commented. "Forged in the abyss by Lucivenus himself."

"If you have battled this demon before, then you must realize the importance in us getting back to Stonewood to stop this Cult. If Lucivenus is freed, he may seek you out for revenge," Dornell reasoned.

Again the lich made a sound as if he were laughing. "He would not dare. I am ten times more powerful in death than I ever was in life. And as I said, it is highly unlikely that the Cult will succeed."

"We do not share in your optimism, my lord. Just allow us to pass through here and we'll be on our way," Dornell said.

"Do you think that the demon will be satisfied with just Stonewood?" Harcourt added. "He will seek to expand his domain and will want this fortress as well."

"Bah! You have amused me so you may leave with your lives. I will keep this intriguing weapon as a trade to allow you passage through my fortress."

Harcourt did not argue the loss of the dagger. He realized Na'Jala was correct, it was a cursed weapon. With a wave of his other skeletal hand, a passageway suddenly appeared to the right of the throne, where one did not exist moments before.

"Leave me," the lich hissed.

Garth finally found the courage to speak. "We are hungry, thirsty and tired. We need some time to rest here before continuing."

"I said leave."

"You have a large fortress, you won't even see us. There are four of us, and only one of you. Think wisely," Garth dared.

The undead wizard raised an arm and pointed a bony finger towards the bald, insolent man. Garth gasped, then made a horrible choking sound. Veins bulged from his throat, his eyes grew wide with horror, his face began to turn blue. He fell to the floor quite dead, a moment later.

"Does anyone else have anything further to say?" the lich asked.

The three remaining men did not even make eye contact with the lich as they hurried into the passageway, eager to put this place far behind them. Harcourt took one glance back at the still body of Garth, but found that he would not miss the man's company.

Not long after the intruders had departed, the wizard spoke the words of a spell. Garth's body began to twitch. The man then slowly rose to his feet, his eyes milky white, devoid of any life. Garth shuffled off awkwardly to patrol the halls of the fortress for eternity.

CHAPTER 18

"How did I know I was going to find you still here? How, I wonder? Come on get up, let's go. I have a job for us," Evonne said to her hulking partner while tugging on one of his shoulder spikes.

The giant half-ogre reluctantly rose to his feet. He was still staked out in the alley across from the temple.

"You stubborn oaf," Evonne continued. "I have explained to you already, our employer here is gone. Time to move on to other opportunities. There is a serial rapist targeting ladies-of-the-night down on Stain Street. I plan to pose as one this evening. The price on his head is pretty decent; dead or alive too. I have a good description to go by from some eye-witnesses."

The blonde bounty hunter turned to leave and found Vrawg still staring out at the temple. "Forget the girl. Yeah, she is pretty, I get it. But we cannot babysit her any longer. Remember the lecture you gave me on sedentary jobs and the effects it has on the warrior's body? Huh? Remember that one?"

Vrawg just shrugged.

"We gotta see some more action. No more sitting in alleys waiting. Now, let's go."

Vrawg frowned, took another look at the temple, then followed his partner.

*   *   *   *

The sun had not long set when the quartet of cultists met in a secluded area in one of the castle's courtyards. It was their favorite spot near a loud fountain, surrounded by tall trees.

"How could they have escaped?" growled an angry High Priest Sarvin. "Explain that to me?"

"Magic, your highness," answered Brother Jaspar, who had just returned to Stonewood that day. "The man we thought was Weldrick was not Weldrick at all. He was ensorcelled with an illusion and managed to trick the guards posted."

The tall pale priest altered the story slightly, shifting blame to the guards. He also made no mention of the magical mask; he meant to keep that priceless treasure for himself.

"But they fled to the opposite side of the Black Peaks, my lord," Jaspar continued. "Even if they manage to elude the wraggoth, it is no easy task navigating around those mountains. They are ill-equipped, and without food and water. I would not worry about them."

"The only way through those mountains is Morgaldrun. If the lich still occupies the fortress as we believe, then that will not be an option for them," added Devi-Lynn.

"I am still not happy about this turn of events. I wanted information out of them, then I wanted them terminated. Now we have no valuable information and they are still alive and on the loose. Both these men know me as a high-ranking member of our order. I cannot have them skulking about," Sarvin fumed.

"Apologies, my lord. I still have agents searching for them," Jaspar said with a bow.

"Count yourself lucky that I consider you an invaluable member of this order. Otherwise I would have had your heart for this. Do not fail me again."

"I have already informed Thelvius to watch for these fugitives in case they attempt to return to Stonewood," Devi said. "Even if they somehow got past the mercenaries, which is unlikely, they would never get through the city gates. We have guards sympathetic to our cause posted at each."

"I will not be satisfied 'til their heads are mounted on pikes," the High Priest grumbled.

"Worry no more about them. We must focus now on our last heart. The King's birthday fast approaches," Devi said, changing the subject.

"The ritual of the royal heart was a success, then?" asked Jaspar.

The raven-haired priestess glowed with excitement. "Yes indeed. The youngest prince proved very worthy."

"He was taken with no problems then?" the pale priest wondered.

"None at all. We got him to leave the city, alone, and there he was no match for Syrena. It will take some time before the royals assume foul play," answered Devi.

"I believe we should leave hints of Guild involvement

in his disappearance. We could get even more support from the King then in our little war," Brother Veral finally spoke up.

High Priest Sarvin waved away the suggestion. "A fine idea but there is no need now. Soon the Guild and the King will trouble us no more."

"So who will provide us our last and most critical heart?" asked Jaspar.

"We are going to strike at the Temple of the One True God," replied Sarvin. "We need a devoted heart, the most devoted. We should find the perfect candidate in that temple of fools."

Brother Veral raised an eyebrow. "Strike the temple? Or simply snatch a priest to suit our needs?"

"Strike the temple. They would see us destroyed above everyone else, so I want them weakened before our glorious day of summoning arrives. We will kill many and find the perfect priest for our final ritual. When faced with death, we shall see who possesses the most devoted of hearts," Sarvin answered.

"Maybe we should consider First Fool Viktor?" Devi suggested.

Sarvin shook his head. "I will not risk keeping him alive until the King's birthday. I cannot say for sure how powerful the old man is. He must be killed during our raid."

"I will do it. Let me lead the attack," Brother Jaspar offered.

"No," Sarvin said. "I need you to aid Brother Veral in another very important matter. Devi, I want you to assemble a strike force of our most trusted members. I want you to lead the group and choose the most appropriate heart."

The priestess beamed with excitement and pride. "I will not fail you, my lord," she said with a bow.

"I know you won't. And do not allow any to realize who you are. Leave no witnesses to your presence."

*   *   *   *

Krestina's heart raced and sweat formed on her brow. She watched in horror as a woman in a black robe with a hood concealing her face approached Brother Havlan, promising to tear out his heart in the name of some vile demon. The priestess struggled to try and aid the man but she was locked in the strong grip of another cultist, forced to watch the macabre spectacle, helpless to do anything to prevent it.

As the robed woman drove a blade into the chest of the priest, Krestina screamed and her eyes shot open. Breathless and disoriented, it took a moment for the young priestess to realize she was sitting cross-legged on the floor of her room. It had just been another vision. The vision was so vivid that it took several long moments before her heart rate decreased.

"Krestina?? Krestina are you ok??" a woman's voice called from outside her door. "May I come in?"

"Yes, you may," Krestina answered in a labored voice.

Her door opened and in rushed Sister Aymee whose quarters were next to Krestina's. Aymee was tall and thin like Krestina, in her late twenties. She was quite attractive with long fiery-red hair and freckles that dotted her cheeks. The two priestesses had become good friends since

Krestina had joined the temple. Her friend now crouched next to her with worry written across her face.

"I am ok," Krestina assured her. "It was just another vision."

"What was it this time?" her friend asked.

"The Cult had attacked the temple again. Aymee, it was so real. I saw Brother Havlan. He was about to….," Krestina did not finish her sentence.

"It's ok. Didn't First Priest Viktor tell you not to worry? He is right, what could the Cult gain from coming here?"

"Then why do I have these visions? Are they not given to me by God?"

"Yes, but perhaps you need more experience to interpret them properly. Maybe you are worrying too much about this Cult and it is causing your visions to become clouded. I think the disappearance and murder of that orphan girl has really taken a heavy toll on you."

"I really don't know what to think. I just cannot shake this feeling that we are in terrible danger."

Sister Aymee wrapped her fellow priestess in a tight hug. "I am here to watch over you. And First Priest Viktor can protect us all, God willing. Let's go sit in the garden. You can use the fresh air and we'll get you something cold to drink."

* * * *

A bejeweled goblet soared across the room and crashed into a wall, spilling its contents onto an expensive eastern rug.

"Nobody can tell me where he is? How can nobody

know??" roared King Stonewood.

His closest advisors and personal guards flinched, fearing the King's wrath. Even Prince Orval lowered his head in shame, not having the slightest clue as to the whereabouts of his younger brother.

"He could have been kidnapped by the Thieves Guild, or even the Cult!" the King bellowed, pacing back and forth.

"He left us a note, sire. I can confirm it was his handwriting," said the elderly Gervas, the closest advisor to the King.

"He could have been forced to write that by his captors!" the King responded.

Edward, the taller of the two personal knights to the King, then dared speak. "My King, no kidnappers or assassins could have gotten into his quarters. He must have left of his own accord."

"I have dispatched men to Bluebarrow to confirm if he indeed went there or not," said Gervas. "They will send messenger pigeons upon confirmation."

Prince Orval spoke up. "Father, it is my belief that Denniz has gone in search of Fezzdin. You know how fond he is of the wizard and he has been most distressed by his disappearance."

"And what of the wizard?" asked the King. "He has not turned up anywhere either? I want his tower searched. Perhaps an experiment went awry and he is in need of help."

"My lord, we have tried," said Captain Gregor, the captain of the castle guard. He was a tall, muscular middle-aged man with black hair and beard, and a long, jagged-looking scar running along his left jaw-line. "We attempted to gain entry to the tower and two of my men were injured by the guardian gargoyle. I believe the doors are sealed with magic and the stony beast will not allow any to touch them."

"There are other wizards in this city. Find someone who knows something about magical seals and gargoyles," commanded the King.

"Yes, my lord," bowed Captain Gregor. "Right away."

"Scour the city! Scour the countryside! I want my son found!"

*   *   *   *

The streets of Stonewood bustled with activity. The King's birthday was less than a week away and the excitement level had visibly risen. City workers were busy decorating the streets and hanging candles that minor sorcerers' would imbue with multi-colored flames. Clothing shops had lineups that stretched out of the stores with folk buying their outfits for the occasion.

Only the very rich and influential were invited to the castle for the actual party, but the whole city from north to south celebrated and were provided free food and wine with music in the streets. It was generally the only time of year when everyone put aside their differences or grudges and just enjoyed a day of festivities.

Serdic, however, did not share in general everyone's excitement; he was only annoyed at how slow his journey through the streets was taking him. He was running late for a meeting with a visiting merchant from Red Lake in the east. His two large bodyguards were doing their best to shove a path through the mob of people before them.

"I see you are in a hurry, but I request a moment of your time," a familiar voice to Serdic's right said.

"Randar," the older thief answered. "Not a good time. I am in a hurry as you are aware. Can this not wait for our big meeting tomorrow night?"

"You have been a hard man to get ahold of as of late. I was hoping to speak with you before that meeting."

"This really isn't the place for it, nor the time. Can it wait 'til later this evening?"

"No," the Guild enforcer said, and his tone told Serdic that it was not up for further debate.

The older thief scanned the crowd around them to make the point that too many ears were about. "People are too busy to take any notice or care about us, fear not," the thug said in a lowered voice.

The two men walked over to the front of a trinket shop and stood in the shade to avoid the bright noon-day sun. Serdic's bodyguards followed them and stayed nearby.

"We are on the brink of disaster," the enforcer said.

"Agreed," the older thief replied.

"We are in need of strong leadership if the Guild is to survive. They got to Weldrick. Who knows who will be next? We are fighting both the Cult and the city which seem to be one and the same."

"This is quite possibly a losing battle," Serdic reasoned.

"What are you saying?"

"Perhaps we should think of alternatives to continuing this fight. Maybe it is time to quit - we are all wealthy - or just lay low for quite some time," the older thief suggested.

"Coward," Randar spat.

"I beg your pardon?"

"Cowards quit. The weak run and hide. You want to let them win?"

Serdic was now becoming very annoyed. "I want to live a long life. When we first began this little war with the Cult, we had no clue what we were really up against. If their funding and resources do indeed come from the city, we cannot win. We are simply outmatched and must accept that truth."

"We can win this," Randar countered, "with the proper leader and with all of our resources combined. You, Serdic, have many men under your own employ and yet you have offered none of them to help."

"I have my own businesses to run and interests to look out for as well. We are not an army, in case you need reminding."

The Guild enforcer glared at the thief. "You are a Guild member first and foremost. Everything else is secondary."

"I am in quite a hurry. Is that what you stopped me for? To tell me that the Guild is in danger? As if this was news to me?"

"We need a new leader," Randar said. "And we need to choose tomorrow."

"Why not a council instead?" Serdic asked.

"What? So we can sit around and debate things endlessly when we need immediate action? No, I don't think so. We need a single leader, a strong leader, to take action."

"So this is the part where you tell me that you are that leader?"

Randar did not like the other man's tone. "I will be leader. And I expect your support. Many members look up to you and respect your opinion, so I expect you to endorse me."

"I grow weary of this battle. The war is costing us, we are not profiting from this," Serdic said, also not appreciating the thug's tone. "Do what you will. Take the Guild if that is what you want. I believe I shall pursue other options while they are still available."

"You are a member of the Guild," Randar growled. "You think you can just walk away like that and leave us behind. Especially at this crucial time?"

"You are choosing to do what you see is the right course of action. I am also doing the same. And I am not looking for permission to do anything."

"So, you are walking away?" the enforcer asked.

"It would appear to be the best course of action for us all at the moment," Serdic replied.

In a blur of movement, Randar suddenly stood face to face with the slightly taller thief. Serdic felt a sharp sting and his breath was stolen. Attempting unsuccessfully to suck in air, the older man glanced down to find the thug holding a blade buried hilt-deep into his chest.

"Nobody leaves the Guild," Randar whispered into his ear.

Nearby, a woman screamed as the bloodied thief slumped to the ground. He was dead before his bodyguards even realized what had happened. The two much larger men advanced but not without concern.

"Your employer is dead," Randar said to the two men, holding the bloodied dagger before him. "You can either join him, or work for me now."

The two large thugs exchanged glances and read one another's minds. There was no sense in throwing away their lives needlessly.

CHAPTER 19

Dornell and Na'Jala sat with their backs to trees in the darkness of the wooded area. There was a chill in the air that caused the former gladiator to shiver, having spent his entire life in the warmer climes of the south. The men felt slightly refreshed after finally finding a stream earlier that day, but they had still not yet eaten. The smell of meat cooking over a nearby campfire was quite literally torture.

"Your friend, he is a good scout then?" Na'Jala asked, referring to Harcourt who had crept off to investigate the campfire.

"Something like that," Dornell chuckled. "Let's just say he is good at not being seen."

"The undead wizard, he referred to him as a thief. And you a guard. An odd friendship, no?"

Again, the former captain chuckled. "Yes an odd friendship indeed. Life has a way of throwing us strange surprises. Some not so pleasant, others welcomed."

"Yes, I am all too familiar with that," Na'Jala agreed. "Most of it not so pleasant."

"You will return south eventually? Find your family again? You are a free man now."

"Yes, I will. This is my dream. My son and daughter must be so big now. I just hope they still remember their father. When I have the gold to pay for passage on a ship, I will find them."

"I have friends in Stonewood. If we can make it back into the city, I will get you the gold right away and you can begin your journey," Dornell offered.

"I thank you. But first I will aid you in your quest. Your friend saved my life. That is no small thing to me."

"You do not have to. Stonewood is probably a much larger city than you are used to, and full of dangers. The people we are after are very powerful. This is no easy task."

"I am no stranger to peril," Na'Jala replied with a shrug. "And besides, if these people you seek are connected to my captors from the mountain, I would very much like meet them too."

Dornell nodded then spun around at the sound of a twig snapping behind. Several more snapped before the thief appeared from the darkness and rested against the next closest tree.

"I thought you were a master of stealth? You would have woken a sleeping drunk," Dornell said to Harcourt.

"It's these stupid sticks. They are everywhere," the thief replied.

"Yes, they are. Welcome to the outdoors," Dornell said, shaking his head.

Harcourt was not used to the terrain outside of a city. He nearly gave away his position several times with some misplaced steps. Within the city, not a soul would have heard him move about. Luckily for him, the men at the campfire were talking very loudly amongst themselves and appeared not to notice.

"There are four men and three horses. They have several wagons as well," Harcourt told his companions.

"Bandits?" Dornell asked.

"I don't think so. They appear to be well dressed. Merchants, I believe."

"Armed?"

"Each has a sword and there was crossbows nearby, though none look much like warriors."

Dornell rubbed his chin. "We need those horses. And food, obviously. We will have to negotiate with them."

Harcourt laughed. "We have nothing to negotiate with and we look like bandits or escaped prisoners, which we are. We may have to be a little forceful."

"I will not allow any harm to come to these people. We may look like bandits but we are not bandits," Dornell said.

"Obviously we are not going to harm them," Harcourt replied. "But I am saying we may have to be a little demanding. We will need to get the jump on them before they can reach for those crossbows."

"Well, try not to step on so many twigs and we might have a chance. And we will try and negotiate something fairly, first."

"I say we just send him in," Harcourt pointed to Na'Jala with a smile. "Were I to see him walk out of the darkness with a sword in hand demanding my horse, I just might give it to him."

Na'Jala laughed but was not sure if that was a compliment or not. "Let us go then, the smell of that food is driving me mad," he said.

*   *   *   *

Dornell urged his mount on faster, he was very eager to get back to Stonewood. Directly behind him, and sharing the same horse, sat Harcourt who clung to the former guard captain tightly to keep from falling off.

The thief was very uncomfortable with his current situation. "We just couldn't take the third horse, eh?"

"I was not going to leave them stranded," Dornell replied. "And besides, you do not even know how to ride a horse."

"How difficult can it be? You just sit on it," the thief said, just trying to be difficult.

In reality, he was quite pleased at how the encounter unfolded with the merchants at the campfire, and they did turn out to be merchants as he expected. Also, as he had guessed, they were not warriors and had no stomach for a fight with the three strange men that had suddenly surrounded them from the woods. They shared their food which the three companions ravenously devoured, and some much-appreciated ale. They took two of the three horses the merchants had. Dornell insisted on leaving them with one horse and offering them gold in compensation if they were to travel to Stonewood. As well, he planned to leave the horses for them to pick up upon their arrival.

Taking the horses did not bother Harcourt one bit. After all he had spent his entire life taking things that did not belong to him. In his mind, they needed the horses more than the merchants. The theft weighed heavily on his friend Dornell though, who despised what they had just done but did realize it was a necessary evil. It was for the greater good when you looked at the grand scheme of things. Na'Jala was no expert horseman but had enough experience to keep up and trailed a short distance behind his two companions upon his own horse.

They followed a main road and worried about running into any patrols of Stonewood troops, or even Cult members who may be still searching for them, but luck was with them. Darkness enveloped the lands again as they slowed their pace at the sight of the city lights off in the distance. What troubled them now were the many campfires spread out across the fields surrounding the great city of Stonewood. The mercenary army still had the city surrounded and would surely stop them before they made the front gates.

The three companions dismounted and crept closer on foot for a closer look to assess their situation.

"Ok, genius," Dornell said, turning to the thief. "You said if I got you to the city you could get us in. So what's your plan?"

Harcourt grimaced. "Well….. if we can make it to a large oak tree on the northeast side of the city then we are in. But I was not anticipating the mercenaries to be so spread out as this. We need to somehow get past them to find that tree."

"Great," Dornell commented sarcastically. "We are convicted criminals of Stonewood, and escaped prisoners of the Cult, both of which would like to see us hang. The mercenaries will just see this as an opportunity to turn us over for more gold."

Harcourt agreed. "And what's worse is Krommel is

the one that has hired Thelvius and his army so he is the one really in charge."

"What did you just say? Whose army is this?" Na'Jala asked very curiously.

"I was told that a man named Thelvius the Great runs this mercenary company. A former gladiator, like yourself," Harcourt replied.

"Yes, this Thelvius was a gladiator and the best Gladenfar had ever seen. He was freed after an unprecedented undefeated career. I know this man. I have even fought alongside him in the arena on a few occasions," Na'Jala said.

Dornell's face brightened. "Do you know him well then? Enough for us to speak with him and perhaps be allowed to pass?"

"I would not say I knew him well, but as I said, we have shared the arena and a few meals together. We could try. I knew him has an honorable man."

Harcourt did not like the sound of this idea. "We would be taking a huge gamble here. This man is a mercenary, out for gold. If we tell him who we are, he could very well turn us over. At the very least, you and I, Dornell. I say we try and sneak past them."

"I could go alone then to speak with him. If things turn sour, then you both are still free to try another plan," the former gladiator offered.

"No," Dornell replied. "We are in this together and we shall all stick together. I say we take this gamble and trust in our new friend here. Our chances of slipping past this army are slim to none. They may be less hospitable towards us if we are caught."

Harcourt looked to Na'Jala who nodded in agreement

with the former captain. The thief sighed. "Alright then, we'll try your plan."

*   *   *   *

Harcourt, Dornell and Na'Jala were stripped of their few weapons and led through the mercenaries' camp by five heavily-armored men. Two of them pointed loaded crossbows at the trio. Harcourt still did not like this idea. They had worked so hard to escape their captors in the Black Peaks only to turn themselves over to the mercy of a man employed by Chief Magistrate Krommel.

This army looked nothing like the army that protected Stonewood. The men did not wear a common uniform save for a small emblem of a bird clutching a bloodied sword in its talons. Some men wore plate armor, some wore chain mail, some wore leather and others wore mismatched pieces of various types of armor. They all looked like seasoned warriors, though, who had seen many battles.

They were led passed several large tents and groups of men sitting around campfires drinking and singing the night away. They halted in front of the largest tent they had yet seen and one of their escorts disappeared inside. Several moments later, he emerged and bid them all enter.

The inside of the tent was lavishly decorated with furniture and paintings depicting great battles. There were several tables with maps strewn about them and golden goblets to hold them in place. Several other men occupied the tent wearing exquisite sets of armor, most likely the army's commanders. Seated in front of them was a man who probably stood about six-foot tall, wearing a gleaming set of bronze armor. He was bald and sported many scars that lined his face and head. His nose looked as though it had been broken many times over. His eyes bespoke of a possible mixed heritage between the far east and the far south. Skin almost as bronze as his armor indicated he had spent much time in the blazing sun of the south.

To the left of his chair rested a great sword with a golden pommel carved into the likeness of a bird-of-prey. To his right sat the largest dog the three men had ever seen. It was bluish-grey in color and was the size of a small bear. What was even more of a curiosity was that it also wore a suit of spiked bronze armor. Razor-sharp spikes dotted its entire back and sides and it even wore a small skull-cap with one large spike protruding from the dog's forehead like a horn. His tongue hung to the side and he drooled from a crooked-looking mouth. He sat up at the arrival of the three strangers and gave a low menacing growl.

"Jag here does not like strangers in our camp," the man seated in the chair said. "Give me one good reason why I should not have him eat you." Then the man took a longer look at the strangely-armored black warrior who stood before him and a look of recognition crossed his face. "I know you, don't I?"

"Yes, the arena of Gladenfar," the former gladiator responded. "My name is Na'Jala and I used to fight for House Firebrand. The last time we saw each other, we fought together with a group re-enacting The Battle of the Seven Stars. Thankfully, we changed history and won that battle."

Thelvius the Great chuckled at that memory, recalling how angry Lord Mylos had been when they won. "A glorious day that was. Seven of us standing against thirty and still we were victorious. As I recall, a sword almost found my back if not for you."

"Good timing on my part was all," Na'Jala said, remembering how he struck the man down before he could deliver a potentially mortal blow.

"The gods smiled on you that day, my lord," said a broad-shouldered man with a brown beard, standing behind one of the maps.

"The gods never smiled on me that day, or any other day in my wretched life," the mercenary leader said with a laugh. "I have faith in my sword and my sword alone. I have won all my battles through my strength-in-arms and not because of the whims of some god. Now tell me, Na'Jala, what brings you here to my camp and why I have been instructed to look out for three men fitting your descriptions?"

First Na'Jala told the tale of his leaving Gladenfar and eventual capture at the hands of the cultists and then of their daring escape from the mountain and the encounter with the Lich Lord which led them on the path to the mercenary camp.

"So my friends here need to gain access to the city to try and put an end to this evil Cult. They have terrible plans that are nearing completion," Na'Jala said, finishing his tale.

"This Krommel fellow, he is the one filling our pockets here with gold. Are you certain he leads this Cult?" Thelvius inquired.

"Absolutely," Harcourt answered. "Without a doubt."

"How long has it been since you have seen any of Stonewood's troops around?" asked Dornell.

"Several days at least. The army has split up and gone off on some training maneuvers. In the meantime we are paid to watch the city for fleeing thieves," the mercenary leader replied.

"Krommel has ordered the troops as far away from the city as possible while an army of wraggoth are on their way here now," Dornell said.

"Wraggoth? What purpose do they have in leaving their mountain homes?"

"The Cult has assembled them into an actual army and even equipped them with weapons and armor. They have something major planned within the city and this wraggoth army is on the way to help them win the city," Dornell told him.

"We received word a short while ago of an approaching host but we assumed it was some Stonewood troops returning," said the bearded mercenary captain.

Thelvius turned to the man. "Dispatch a scout. I want to know if this is the wraggoth army and how many they number."

"You see?" Dornell said. "The pieces on the board are moving. My guess is that you are expected to fall in line and aid them, or be destroyed along with everyone else."

"We were told about none of these plans," Thelvius said, anger creeping into his voice.

"Thelvius, these men are evil and responsible for many atrocities," Na'Jala cut in. "Worse even than the slave owners of Gladenfar."

The mercenary leader sat in his seat rubbing his chin in silent contemplation for several long moments before speaking again. "If we confirm that an army of wraggoth are indeed marching on the city, then I will withdraw my men. We shall leave."

"You would abandon the city at this crucial time?" Dornell asked.

"We are not heroes, we are mercenaries. I do not risk my life and the lives of my men for nothing. If there is nobody to pay us then we must leave. I am sorry if that is difficult for you to hear."

"Believe me there will be mountains of gold for you if you aid the city in the coming battle. I am sure the King will be very grateful to anyone helping in the city's defense. The Cult will be dealt with from within the city, but we will require aid outside the walls," Dornell said.

"You seem like a good man but I apologize if I cannot go by your word that the King will pay for our help."

"Pull your men away from the city then. Let the wraggoth believe that you have left but wait a safe distance away. We can then get word to you that your help is required and you will be compensated," Dornell suggested.

"Well again, we need to confirm what you say is true. If it is an army of wraggoth approaching, we will pull back and wait. If we hear nothing from you after a period of time, we are leaving and Stonewood can deal with this on their own," Thelvius replied.

"So you will let us go then?" Harcourt asked.

"Yes. You are free to go and do as you wish. I trust that the tale Na'Jala told me is true. I have no love for demon-worshippers. If this Krommel is in league with them, then you have a mighty task before you. But expect no further help from me unless the gold matches the risk. You are welcome to food and drink and some supplies before you go. This much at least I owe you, Na'Jala.

Good luck my friends."

*　　*　　*　　*

Na'Jala had been correct, Harcourt thought. Thelvius had turned out to be a very decent and honorable man. They had been provided with all they could eat and drink, they were each given a sword of excellent quality along with two extra daggers for Harcourt, and a change of clothes which included dark cloaks for each of them.

The three men crept through the darkness outside the city walls undetected. City guards patrolled the top of the walls but it was a cloudy night; not even the moon shone through, which provided excellent cover for the trio. Not long after leaving the mercenary camp, Harcourt had found the large oak tree he had sought and memories flashed through his mind of that memorable night he stood there with Warden and was gifted the magical mask. It seemed like a lifetime ago to the thief. So much had changed since then.

"Ok, so it's a large tree. How does this get us inside the city?" Dornell asked.

Without reply, Harcourt began moving some small bushes out of the way which revealed the handle to a wooden door set into the ground near the tree. From years of disuse, the thief struggled at first to open it, but it eventually gave in and cooperated. The door opened. He produced a small lantern given to him by the mercenaries and it revealed many thick cobwebs in the tunnel below.

"This is an old smuggling tunnel of mine. It will lead us to the basement of a tavern in the upper west district." Harcourt then waved a finger at Dornell. "Filbur, who owns the tavern there, is a good man, Dornell, so you must forget you've seen this tunnel."

"Lead on," was all the former captain said.

CHAPTER 20

Evonne and Vrawg quickened their pace as the rain began to fall a little harder. The combination of the late hour and the falling rain had kept most of the city streets empty. They did not mind the miserable weather so much since they had just picked up their latest bounty and they were still living high off the payment they received from Weldrick of the Thieves Guild. Even so, Evonne insisted that the pair stay busy. The south-side rapist proved an easy catch and should end up with a lengthy stay in the castle dungeon, along with the two broken legs Vrawg had given him. Now they were on their way back to the inn where they were staying for some much deserved drinks to celebrate.

Evonne was trying her best to stay behind the hulking half-ogre to block the wind and blowing rain. In their time spent in Stonewood, she had become quite familiar with a large portion of the city but she felt it was taking much longer to reach the inn this evening than it should have.

When her large partner turned down an all-too-familiar alley, the former pirate stopped in her tracks, hands on her hips. "You sneaky bugger, you! I thought this was taking longer than usual. You deliberately took the long way so we could pass by that damned temple again, didn't you?"

Vrawg shrugged his shoulders, maintaining a look of innocence.

"Has to be that pretty lass that has gotten to you, 'cuz I know you don't give a damn about that temple and their god. How many times have I listened to you go on and on and on about the falseness of the gods, how all the religions were created to manipulate the masses and line their coffers with gold? Eh? How many times?" Evonne ranted.

Again, her partner only shrugged. He turned and walked to the other end of the alley, stopping to peer around the corner at the temple. Evonne stood defiantly in the rain, not wishing to follow.

The night was extraordinarily dark. There were no moon or stars visible and the rain had extinguished most of the torches and lanterns that lit the streets and temple. A loud clap of thunder boomed overhead and a streak of lightning momentarily lit up the sky like the sun. It was in that brief moment that Vrawg noticed several strange figures enter the front doors of the temple. Vrawg had watched the temple long enough to know that all its members wore brown robes, and brown robes only. These figures wore jet-black cloaks with pants to match. Swords hung from their belts. Even the holy warriors that protected the temple did not wield swords and the edged weapons were not permitted inside the temple.

Warning signals went off in the half-ogre's head as his

partner finally began pulling on his belt.

"I am getting soaked here. If you want to put me in a miserable mood, you are on the right path," she said very annoyed.

Then a woman's scream from within the temple gave the two a start. There were some muffled shouts followed by a second scream. Vrawg looked down at his partner then turned to run for the temple.

"Whoa, whoa, whoa!" Evonne shouted desperately, still hanging onto his belt. "Let's think about this first. We can't just go running in there, we don't know what's going on. We don't do charity work, remember??"

"Bad Cult," Vrawg said in a very deep voice.

"You don't know that! And it's not our fight. We'll go alert the guards if that makes you feel better. Come on."

"Bad Cult," her partner repeated and broke free of her grasp and ran for the temple's entrance.

"Curse your soft heart," Evonne said, pulling the crossbow off her back, and ran to catch up.

Vrawg attempted to open the double doors leading into the temple but found them locked, barred from the inside. He rammed them with his massive spiked shoulder but these doors were solid and strongly built; they did not budge. Muffled shouts of alarm could still be heard from within the temple.

The giant bounty hunter grabbed his warhammer and was about to batter the doors down when his blonde partner nudged him from the side. "Come on, let's go find another door or even a window. I would prefer to use another route in."

*　　*　　*　　*

A middle-aged priest stepped out of a private prayer chamber into the main hallway of the temple and was greeted with a horrific sight. Blood lined the walls and floors and three fellow members of the temple lay dead before him. A cloaked figure brandishing a bloodied sword advanced on him. Brother Fron attempted to shout for help but not a sound was heard. In fact, he could hear nothing at all. He was surrounded by an eerie silence.

The sword plunged into his chest and he died without a sound. Nearby, Devi-Lynn smiled at her handiwork. She had cast a spell of silence on the area so as to minimize knowledge of their presence. She still felt as though this move on the temple was too bold. She wanted to find her worthy heart, eliminate First Priest Viktor, and get out of here as quickly as possible.

*   *   *   *

Sister Krestina bolted upright in her bed, wakened from her sleep. She thought she had heard a scream but now there was nothing but silence. Perhaps it was just a dream, she thought. She waited for her eyes to adjust to the darkness before sliding out of bed and walking across the room to pour a glass of water. She let out a loud sigh when she realized her pitcher was empty. Frustrated, she threw on her robe and set off on her long trek to the well on the other side of temple.

*   *   *   *

As Evonne turned the corner of a narrow hallway, suddenly she could not hear the sound of her own footsteps, or those of her hulking partner who possessed no ability of stealth whatsoever. She looked back to the half-ogre who was rubbing his ears, apparently experiencing the same deathly silence. Rounding the corner of the next hallway, she stopped short at the sight of two cloaked men; an elderly priestess lay on the floor in front of them. She appeared to be pleading with her attackers and yet no sound escaped her lips.

It became clear to the petite bounty hunter that her partner was right. The temple was under some kind of attack and it could very well be that vile Cult that was behind it. Well, she thought, this mysterious silence was going to work to their advantage.

She quickly crept up behind the pair of cultists and as the one on her right raised his sword to end the life of the pleading priestess, she pulled the trigger of her crossbow. The bolt embedded itself in the man's skull and killed him instantly. As he fell forward, the other cultist turned in surprise not realizing what had caused his partner to stumble. He did not have time to ponder that question as a knife found his throat.

Evonne pulled the priestess to her feet and shoved her off in the direction from which they had just come. The older woman paled at the sight of Vrawg but realized this pair had just saved her life. With a silent thank you, she took off running.

*   *   *   *

Still half asleep, Krestina shuffled down the winding corridors of the temple, her eyes more closed than open. She did not really need to see where she was going since she had made this walk so many times before. She had not slept very well lately, but this night she had passed out very early in the evening. She heard a crack of thunder boom overhead and now worried the storm would keep her up the rest of the night. She had always been frightened of storms; living in the orphanage, she never really had anyone to make her feel safe and tell her everything was going to be alright. So now, even as an adult, storms unnerved her.

Suddenly, the beautiful priestess slipped and scraped her elbow against the stone wall trying to remain upright. She stepped into something slick and her foot nearly slid out from under her. Looking down, her eyes went wide with horror as she realized she stood in a pool of blood; a trail of it led around the next bend.

Nervously, she proceeded down the hall and peeked around the corner, afraid of what she might find. It was worse than she imagined. Instead of finding one body, there were several bodies lining the hallway, all brothers and sisters of the temple, all apparently dead. She closed her eyes tightly and shook her head. Desperately, she hoped this was a dream, or even just a vision. Upon opening her eyes, she realized that it was real, that her visions of the temple coming under attack had come true.

Instinct told her to flee in the other direction. But against better judgment, she continued down the hall of horrors, trying to tip-toe around pools of blood. There could be others in need of help and Krestina could not abandon them.

*　　*　　*　　*

229

Evonne sprinted full speed down the corridor away from the main meeting hall. On her heels were three cloaked cultists, bloodied swords in hand and intent on catching the strange woman who was clearly no priestess. There was no mysterious silence in this area and the bounty hunter heard the curses these men spat at her.

The cultists whooped with delight as they neared their catch, almost on top of the blonde woman. The fastest of the three reached out to grab her ponytail but just missed as the woman skidded and disappeared around a bend. He too turned the corner in full pursuit only to have his skull caved in by a massive warhammer.

The second man witnessed the grisly attack but not in time to turn and flee. Vrawg backhand-swatted the cultist with his hammer like a bug and the man flew into the wall with a crunch, bones broken. The last cultist skidded to an abrupt stop and began backing up. A crossbow bolt found the center of his forehead and he dropped, lifeless, to the floor.

"There is a lot more of this scum than we anticipated," Evonne said to her partner as she reloaded her crossbow. "I think we need to consider leaving now and alerting the city guard. We cannot fight this whole Cult."

"Bad Cult," was all Vrawg said in reply and stormed off in search of more men to smash, and a certain priestess to save.

With a sigh, Evonne followed.

* * * *

"Oh my god! Brother Antony!" Krestina cried and

knelt next to the priest who sat against the wall of a study.

She gently pulled his hands away from the wound he grasped at his stomach. She gasped. It was a deep gash and she knew from his labored breathing and the distant look in his eyes that his life was fading. He did not even seem to register the presence of the priestess.

Tears streamed down her face. Brother Antony was a kind, middle-aged priest who had been one of the first members of the temple to welcome Krestina and get her moved into her quarters. She placed her hands against the wound and pleaded with God to hear her prayers and grant her a spell of healing.

She almost jumped back in shock as her hands began to glow with bright silvery light. She held them in place against the wound and watched as the gash slowly close before her eyes. Vigor returned to the older priest's face and he turned to his savior and smiled.

There was no time to rejoice as the sound of booted feet caused her to stand and turn. A cloaked cultist advanced on her and raised his sword. There was nothing else Krestina could do except hold up her hands in a feeble defense and screamed, "STOP!"

The Cult member suddenly froze in place, totally immobile, a statue standing before her. "It worked," the priestess said in a quivering voice. "My prayers were answered. My spells worked."

Brother Antony stood and placed a hand upon her shoulder and spoke with a sense of urgency. "Come, my child. I believe they are looking for First Priest Viktor. We must find him."

*   *   *   *

First Priest Viktor ushered the small group into the dining hall before him. It was a large room with space to spread out and possessed several points from which to exit. The group of priests and priestesses were pale with fright. They had just witnessed four of the temple's warrior protectors cut down by evil demon worshippers. The armored quartet was assailed by spells from a couple of Cult priests before they were butchered by sword-wielding cultists.

The ancient First Priest turned to face the door they had entered and backed up, shouting, "Pyrim victus!"

Two unlit torches that hung from the wall on either side of the doorway blazed to life. It was not long after, that the first of the pursuing Cult members strolled arrogantly through the same doorway. He had greying hair and wore the black robes of a Cult priest. First Priest Viktor wasted no time in shouting the words, "Pyrim Attackus!"

The flames from both torches roared towards the evil priest as if they had a life of their own. With a scream of agony, the priest cooked to death where he stood, his charred body crumbling to the floor. The other cultists who were about to enter the dining hall stopped and backed up, reconsidering their course. That bought Viktor and the others a little time.

"Sister Amberlyn, if you wouldn't mind, please check the southern door and see if our path is clear," the elderly priest asked.

First Priest Viktor's attention was then brought back fully to the other doorway as a fanatical axe-wielding cultist leaped over the burnt body and charged forward into the room, looking to behead the elderly priest.

"Invisiblem!" Viktor shouted and the cultist appeared to run straight into a wall.

The man's nose exploded with blood and he stumbled back onto the floor in a daze. The First Priest had erected an invisible wall that blocked off access to him and the others. Impenetrable, it was as hard as stone and nothing, not even spells, would be able to pass through.

"How long can your force wall keep them at bay First Priest?" Brother Havlan wondered.

"For as long as I stay and concentrate on it. Now everyone out the south door, quickly. Be careful. I will hold these ones off here. Get outside the temple. Worry not about me I shall follow shortly."

The others hesitated, not wishing to abandon the First Priest, but he assured them again that he would be right behind them.

"I, at least, will remain by your side," Brother Havlan said as the others quickly fled from the hall. Havlan knew the First Priest was powerful and preferred his chances by his side.

The two priests turned to regard the eastern door into the hall which suddenly swung open, but to their relief it was two other members of the temple. Sister Krestina and Brother Antony rushed over to join them.

Tears streamed down Krestina's face. "My visions came true, First Priest."

"Indeed they have, my dear," he replied. "A fool I was not to take heed. God was sending his warnings through you but I have failed to prepare for this disaster."

"It is not your fault," Brother Havlan said. "Who could have really foreseen this nightmare?"

"She did," the First Priest answered motioning to the

priestess. "Several times she told me of her visions, but I thought her young and inexperienced. A costly mistake."

As the dazed cultist lying on the floor beyond the invisible wall began to regain his senses, a heart-wrenching sound startled the group. From beyond the northern doorway, a woman's voice could be heard pleading for her life and sobbing. It sounded as though it was getting closer and closer.

First Priest Viktor turned to Brother Antony. "Brother Antony, when our sister reaches this room, I will drop the wall. See to it that this fellow on the floor does not follow her, then I will raise the wall yet again."

Moments later, a woman in brown robes ran frantically into the room, the sounds of pursuit closely behind.

"Behind us, Sister, over here. Now Brother!" Viktor shouted while mentally willing the invisible wall to drop.

The priestess leaped into the air as the cultist on the floor reached for her leg. A beam of silver energy shot forth from Brother Antony's hand and struck the vile man in the chest, forcing him back to the floor. The sobbing priestess scrambled behind the First Priest as he once again raised the invisible wall as more cultists began to fill the room. Five of them were armed warriors, the sixth a dark-robed priest.

"Greetings, First Priest. Thank you for waiting here for us to arrive," the evil priest said calmly.

"You will not find any easy victims here I am afraid. And you shall not pass my wall," Viktor replied confidently.

The Cult priest chuckled. "Your wall will not protect you."

Before the First Priest could tell the man he was wrong, he felt a sharp pain in his back. He looked to his chest to find the tip of a long dagger protruding through. Sister Krestina screamed as Devi-Lynn, wearing the brown robes of a temple priestess, withdrew her dagger and Viktor fell to the floor; his invisible wall no longer existed.

The other cultists swarmed the group, throwing them roughly to the ground, kicking and punching them into submission.

"A fine plan, Sister Devi," the Cult priest said.

"Thank you, Brother Alvyn, I told you the First Priest was a fool," Devi replied, tossing aside the brown robe to reveal her black one beneath.

"I suggest you choose your heart quickly. I fear city guards will be storming this temple very shortly," Alvyn said.

"I believe he will do," the priestess motioned to Brother Havlan.

The priest paled. "No no no no no no no no," he pleaded, his hands waving in the air. "I have seen the errors in my judgment now. Clearly, God is not all powerful as I once thought. Our defeat here is proof of this. Your Lord Lucivenus is obviously much more powerful. I pledge myself to your order. Just let me live."

Devi-Lynn shook her head in disappointment. They required a devoted heart, the most devoted. This priest was not so devoted after all, seeking to switch sides to save his pathetic life. "On second thought, you will not do," she said, walking over, then cutting the priest's throat with her dagger.

Krestina struggled but was helpess to do anything under the strong grasp of the Cult warrior who held her.

"You evil witch!" she screamed.

Her outburst then brought the evil priestess's gaze fully to her. "So, you little tramp. You do not also wish to beg for your life and offer to join with us? We are actually in need of more female members. Especially those that look like you. What do you say?"

"To the abyss with you!" Krestina shouted in reply. "Go down and rot with your vile demon lord."

"Oooh, I like this one's spirit," Devi said, walking over to the priestess who was forcibly held on her knees. She waved her bloodied dagger in front of Krestina's face. "Are you absolutely sure I cannot change your mind? Otherwise, I can send you to meet your God right now."

Krestina closed her eyes and calmed her breathing. "Do it then, you witch. God will look after my soul. I do not fear you or your threats."

Devi smiled. Now here was the devoted heart that she sought. Yes, this pretty priestess would serve their purposes well. "Bind her and gag her. She is the one."

*   *   *   *

There was a sickening crunch as the cultist's head split open and he collapsed to the floor. Sister Aymee dropped the heavy mace that she had found by the body of one of the temple's holy warriors. The cultist had his back to her and never saw her coming. She sprinted into the dining hall at the sight of First Priest Viktor laying on the floor with other members of the temple. She began to weep when she found the First Priest to be dead. Movement to her left caught her attention. Brother Antony stirred, struggling to speak.

Aymee moved over to the other priest and noticed the stab wounds to his chest. They were deep and he had already lost much blood. Tears streamed down her cheeks.

"They......took......Krestina," he managed to say before his eyes closed forever.

Aymee wept and wept. She could not imagine what fate was worse, being butchered here in the temple or being taken prisoner by the evil Cult. She could only imagine how terrified her dear friend must be. So distraught was the priestess that she had not even noticed the two people who had walked up to stand behind her.

"Come on, Sister, get up. Let's get you out of here," Evonne said.

The priestess recoiled at the sight of the strange blood-soaked warriors, especially the hulking giant that stood next to the woman.

"We are not with the Cult, fear not," the bounty hunter tried to reassure her. "But it's not safe here. Come with us, we are leaving."

Aymee took the extended hand of the blonde woman and was pulled to her feet with amazing strength for such a petite person.

"Hear the horns?" Evonne said to Vrawg. "The guard has finally arrived. Let's go before we have to answer too many questions. You owe me that drink we were supposed to have earlier."

CHAPTER 21

Meanwhile, as the temple was under attack, a certain weasely-looking master thief wound his way through the dark streets on the other side of the city. The storm ensured the streets were virtually empty, but Zenod clung to the shadows anyways. It would take a trained eye to ever know that the thief had passed you by.

Zenod felt quite distressed and was uncertain about his future. The man had very few people he would consider a friend and Serdic had been one of them. Serdic was now dead though, murdered on a busy street. By all accounts his murderer was Randar, though it was difficult to find anyone to speak up and admit to that. It made complete sense though. Serdic was the only man with enough men and influence to stand up to the Guild enforcer. But what did not make sense was why he needed to be killed since Zenod knew that Serdic had no designs on Guild leadership.

That troubling question had been bothering the master thief. He was now on his way to a special Guild meeting that had been called by Randar. It was a mandatory meeting with all senior members. Zenod could not help but wonder if the thug planned to clean house before claiming the Guild leadership for himself. Ever since the news of Serdic's murder reached his ears, Zenod had gone into hiding, until now. He had spent so long arguing with himself as to whether he would attend the meeting that now he was late.

Zenod froze in place against the wall of a shop as movement on the street caught his eye. A woman with a perfect body, which was evident from her tight-fitting clothes, sauntered down the middle of the street seemingly not caring about the rain that fell. Women-of-the-night were quite common in this area, but they always travelled in pairs, or larger groups, for safety. A quick scan of the street told Zenod the woman appeared to be alone but walked with a certain confidence, a confidence that Zenod had seen many times.

"A fine wig, my lady," the master thief said once he stood behind the woman.

"I was beginning to wonder when you were going to finally slink out of those shadows," Feylane replied, turning to face the man.

"A change in profession?" Zenod teased.

"Don't be a fool."

"Well, you are travelling in the opposite direction of our meeting, which it appears you are late for as well."

"I have a job tonight, I have no time for meetings."

"But it is mandatory."

"Says who?"

"Says Randar."

"And since when did Randar become Guild leader to

bark out orders for the rest of us?"

"He is soon to be leader, in case you have not been paying attention."

"I have been busy."

"Yes, well, with Serdic out of the way, Randar is sure to declare himself Guild leader tonight, and woe to any who oppose it."

"What do you mean 'with Serdic out of the way'?" Feylane asked, genuinely concerned.

"You have been busy, haven't you?"

"That's what I said."

"It would appear our thick-headed friend has eliminated the only threat to his claim for leadership. Serdic was murdered. I believe tonight is the night he makes his claim official."

The beautiful assassin felt a pang of sorrow. She liked Serdic, in fact everyone did. "If Randar is the one that killed him, then he must be held accountable. Members do not murder other members, especially senior members."

"And who is going to discipline him, eh? You? Me?"

"The Guild. We must all stand against him."

"Not bloody likely. And especially not now without Serdic's backing."

"The Guild be damned then."

"Oh the Guild is damned, of that I am certain. Randar will turn us all into street thugs and soldiers fighting a gang war with the Cult, a war we cannot win, I am afraid."

"That disgusting Cult needs to be eliminated."

"Oh, I do not disagree. But we do not have the resources to succeed. Think wisely, my pretty friend. Do you really wish to see our Guild in ruin?"

"We always find a way to survive. Now if you don't mind, I am soaked and still have a certain person I need to locate."

The master thief nodded to the beautiful assassin and left in the opposite direction. His soaking-wet cloak felt ten pounds heavier from the rain and he was looking forward to getting somewhere warm and hanging it up to dry. First though, he figured he should get to that meeting and learn what fate would befall the Guild.

*   *   *   *

Randar paced angrily within one of the Guild's many secret meeting chambers beneath the city. He hated being made to wait. One of his first duties as Guild leader would have to be to remind people to be on time when he calls a meeting, he thought to himself.

One of the eight entrances to the chamber, the one that led from the basement of a nearby tavern, opened and in walked a man known only as Patch. Patch was called Patch for obvious reasons - he wore one over his right eye. But the lean, six-foot, dark-haired man was not missing an eye as he led everyone to believe. He, in fact, had two very well-functioning eyes. Patch was a former bandit leader whose gang was eventually tracked down and destroyed. There was a very large price on his head in many of the territories surrounding Stonewood. Being a man who had been born with two different-colored eyes, he was easy to pick out in a crowd. He chose to display his brown eye, and hid his blue eye behind a patch, having told the tale of losing his eye in a tavern brawl. Nobody knew his real name aside from the nickname and he preferred to keep it that way.

"You are late," Randar barked.

"My apologies, I was held up with this storm. As you know, the gambling house I run is on the far side of the city," the former bandit said, taking a seat at the table with the others who were present.

"Considering we are still missing a few others, you are kinda early," said the silver-haired Yanzul, the oldest member of the Thieves Guild who had to be pushing seventy.

Next to Yanzul sat the black-skinned thief Jorold. Across from Jorold sat Jewel. Her abilities in appraising precious gemstones were second to none, which was where her nickname originated. Beside her sat Pitor, or Brother Pitor, as others called him. He wore the brown robes of a priest of the One True God. Only Pitor was no priest or a believer in any of the gods. He was the Guild's inside man at the largest temple in Stonewood and skimmed much gold from their treasury. He had been stealing gold from others his entire life until he learned that when you wore the robes of a priest, folk handed it over freely.

Another of the eight entrances opened, this one from a sewer tunnel, the same as four others. "Got here as soon as I could, only started my duty not long ago," said Myrvold, who was also a member of the city guard, as was evident by the armor and tunic he wore. He hung his soaking-wet cloak on a nearby hook.

Randar scanned the table at those assembled. Serdic was missing, of course. Zenod and Feylane were both running late. And there was another who Randar deemed worthy to sit at their table. That insulted the Guild enforcer the most, that man should not have been late, given that this was the first meeting to which he had been invited.

Then another door opened, and there stood the young thief Norvil, a puddle of water pooling on the floor beneath him, dripping from the curious black robe that he wore.

"You of all people I expected to be on time. Do not make me regret having promoted you," Randar growled with anger.

"Shut up, you lowly worm. Your time to regret that decision is at hand," replied the young thief in an unwavering voice.

Randar stood slack-jawed for several long silent moments, not believing his ears. Once he recovered, he spoke not a word. The Guild enforcer drew his short sword and marched around the table towards the upstart thief.

Norvil, or Brother Veral, was still a young priest and not one of any real power as of yet. So High Priest Sarvin had sent one along that was. Veral stepped into the chamber and moved to his left, making room for Brother Jaspar who took his position in the doorway.

The tall pale priest spoke an indecipherable word and pointed a finger at the advancing thug. A greenish glob flew from the priest's hand to splash against Randar's chest. The Guild enforcer had elected to wear a steel breastplate under his shirt this night, which turned out to be a wise decision. The glob of acid burned through his shirt and began to smoke as it ate its way through his armor. In a panic, the thug dropped his sword and fumbled with the straps to strip-off the breastplate before the acid could reach his skin.

The other Guild members jumped to their feet in shock, drawing weapons. It was then that three other doors to the meeting chamber burst open and in rushed screaming cultists wearing mailed shirts and brandishing long swords.

Patch impaled the first cultist through the nearest doorway with his curved sabre. He preferred the favored weapon of pirates and had taken this particular sword from the dead grasp of one in Port Bayswater. With blinding speed he pulled the light blade free of the man's chest and slashed the throat of a second as he entered the chamber.

Yanzul was quite the fighter in his younger days but age had caught up with him. He drew a knife from the top of his boot but received a sword-slash across his chest. He was too slow. He fell to his knees where he was hacked to death by a crazed Cult member.

Sparks flew as Myrvold battled fiercely with one cultist before a second joined the fight. The Guild member was heavily armored and took several strikes that fortunately did no damage.

Jewel drew a small throwing knife and launched it with amazing accuracy at the tall priest. The blade would have found the man's throat but bounced harmlessly off some invisible barrier. Before Jaspar could speak the words of a spell he planned to direct at her, a sword found her back and came out through her stomach.

Jorold ducked under a decapitating swing and came up with a vicious attack of his own, removing the cultist's arm at the elbow with his short-bladed sword. The Cult member fell to the floor without even a grunt. Another member took his place and nicked the thief on the shoulder drawing blood. Jorold backed up parrying the next two attacks before Patch's sabre tore open the cultists right side. As the wounded man fell forward, the thief split open his skull.

Randar finally threw his breastplate to the floor, receiving only minor burns to his chest. A cultist lunged for the thug thinking him an easy, unarmed target. With lightning-speed, Randar drew a dagger from his right boot and plunged the blade right up under the cultist's jaw. He kicked the dead man in the chest, sending him flying away, not even bothering to retrieve the dagger. He pulled a second, smaller blade from his left boot and buried it in the throat of the next closest cultist. The Guild enforcer was beyond furious – he was filled with rage. He snatched up his fallen sword and began to hack his way to Brother Veral.

Veral had not been idly standing by. He slipped past Jorold to where Pitor desperately tried to keep a swordsman at bay with a long dagger he had hidden under his brown robe. At the last moment, the thief noticed the black-robed man moving behind him. He attempted to turn but Veral was too fast, sliding a blade into his ribcage. He gasped, then a sword found his shoulder.

Jorold cut down another cultist before lunging at the tall priest. Jaspar spoke the words of a spell and a gust of wind blew the thief backwards, slamming him hard against a wall. Winded, he took a slash to the stomach. He blocked the follow-up attack and countered with a slice of his own across the cultist's cheek. A second blade from his right cut open his sword-arm. He spun on that man, driving his sword into his shoulder. A blade then pierced the thief's back as a second found his chest. Choking on blood, Jorold collapsed to the floor.

With a roar of rage, Randar swung for Veral's head. The smaller man side-stepped out of range but then nearly tripped over a dead cultist. The thug capitalized on the priest's momentary distraction and drew a line of blood across his forearm. Another cultist then stepped in between the pair but found Randar's sword buried in his chest before he could raise his weapon to block. The thug body-checked the dying man aside and lunged again for the priest.

Brother Veral again moved out of range but this time he did stumble to the floor, tripping over the body of Pitor; bodies littered the floor of the meeting chamber. With a cry of victory, Randar raised his sword and brought it down towards Veral's head. Thinking fast, Jaspar mouthed another spell and Randar's blade stopped short of its target, hitting some invisible barrier. The thug growled and hacked at the barrier like a crazed berserker but his blade bounced off harmlessly with each strike.

Patch felled two more cultists and panted with exhaustion. He found himself standing next to an open doorway leading to a labyrinth of sewer tunnels, a labyrinth he happened to know very well. He surveyed the carnage around him and his mind was made. He disappeared into the tunnel.

Myrvold barely blocked a strike to his face. His armor had saved him from countless hits, but his counter-attacks were getting slower and slower. The pale priest looked at him with glowing-red eyes and the Guild member's head exploded with pain. Nothing had actually hit him but he was forced to his knees, unable to lift his arms. Suddenly the room went upside-down. Confused, Myrvold glanced around and saw his headless body, then he knew no more.

Randar burned with a deep hatred inside, but he was smart enough to realize this battle was lost. With his free hand, he pulled three small spheres from a belt pouch and threw them against the floor. The spheres exploded with blinding light and the room filled with thick smoke. The thug cut one more cultist's throat before exiting through the door that led to a tavern.

When the smoke finally cleared, Brother Jaspar found Brother Veral still lying on the floor. The younger priest looked pale, having come so close to death at the hands of the enraged Guild thug. Jaspar was not happy, though. They had taken heavy losses and two thieves had escaped, one being their main target. But now the Guild was crippled, he supposed. Many senior members lay dead before him and now the Guild knew they could be found. They would be forced to scatter or flee the city. He wondered how Sister Devi had faired over at the temple. If she was successful, there would be nobody left to stand in their way.

*   *   *   *

Zenod peered into the meeting chamber and his heart thudded inside his chest. What he beheld was an absolute massacre. Bodies of Guild members lay butchered about the room. It appeared to have been all quite recent. He swallowed hard and thanked the dark gods for his tardiness. He risked entering the room to scan the bodies of those present. Randar, it seemed, was not among them. So now the mystery deepened. Was this Randar's doing?

Or was it some surprise attack by the Cult? There were no other bodies aside from Guild members.

Further investigation revealed that Patch's body was also not among the dead. The master thief wondered if the man had also chosen not to attend or had managed to escape. Zenod figured he should look for Patch first before deciding his next course of action. He would also need to find Feylane and inform her, but she was not so easily found when she did not wish to be.

CHAPTER 22

Dawn was upon Stonewood though you would not know it. The sky was dark as the terrible storm from the previous night still raged on. Lightning lit up the city frequently and thunder rattled windows.

High Priest Sarvin stood on a balcony high up in Castle Stonewood, reveling in the storm. Heavy rain had thoroughly soaked his robes but he did not care. They had scored a major victory that night. His enemies were now broken and scattered. They knew fear.

His lovely assistant Devi-Lynn had performed her duties marvelously at the temple. The First Priest was dead along with many others and they had a worthy heart for the last ritual. The beautiful priestess's heart would be used at the King's birthday ceremony, right in the throne room. Lord Lucivenus himself would be wishing the King a *happy birthday*. Sarvin smiled at that thought.

Brothers Jaspar and Veral had also done exceptionally well at wiping out many of the Guild's senior members. Randar had managed to slip away but it was no matter. He would be hunted down and eliminated in time. Now the Guild could not relax. They knew their enemies could find them. Sarvin knew that most thieves had little stomach for a street war and he considered most of them cowardly scum. The Guild was no longer a threat to them.

"Do you want to catch a cold? Come back in here," Devi-Lynn purred from just inside the balcony door.

"What news of the mercenaries?" Sarvin asked.

"Gone," she replied. "They have left."

"Thelvius was well paid. Why would he leave?"

"They are mercenaries, they cannot be fully trusted and have no allegiances to anyone. Perhaps they were frightened off by our army of wraggoth that are now camped a half day's travel from the city awaiting further instructions."

"Excellent. Tell them to remain there. They are not to surround the city until the evening of the birthday celebrations. Once we have completed our goal, we will deal with those wretched mercenaries."

Sarvin then accepted the extended hand of the priestess and went back inside.

*   *   *   *

Dornell flexed his fingers on both hands, then made tight fists. "They feel great, my thanks."

The former guard captain sat on a stool within a small prayer chamber at the Temple of the One True God. Sister Melina had just prayed for a spell of healing and her prayer was answered.

Harcourt leaned against the wall, head down, feeling very distraught. They had just been given an account of the attack on the temple the night before. In a brave move, the Cult had actually sent a force into the temple and most troubling of all, took a prisoner. And not just any prisoner, but the only person there that Harcourt cared about. He did not understand why Krestina had been chosen by the Cult but whatever the reasons, they did not bode well for the priestess.

Harcourt felt as though he had failed again. He had failed to protect his first love, Jalanna, and now he had failed in his duty to protect Krestina. The bounty hunters were paid well to watch over her but Harcourt did not fault them for not protecting her. For all they knew, he was gone from Stonewood forever, so why continue to work for a dead man. It was his fault for getting caught and being sent away. Had he have been here in the city, he would have got her out of the temple to safety.

"I have to find her," Harcourt said after Sister Melina left the room to fetch the pair some water.

"What is so important about this priestess? To you and them?" Dornell asked.

"She is…," the thief paused, thinking of a way to explain it, "…an old friend of mine. The Cult obviously knew Weldrick was the Guild leader, so it is possible they targeted her for being an acquaintance of mine. I really do not know any other reason."

"There is a good chance she is still alive. They could have just killed her here like the others but they took her alive. But where would we even begin to look?"

Harcourt had no answer for that. "They took her alive so that they could rip out her heart for some sick ritual, of that I am certain. But where and when is anyone's guess."

"I need to find Captain Flannis," Dornell then said. "He is one of the few men I know I can trust."

"I suggest we split up for the time being. Take Na'Jala with you and find Flannis. I need to speak with Fezzdin and then attempt to make contact with the Guild. And before you roll your eyes, we need any help we can get right now and there is no love between the Guild and the Cult."

For once, Dornell did not argue. "But your mask is gone, you are no longer Weldrick."

"I will deal with that at the time."

*   *   *   *

"If your mother was still alive, she would have this entire city torn to pieces looking for your brother. I feel we are not doing enough," King Stonewood said, his voice sounding exhausted.

"Father, we have all the resources at our disposal looking for him. I think the Cult has him and that he is still alive. They are not shy about leaving heartless bodies to be found. Since there has been no sign of Denniz, it might be a good sign that he is being kept prisoner," Prince Orval reasoned.

"The Prince may be right," Chief Magistrate Krommel commented as he entered the council chamber. "They also took a prisoner during that disgusting attack on the temple. It might be wise to show some restraint. I feel they may be looking to ransom off prisoners. I would think we should hear something from them soon."

"And how long are we supposed to wait?" the King asked, his patience already stretched thin.

"Your birthday is in two days, my lord. I feel we may hear something from them by the time that passes. They most likely are hoping that your grief will disrupt the celebration. And if you call off the festivities then the common people will be angry. I believe we must carry on and be strong. Let us not give into despair as they would have us," Krommel answered. "I have seen to it that there will be much added security here at the castle during the party that night."

"Oh, how I wish this cowardly Cult was brave enough to meet me face to face to make their demands," the King said angrily.

"You never know, you may just get that wish," Krommel replied with a slight grin.

*   *   *   *

Evonne sat nervously on a bench outside an office within Castle Stonewood. Four castle guards had escorted her inside and stood nearby keeping an eye on the bounty hunter. The guards had visited the inn where she was staying and told her that Devi-Lynn demanded an audience with her. Evonne was fairly confident that she and Vrawg had left no cultists alive in the temple to place them there during the attack. If the Chief Magistrate was the leader of the Cult, then it was a good bet that his assistant Devi-Lynn might also be in on it. That was why Evonne elected to come to this meeting alone. If Vrawg believed that the woman was involved with the Cult, there would be no controlling him. Since Evonne could not be entirely sure, she decided to investigate herself. She fervently hoped this was not the wrong decision.

The office door opened and another guard, one dressed in black platemail, bid her enter. Evonne cautiously did as instructed and took a seat across from the raven-haired assistant of the Chief Magistrate.

"It is a pleasure as usual to see you, Evonne," she said.

"And you."

"Now, I have to say that you and your partner, whose services are extremely expensive, have not quite lived up to your reputation lately. Compared with the other bounty hunters, you have not fared so well in dragging in Guild members in quite some time."

Evonne did her best Vrawg imitation and shrugged her shoulders. "What can I say? Slippery lot them thieves."

"Yes, well we would like to enlist your help again, a different job this time."

"Do tell."

"As you have probably witnessed, the city is preparing for the yearly birthday festivities for the King, which take place in two days. We have a large party in the throne room and this year we would like to increase our security measures. The Chief Magistrate has become increasingly concerned about this Cult, more so since the brazen attack on the temple. We are willing to pay you five-hundred gold pieces for the evening, to be inside the throne room and watch for any trouble."

"That is a possibility," Evonne replied. "You are expecting trouble in the throne room?"

"We have reason to believe that the Cult has infiltrated some of the castle guard."

I bet you do, Evonne thought to herself.

"The King's birthday ceremony would be the perfect

setting for them to try something. So no matter what happens, we ask that you protect the Chief Magistrate at all costs, especially against traitorous guards."

"Don't you mean protect the King at all costs?" Evonne asked.

"The King has his own personal trusted guards, I am hiring you to protect the Chief Magistrate. It is whispered that he may be the Cult's next target. If these traitorous guards reveal themselves and move against him, do not hesitate in cutting them down. I will quadruple your fee if he is alive and well the next day."

So there it was, Evonne mused, the Cult must be planning something big the night of the King's birthday. They are bold indeed if they plan to move against the King himself in his very throne room. The bounty hunter figured this might be a good time to leave Stonewood behind and seek other jobs elsewhere. But she thought it best not to reveal those plans.

"We have a deal," Evonne responded.

"Excellent. See the clerk on your way out, she will give you two special passes to get into the castle for your duties that night. And do not be late."

*   *   *   *

Harcourt finished suiting up in a set of studded leather armor, and strapped on two daggers and a short sword that were crafted by the dwarven smithy Wendall. He was fortunate that nobody had known where Weldrick lived, so he had snuck into his own home and found everything still intact. He double-checked his hidden safes and found every coin and every gemstone accounted for.

Every once and awhile luck was with him; it was just not consistent.

The thief threw on a thick, black cloak, pulled the hood around his face and ventured back out into the streets. Many folk were about, now that the storm was relatively over. The skies were still dark but the rain had stopped for the time being. Even though Harcourt did not really feel as though anyone would recognize him - after all he was supposed to be dead - he still kept his head down and his hood pulled tight.

The thief needed to speak with Fezzdin the Fantastic, but he was unsure how he would get anywhere near the wizard's tower. Fezzdin's tower resided in the north district and nobody came and went through there without a guard escort. Harcourt had never attempted sneaking into the district before; it was walled off from the rest of the city and heavily patrolled. Getting over the wall was near-impossible now, given the time of day and the number of people about.

After much internal debate, the thief decided to take the direct route and approached one of two guarded gates that led into the north district.

"State yer name and business," asked one particularly large guard, who seemed annoyed that he had to get up off his stool and do something.

"My name is Samwell. I am an associate of Fezzdin and need to speak with him immediately," Harcourt replied.

"Are ye now? Ye don't look like someone who associates with the wizard. Very few people do."

"I can assure you we are friends. He can tell you himself if you would just escort me to his tower."

"Oh, I could take ye there, but ye would be waiting there a long time me-thinks. Wizard's been missing for awhile now. Nobody knows where he is and nobody can get into his tower. So best ye just run along, then."

Harcourt turned and left, figuring he would get nothing more of use out of that guard. If the wizard had been missing for quite awhile, that might explain why he was not around to lend a helping hand when he was most needed at the trial. Surely he could have spoken up for the thief or at least Dornell. But this was troubling news indeed. What if Krommel had got to Fezzdin? The thief had been counting on the wizard's help to figure out his next steps. He was hoping that Fezzdin might have some idea where to begin looking for Krestina. Harcourt knew the Cult would not keep her alive for much longer, if she even still lived.

Harcourt shook that terrible thought from his head and quickened his pace, but where he was headed now he was not sure. Suddenly, he tripped over something and nearly tumbled to the cobblestone street. Glancing down, he noticed a familiar-looking orange cat who must have purposely attempted to trip him.

"Lex? Is that you?"

The orange cat rubbed his head against the thief's leg.

"Where is your friend Fezzdin? Do you know?" Harcourt felt silly asking the cat a question like that but something had told him there was more to this cat than one might think.

Lex then trotted off down a street, pausing only to look back to see if the thief was following. Harcourt did his best to keep up with the cat who wove his way so easily through the crowded street.

Lex turned down an alley that led to a narrow road behind several shops. He leaped up upon a stack of empty crates and stared off into the direction of Castle Stonewood which could be seen clearly off in the distance.

"He is in the castle then? Is that what you mean?"

The cat then bumped his head into the thief's arm. Well, Harcourt figured that if Fezzdin was reported as missing, but he was in the castle, then it was a safe bet that Krommel may have had him locked away somewhere. It might also be possible then, that Krestina could be held in the same place as Fezzdin.

Harcourt sighed in despair. How would he ever be able to get into the castle? And even if he could, where would he begin to look? The castle was massive. If he still possessed his magical mask, he might have been able to pull it off.

The thief scratched the cat on the head. "I don't know how yet, but I will find your friend."

*   *   *   *

By the third knock at the door, Evonne knew that this person was not just going to go away. The bounty hunter slid out of her bed and scooped up her loaded crossbow which she always kept within reach. She padded silently over to the door and stood motionless, listening. A fourth time, someone banged loudly. It came from midway down the door. A child, she thought, or a dwarf. Or someone wanting her to think that.

In one swift movement, she unlocked the door and pulled it open, leveling her crossbow in the appropriate spot. A young boy then sprinted off down the hall as quickly as his legs could carry him. As soon as the idea of a diversion came to her mind, she felt the sting of a blade pressing into the back of her neck.

"Lay the crossbow on the floor, so nobody gets hurt," the voice from behind said.

Even dressed for bed, she was not without a few tricks, so she did as she was instructed.

"Do you always sleep with the window unlocked?" the man asked and suddenly she felt she recognized the voice.

"Harcourt?" she inquired, turning to face the man.

CHAPTER 23

The tall guard captain of the south district was returning back to the guardhouse after a long shift. He had arrested four people and broken up five separate fights this day. He rubbed the knuckles on this right hand which were still sore after breaking a man's nose several hours earlier for vandalizing decorations for the King's birthday. Captain Flannis always dreaded that day where the streets would be packed with partiers from dawn til dawn, and was almost impossible to control.

"A moment of your time, please," said a cloaked man leaning against the wall of the guardhouse.

"How many times I have told you beggars to stay away from here? Now get lost," Captain Flannis replied.

"Is that any way to speak to an old friend?" the man said, pulling the hood of his cloak back just enough to reveal his face to the guard captain.

Captain Flannis stood slack-jawed before he could compose himself. He looked about suspiciously then said, "Inside quickly, before someone sees you."

Dornell followed the captain inside and signaled to Na'Jala to wait nearby.

*   *   *   *

"We never thought we would be seeing you again," Evonne said to Harcourt, after she put on some clothes and fetched her partner.

The trio sat inside the blonde bounty hunter's room at the inn. Vrawg wore the same shocked expression that was on Evonne's face.

"I didn't think so either but sometimes, on occasion, I get lucky," Harcourt replied.

"The Cult took your friend. We're sorry, we tried to help but we were too late," she admitted.

"I figured you both would have given up on that job as soon as I was arrested and sent from the city, and I wouldn't have faulted you for it."

"Don't think I didn't try to convince this oaf here of doing just that, but he is a stubborn one."

"My thanks for your efforts," Harcourt said to Vrawg.

The huge half-orge nodded but frowned at remembering his failure to protect the priestess.

"I have to find her. I am hoping she is still alive. I have a hunch that she might be in the castle. The Cult is probably planning some ritual where they will take her heart, so time is running out."

"I think I might have an idea when this will be," Evonne mentioned.

"Oh? What do you know?"

"That raven-haired assistant to the Chief Magistrate

invited me in to meet with her this afternoon. She wanted to hire us to work security in the throne room for the King's birthday party. She said she feels the Cult may try something that night and we were to protect the Magistrate at all costs, especially against traitorous guards who may attack him."

"So they are planning something big for that night," Harcourt figured.

"That would be my guess. Pretty bold, if you ask me. Vrawg and I were going to leave the city tomorrow."

"I have to get inside that castle somehow. If what you say is true, they may be using Krestina for their nefarious plot. I have to try and find her before the party."

"If you want inside the castle, that woman issued us these," Evonne said pulling out two copper medallions from a chest on the floor. She tossed them to the thief. "These are our passes into the castle as hired security."

Harcourt wondered if he would be allowed entry posing as a hired bounty hunter. It was worth a try, it was his only option. The only problem was that it would have to be on that very day, which did not give him much time to find Krestina.

"I would very much like to have you both in the castle as well, if things turn sour. Can I pay you to go ahead with Krommel's plan and have you both in that throne room that night?" the thief asked, producing a diamond from inside his cloak.

Evonne was very fond of diamonds and liked the way this one sparkled. Vrawg nodded in agreement with the plan but then held out his massive hand to wave away the diamond, indicating that it was not necessary. The blonde bounty hunter was about to protest but the look on her partner's face told her that it was not open for debate.

"Curse your soft heart," she whispered under her breath.

"Thank you," Harcourt said addressing the half-ogre. "You are very kind and honorable."

Evonne rolled her eyes. "Oh, do not get him started, I beg you. Once he starts he won't shut up."

Harcourt looked curiously at Vrawg, who he had never heard speak a single word. The huge bounty hunter just shrugged.

"But if I have these," the thief held up the medallions, "How will you both get into the castle?"

"Leave that to me," Evonne replied confidently.

*   *   *   *

"Your position of Captain of the Investigations Unit has already been filled and I have never heard of the man who holds it now. Krommel appointed the man only a day ago," Captain Flannis said as the two men sat inside his personal office, which was once Dornell's for many years.

"Krommel has spent years promoting Cult members to positions of power within the city. God only knows how many men are under his control," Dornell replied.

The former captain had filled in his friend on all the events that took place from the time of his arrest, to his arrival back in the city. Flannis could not believe what he was hearing.

"It is not safe for you to remain here," Flannis said. "There are many guards here that I certainly do not trust, many appointed to this post only recently as well."

"I will not be staying. I wanted to get some armor

and weapons from you. I have to meet with Harcourt in the morning and then figure out a way to get to Krommel and find this priestess that they took prisoner."

"You know, Krommel has some cells where they hold special prisoners separate from the dungeons. Underneath the east wing. I had arrested a thief of note once and Krommel bid me deliver the man there for questioning. That might be worth looking into, if you managed to get inside the castle," Flannis suggested.

"My thanks, old friend. I knew I could count on you."

"You know I will do anything to aid you. Help yourself to anything in the armory. Take a uniform as well, it will help you move about the streets, just keep your face hidden. News of your escape has spread and folk are on the watch for you."

＊　　＊　　＊　　＊

It was very risky, but Harcourt decided to pay a visit to one of the Guild's hideouts. He needed all the helpful information he could get about the castle and the possible dangers inside on the night of the party. The Guild employed several city guards, so the thief hoped he might be able to speak to one of them.

The major problem, as pointed out by Dornell, was that he was no longer Weldrick. The thief had gotten so used to life with the magical mask that it actually felt weird just being Harcourt again. At least his face was not one of a wanted fugitive like Dornell's.

The thief turned down a particularly dark alley next to Shashi's Books and found it strange that he was not greeted with the barking of dogs. The Guild used several large dogs that wandered this alley to alert them of anyone approaching the hidden gambling house. This night there was not a one. He made a right-turn down an even narrower alley that was only wide enough for one person. Harcourt then knocked four times on a stack of boxes that appeared to be just stacked against a plain wall, but they were actually blocking the door to this particular hideout. Normally, a thug was posted inside the door to keep watch but nobody answered. Again, odd.

Harcourt drew his short sword and pulled open the secret door. He found the stairway leading below this building unoccupied. On an average night, at this hour, there could be anywhere from ten to twenty Guild members here playing a variety of games with the intent of taking the other's gold.

He silently descended the stairs but stopped short of entering the room below when he heard two voices.

"Word has spread quickly. There weren't nearly as many thieves here as I would have expected. I believe we'll find even less at our next target," he heard one of the voices say.

"Don't be so sure. The Guild should not even be aware that we know of their hideout in the abandoned stables near the cemetery. We should catch them once again, completely off-guard," the other voice replied.

"I hope you are right, Brother Thomas, these thieves have proven themselves quite dangerous. They have ruled these streets for a very long time."

"The city is theirs no longer. Lord Lucivenus will be returned shortly and reclaim what he had once taken. Stonewood will be his and we, his loyal followers, will reap the rewards."

Harcourt had heard enough and entered the room. The scene before him looked as though a battle had played out not long ago. Many of the card tables were overturned and scattered about the room. The bodies of four men were strewn about the floor, hacked to pieces. In the center of the room stood two men, one brown-haired wearing the black robes of a Cult priest, the other a bald man wearing a set of chain mail armor, a sword hanging from his belt.

Harcourt had never killed anyone until that cursed red-bladed dagger had compelled him to. Once the Lich Lord had taken the weapon from him, the thief had felt remorse for his actions but he realized it was necessary. These Cult members were evil and capable of terrible things. He told himself it would be a huge mistake to let them go.

Holding his sword in his right hand, Harcourt drew one of his daggers with his left and threw it with superb accuracy into the lower back of the priest, who grunted and fell to his knees, attempting to reach back for the blade.

"You should have fled like the others," the second cultist said, drawing his sword and advancing on the thief.

Confident in his swordsmanship, Harcourt engaged the man. The cultist swung for his neck and the thief easily parried, then countered. The man stepped back just out of range of the thief's shorter sword which met only air. The pair circled each other before the cultist attacked again. Harcourt blocked, then spun in a three-sixty circle slashing the cultist across the shoulder drawing blood.

The man stumbled back, his confidence shaken. He

glanced over to the priest who writhed on the ground, still trying to pull the dagger free of his back. Harcourt pressed the attack with a series of slashes to the head and body. To his credit, the cultist blocked each attack but this time there was no counter coming.

The thief then knocked the man's blade out wide and stabbed forward but could not penetrate the mail-shirt. The cultist brought his blade back and nearly took off the thief's hand as Harcourt twisted to stand beside the man. The thief then drove his sword into the cultist's side, below his arm where there was a gap in his armor.

With a gasp, the cultist stumbled backwards and fell to the floor, tripping over the priest. Harcourt kicked the man's sword out of reach, then stood over him for the killing blow, but paused. A moment ago, it would not have mattered to skewer the man, as Dornell had once put it, it was him or me. But now the man lay below him, wounded and unarmed. Now it just seemed like a slaughter, and Harcourt was no butcher like these cultists.

While the thief struggled with what to do, a small knife flew into the cultist's throat and he thrashed about for a moment before laying completely still. Harcourt whirled, pointing his sword at the chest of the figure that stood behind him. He was surprised to find the beautiful assassin Feylane standing there, a throwing knife in each hand.

If he had been surprised to see her, then words could not describe the look on her face upon seeing him. She paled slightly, as though she had seen a ghost.

"It's me, Harcourt, your eyes do not deceive you."

"But…..how?"

"That is a very long tale, but I am very much alive as

you can see."

"A curse upon you both," spat the priest.

With lightning speed, the assassin launched both knives which buried themselves hilt-deep into the man's chest and throat. He too, then lay very still.

"No!" Harcourt shouted. "I needed to question him about something very important!"

"Trust me," Feylane replied. "You would have gotten nothing of value from him. They do not succumb to torture. We have tried."

"How did they find this place? How many other hideouts have they hit?" Harcourt asked.

"Firstly, how about you tell me how YOU found this place. And what do YOU know about our other hideouts?"

Harcourt was not sure how best to answer those questions. "Let's just say that I was very close with Weldrick, your former leader."

"Interesting," the assassin replied.

"Look, Feylane, I hate this Cult even more than you, as impossible as that is to believe. I will stop at nothing to see them eliminated. A good friend of mine was taken prisoner during their assault on the temple. I have information that leads me to believe that the Cult is planning something big on the night of the King's birthday and I believe her heart is the one they plan to use. I think she is being held in the castle. Now, I have a way into the castle but I was hoping to speak with some of the guards that the Guild employs. Maybe get some kind of layout of the castle to aid in my search."

"You have a way into the castle?"

"Yes, I do."

"How? I have been trying for years to find a way in to get to Krommel. If you knew Weldrick, then you must know that Krommel is the suspected Cult leader."

"Yes, I know he is. That's why I believe he is holding my friend in the castle. I have acquired two passes into the castle the night of the party, if I can convince the guards I am a hired bounty hunter there to help with security."

"Two passes?"

"Yes, two."

"Take me with you."

"What?"

"Take me with you and I will help."

"Feylane, this is very dangerous."

"You do know who I am, right?"

"Yes, of course I do."

"Then take me with you. I will find Krommel and I will end this once and for all. I will sever the head of this Cult."

Harcourt thought about the offer. He definitely could not bring Dornell with him, he was too easily recognized at the castle. Na'Jala he felt would stand out too much. Harcourt needed to rely on stealth, and Feylane was the very essence of stealth.

"Alright," Harcourt said. "But we make finding my friend the priority. Then we can deal with Krommel afterwards."

"You have a deal," the assassin replied.

CHAPTER 24

Krestina drifted in and out of consciousness. Her wrists were chained to the wall of a tiny cell and she had been gagged to prevent her from speaking the words to any spells. She must have been dreaming again, she thought. She had seen Harcourt looking for her. The priestess took that as a sign that the end was near. The thief she had fallen in love with was dead; perhaps this meant she was soon to join him.

The image of the thief was replaced with another, only this time it felt very real. Standing at her cell door was a large man dressed in the robes of a city official. She thought she had seen this man somewhere before, a magistrate perhaps. She was certain that she was actually awake so a feeling of excitement washed over her, someone had found her and was here to rescue her.

Her feeling of joy was short-lived as an evil chuckle came from the man staring at her. Suddenly, she knew he was not her savior.

"You should feel proud of yourself my dear, that you

were chosen over so many others," the man said to her in a sinister voice. "You will not have to remain in this cell much longer. You are going to attend the King's birthday celebration with me tomorrow night. We are going to have a special surprise for the King."

And then High Priest Sarvin left, leaving Krestina alone and wondering what surprise he could have meant.

*   *   *   *

Ruggard Bloodaxe downed his sixth consecutive mug of ale as if it was a single shot. The huge red-bearded northman signaled for the barmaid to bring more. Since leaving his home in the icy north, Ruggard had become a sellsword and bounty hunter, a very successful one. The man had a lust for gold that could not be sated in the frozen lands where he was born. Coming to Stonewood was his best decision yet; his pockets and belly were always full.

Ruggard turned to face the woman standing to his right and frowned when it was not the barmaid he was expecting with more ale. "What do ye want, lass?"

"May I sit?" Evonne asked.

"And if I told ye no?"

The petite blonde bounty hunter promptly took a seat at the northman's table. The pair knew each other's reputations well but had never before met face to face. Ruggard glanced around the room until he found Vrawg seated at a table near the door. He knew her large partner was never too far away.

"So let me ask again, what do ye want?"

"I imagine a man of your reputation must have also

been hired to work the King's party tomorrow night, eh?"

"Aye. What of it?"

"How much do you know about our employer and the goings-on within this city?" Evonne asked.

"I know I get paid well here. Never has the gold flowed more freely. Cities with problems are very profitable for our kind, no?"

"You were instructed to protect the Chief Magistrate at all costs? Especially against any traitorous castle guards who may try to attack him?"

"Aye."

"Keep your eyes open tomorrow night. All might not be exactly what it seems."

"Why do ye speak in riddles, lass?"

"That Cult of demon-worshippers is mostly likely going to make a move tomorrow night. Just don't get caught on the wrong side, that's all I am saying. Think carefully before you react."

Evonne got up and left the table as more of the northman's ale arrived. She knew what Ruggard was capable of and did not wish to find him on opposite sides of a battle. She hoped the barbarian was smart enough to determine friend from foe if things got ugly.

*　　*　　*　　*

"I don't like this idea at all," Dornell said with his arms across his chest. "You plan on just walking into the castle alongside a Guild assassin?"

"Can you think of a better plan? Our time has run out. The Cult is going to do something big tomorrow night. I have to get in there and find Krestina and then put an end to Krommel," Harcourt replied.

"Then take me with you and not some damned assassin that cannot be trusted," Dornell pleaded.

"You would never get passed the first set of guards, my friend. Your face is very well known and Krommel's people are looking for you, and for Na'Jala I might add. I, on the other hand, no longer wear Weldrick's face, so I have the best shot of getting in."

"He has a point," Na'Jala agreed.

The trio stood in a wooded section of Stonewood's cemetery. It was dark and the best place to have a private conversation at night, given that most avoided the place after the sun had set.

Dornell knew the thief had a point. He just did not like being left out of the plan, especially knowing the danger his friend would be in.

"So we are just supposed to wait for you to make some miraculous escape?" the former captain asked.

"I am afraid so," the thief answered. "There is no other way."

"Look, what is that?" Na'Jala said pointing to a building that was ablaze not far away from the cemetery.

"Our first strike back against the Cult," Harcourt replied.

*   *   *   *

Two cloaked men approached the back door to the apparently-abandoned stables. The front doors had been boarded shut; to all outside eyes the place appeared empty. The Cult, however, knew it was a favored hideout for the Thieves Guild. All the windows had also been boarded up, this back door facing the cemetery was the only way in or out.

The shorter of the two cloaked men pressed his ear to the door listening carefully, then signaled for others to join. Eight more cloaked men brandishing swords joined the first two, along with two others wearing the robes of priests.

"The demon god willing, we will find Randar inside and end his miserable life," Brother Bandor whispered to Brother Pullo.

The other priest grinned wickedly at the thought of slaughtering more thieves where they thought themselves safe. He gave the signal with his hand, one of the cultists flung the door open wide and all of them rushed in.

A moment later, two figures emerged from the shadows around the stables and began pushing large heavy crates towards the back door. Just before blocking the door completely, Patch and Randar ignited two torches and tossed them inside the stables where they had dumped buckets of lantern oil only an hour earlier. As shouts of alarm erupted from within, the two men grunted as they pushed with all their strength to seal the door with the crates filled with stones.

Shouts and curses could be heard behind the barricade, as well as the sounds of boots attempting to kick their way out.

The two Guild members backed up far enough away, then stood and watched the building as it was engulfed in flames.

A satisfying smile spread across Randar's face. It was only a small victory and therefore only a temporary joy, but he would take whatever he could get. The Guild enforcer had not yet fully forgiven the man standing next to him for fleeing the last battle and leaving him in that meeting room, but right now Randar needed all the men he could find.

*　　*　　*　　*

Nearby, Feylane and Zenod also watched the stables go up in flames.

"Harcourt is really alive, eh?" the weasely master thief asked.

"Yes, he has managed to cheat death somehow. He gave me this tip that the Cult was going to hit the stables," the beautiful assassin replied.

"Interesting. And you are really going through with this plan then? You and he, assassinating Krommel right in the castle?"

"Yes, I am. This little war has raged long enough. I am going to end it. After I deal with Krommel, I am going to hunt down that traitorous wretch Norvil," Feylane said confidently.

Zenod thought the plan had sounded fairly crazy, but then he had never known Feylane to fail with a mission. Thieves were dropping like flies so something drastic needed to happen. If the Cult was actually eliminated, there was still the issue of Randar and the Guild, but Zenod figured he would stick around long enough to see how this all played out.

CHAPTER 25

Harcourt and Feylane nervously approached one of the gates leading into the north district. The thief was decked out in his studded leather armor with a variety of daggers and knives strapped to his body accompanying his sword. The stunningly attractive assassin at his side, her hair dyed jet-black, wore a very tight-fitting black leather outfit with a series of throwing knives strapped across her chest, and a long dagger strapped to her right thigh. The thief was positive those were not the only weapons available to his resourceful partner.

Feylane had convinced Harcourt to let her do all the talking; men tended to listen to whatever she had to say.

"State your names and business," said one of six guards posted at the gatehouse.

Today was the King's birthday and the entire city was alive and celebrating in the crowded streets. Wine flowed freely and bread and cheese were handed out to all. As a result, extra security was everywhere. Every guard within the city was on duty this day. The sun had still not fully set but Harcourt and Feylane thought to arrive early for their throne room duty which was set to begin in several hours.

"We are here to report to the castle for our security duty. We have been hired by the Chief Magistrate," Feylane answered. She and Harcourt both flashed their medallions.

"You don't look like a bounty hunter or mercenary," the guard said, looking Feylane up and down hungrily. "What are your names?" he asked, looking around through a pile of papers he had resting on a stool.

"I have many skills," Feylane purred in his ear. "When the party wraps up in the throne room, maybe I will come looking for you later."

The guard lost his train of thought and grinned like a child. "Harvey and Dax there will escort you two to the castle. I will be here waiting later."

Feylane winked at the guard and followed her escorts through the gate. Harcourt shook his head. Life could have been much easier had he been born an attractive woman. Even though nobody would be looking for him specifically, he still kept his hood pulled low over his face just in case any of the guards were to recognize him, since he had made many trips to the dungeons throughout his life.

The streets in the north district were not crowded with revelers like those of the other districts this day. The wealthiest folk in Stonewood lived in the north district, many of whom would have been invited to the party within the castle. Still though, many patrols passed them by on their way to the castle.

Their escorts led them through the front gates of the castle where another six heavily-armored guards stood. Now they were on the grounds of the castle itself and Harcourt looked around in awe. The sheer size of the castle was awe-inspiring. Harcourt was always led down a different route when brought to the dungeons located below the castle, so this was his first time ever on the grounds and this close to the castle itself.

He would have been completely lost as to where to begin looking for Krestina, but Dornell had received some information about a detention area below the east wing of the castle where Krommel had kept special prisoners. The thief was hoping that was where Krestina could be found. Alive.

Their escorts left them alone as they now approached the main doors to the castle lobby. The doors were wide open as guards and staff rushed about with final last-minute party duties. Again, they were stopped and asked to produce their medallions.

"We have urgent news for the Chief Magistrate," Feylane lied to a blonde-bearded guard. "His office again, somewhere on the first floor, if I am not mistaken?"

"No, it's on the second floor of the east wing, but he is not to be disturbed. That was his order. You can speak with him in the throne room when he arrives," the guard responded. "Now straight through the lobby and follow the main hall right down to the throne room. You are not to wander anywhere else. Got it?"

"But, of course," Feylane replied with a nod and the guard all but drooled as she passed him by.

The thief and the assassin now stood in the main
lobby of the castle which bustled with activity. Staff
members hurried in all directions carrying trays of food
and decorations that still needed to be hung. A grand
chandelier hung from the ceiling and Harcourt could not
even begin to guess the worth of it. A lush red carpet
covered the floor running down the main hallway and
lavish paintings and sculptures dominated every wall.

Harcourt, who had lived in absolute poverty his entire
life, had to be shaken by the assassin to wake from the
trance that befell him while drinking in the scenery around
them.

"Keep focused," Feylane whispered. "You can admire
the décor later. By the sounds of it, Krommel is in his
office. Let's find that now and put an end to him."

"I need to find Krestina first. That is the priority.
Then Krommel."

Feylane hissed in frustration. "Either way, we have to
slip down that hall," she said, motioning in the direction
that would lead to the east wing of the castle.

Guards were all about the lobby. Before he could ask
what she had in mind, the assassin tripped a woman
carrying a large covered tray of food. As the woman went
down, she fell into another staff member carrying a similar
tray. The trays, along with all the food contained within,
ended up on the floor with a noisy clatter. Staff and guards
rushed over to view the minor disaster and help the pair
get back to their feet.

Feylane grabbed Harcourt's arm and the two slipped
out of the lobby and into the eastern hallway without being

noticed.

*   *   *   *

Brandyn spurred his horse on as fast as it could run, only slowing as he approached the western gate into the city of Stonewood. The guards began opening the gate as soon as they spied the rider off in the distance and recognized him as one of their own.

Brandyn dismounted quickly as soon as he was out front of the gatehouse. "Where is Captain Landos? I have urgent news."

"I am here, Brandyn, what is it that has you so spooked? Please come in so we can discuss," Captain Landos said.

The guard followed his captain into the gatehouse and then into the captain's office where the pair could have some privacy.

"Sir, there is some sort of army that is almost upon us! They do not seem to move as humans do but I could not get a very close look. Someone needs to inform the King of this immediately. Stonewood is in peril!"

"Yes, I know of this already," Captain Landos replied calmly. "They are Stonewood's new army."

"What? New army? I am sorry, I don't follow sir."

"No, I didn't think that you would," Captain Landos said, producing a knife which found Brandyn's throat.

*   *   *   *

"Hey, Yoran, come here for a moment," shouted a guard that stood watch on one of Stonewood's battlements peering through a spyglass.

"What is it? You spot some wolves again?" Yoran asked.

"No, not wolves. I can't tell for sure but I see a lot of movement over past those hills there. I thought our troops weren't due back for another week or so. But it's too dark to get a good look. We need to send out a few scouts."

"Wait a moment. What's that on the ground below us?" Yoran asked, concerned.

The guard with the spyglass leaned over the wall to take a look and Yoran shoved the guard over the side. He landed with a crunch before he even had time to yell.

*   *   *   *

Harcourt and Feylane dragged two dead-weight guards into a stairwell where they sat the bodies up against a wall. Both guards slept soundly, a tiny needle protruding from both their necks.

"You will have to teach me that recipe," Feylane said, referring to the poison that coated both needles.

Harcourt ignored the comment. "Hopefully, this stairwell will lead down to those cells I was told about."

"I think here we shall part ways," Feylane glanced upwards. "I am going to find Krommel's office. You be the hero and save the damsel in distress."

"We should probably confront Krommel together. You do not know how many guards he may have with him," the thief suggested.

"Nah, I am willing to bet he feels fairly secure inside this castle. We do not have much time so it would be wise to split up. Besides, I work best alone. You take care of yourself and I will see you on the outside." The assassin kissed Harcourt on the cheek and disappeared up the stairs as silently as a cat.

Harcourt knew there would be no changing the assassin's mind and he could not argue her logic. As assassins go, there were none better than Feylane. He had to trust in her to get her job done, while he needed to find Krestina.

Luckily for the thief, the stairs did lead him to what seemed to be below ground. There were no more windows and it felt cooler than the other parts of the castle. Harcourt found it strange that he had not run into any more guards but with the birthday celebrations, most guards were dealing with crowd control; they most likely had no thoughts of someone being fool enough to break into the castle. And that suited him just fine.

He passed several locked doors, none of which appeared to lead to prison cells, so he continued on. Sparsely populated torches illuminated the hallways here, but not by much. That also suited the thief just fine. The fact that the torches were even lit at all told Harcourt that these hallways were at least used for something during the evening.

The thief reached one dead-end, and had to double back. A second dead-end had him growling in frustration, but he ducked back down that hall as a pair of guards passed him by. The two were complaining about being stuck down here while others were at least enjoying the sights and sounds of the party. It gave Harcourt hope that there was something worth guarding down here.

Harcourt's sense of direction was excellent when out on the city streets but down here he did not know north from south and found himself looking at some of the same doors he knew he had passed before. Just when he began to feel dizzy, he spotted a new hallway, very long and very narrow. A single guard stood at the midway point and Harcourt's heart skipped a beat when he realized the hall was dotted with prison cell doors.

Without even a second thought, he marched straight down the hallway with unwavering determination. The guard, finally registering the movement, shouted "Halt, who goes there?"

Harcourt did not answer, only kept marching towards the guard. "I said halt! Who are you and what are you doing down here?"

The guard was reaching for the hilt of his sword when he felt a strange stinging sensation in his neck. Ignoring it, he drew his sword but then staggered back. Suddenly, the hallway began to spin.

*　　*　　*　　*

Feylane had thrown a copper coin to distract two guards who marched off in search of the noise, which allowed her to slip past down another hall. It appeared that many offices were housed in this part of the castle as each door she passed had a name etched into it, along with the person's title below. She scanned each door searching eagerly for the one that said Chief Magistrate.

The assassin pressed her body against a wall as she peered around the corner down the next hall. She stopped breathing altogether when she witnessed Chief Magistrate Krommel himself, unlocking a door and entering a room.

She closed her eyes and steadied her breathing. She silently thanked the dark gods above, then crept down the hall.

*   *   *   *

"State your names and business," the guard at the north district gate said.

"Are you serious? Like you haven't seen us before? My friend here, is he that easily forgotten?" Evonne said, pointing to her monstrous partner.

"Look, I have to ask that of every one, it's protocol," the guard said in reply.

"Well it sounds foolish because you have greeted us here many times before. Now are you gonna unlock the gate or not?"

"What business do you have tonight?"

"What business? We have security duty in the throne room."

"Show me the medallions."

Evonne rolled her eyes. "This one here misplaced them last night in his drunken stupor. Didn't you, you foolish oaf?"

Vrawg just shrugged his shoulders.

"We cannot let anyone in without those medallions. It's…"

"It's protocol, I know," Evonne cut him off. "Well then, I suggest you march right over to the castle and tell the Chief Magistrate that he will be two people short helping to protect his ass tonight. Don't worry, we'll wait. We'll wait right here while you go tell him."

The guard looked to his companions who offered no support. "Fine, you may pass."

*   *   *   *

Harcourt ran from cell to cell, finding each one empty. As he reached the seventh, he sucked in his breath and froze. There, on the floor of the dark cell, sat a disheveled form, a tall woman with long brown hair wearing only the tattered remains of a brown robe.

"Krestina," the thief said as he fumbled with the guard's key to unlock the cell.

He flung open the door and rushed to her side. "Krestina, are you hurt?" he said crouching down and running his fingers through her hair.

Or what he thought was hair. Before he had time to consider why his fingers passed through her hair like there was none, he felt the sharp sting of a blade penetrate his armor and find his belly. He looked down to find a dagger piercing his skin. Krestina raised the palm of her other hand and spoke a single word. Harcourt flew back out of the cell as a gust of wind slammed him into the wall across from the cell. Wounded and winded, he slumped to the floor watching the priestess rise to her full height.

Krestina appeared much taller than she should have been. Then she spoke the words "Argon Dol" and peeled away her face. In her place now stood the tall pale priest Jaspar, a wicked grin playing across his face.

"Your little toy here comes in quite handy," the man said in his soothing, melodic voice. "I had a feeling you would be coming here tonight. Forever the thorn in our side. But not after tonight. I am going to remove this thorn."

"Where is Krestina?" the thief shouted, holding his stomach in immense pain.

"Oh, the wench still lives. For now. But her heart is that last one we need. It will be taken and offered to the demon gods right in the throne room before the King. Lucivenus himself will be wishing the King a happy birthday very shortly."

That was all Harcourt needed to hear. Krestina still lived. That gave him the strength to stand despite his pain and he drew his sword through gritted teeth.

Jaspar just laughed and tossed the magical mask to the floor. He spoke a few words and a strange misty mace appeared out of thin air into his hand. It looked just like the blunt hammer-like weapon favored by warrior-priests, only it was made of swirling black mist. It did not even appear solid, though when Harcourt blocked the first attack from the priest, the weapon felt as solid as stone.

The thief backed up, doing his best to block attack after attack from the pale priest. Jaspar was faster than the thief would have thought. The mace was solid enough but it seemed to weigh next to nothing in the tall man's hand.

Harcourt could feel the blood flowing from his wound which hindered his movements. The force of the last attack caused him to stumble back and prevented him from blocking the follow-up swing. The thief took a solid hit to his left shoulder. To his horror, the strange mace burned right through his armor and blackened his skin. It felt as though a thousand wasps were stinging him all at once.

Jaspar laughed at his obvious distress and spoke the word of a spell. Harcourt was again blown back and slammed into a wall and this time his sword flew from his grasp as he hit the floor. He desperately gasped for air as the priest casually approached. Strange misty tentacles began rising from the floor to grab at the thief but he managed to tumble aside out of reach.

Harcourt twisted to his right side as the mace slammed into the floor where his head had been a brief moment before. Through terrible pain, he leaped to his feet and drew the two daggers strapped to the back of his belt.

Jaspar lunged in with a wild swing but this time took a slash across his right forearm in return. He hissed and swung again with a backhanded motion which the thief managed to duck under. Harcourt slid to the priest's side and slashed him across the hip.

The priest growled with anger then his eyes glowed a deep red. He spoke a word and Harcourt's head exploded with pain. The thief dropped his daggers and fell back against a wall to keep himself upright. He bent forward, doubled-over with a wave of nauseating pain.

Jaspar stood before the thief and raised his deadly mace. A vision of Krestina flashed into Harcourt's mind. He saw her standing, with a beautiful smile. It was replaced then with Jalanna's face, a reminder of his failure.

Ignoring the pain, the thief pulled a knife from the top of his boot and drove it with many years-worth of pent-up fury into the heart of the evil priest.

Jaspar blinked, a look of shock upon his pale face. His misty mace winked out of existence and he stumbled back, falling to the floor, the knife buried to the hilt in his heart.

Harcourt stood there watching the priest until he breathed his last breath and closed his eyes forever. The thief then staggered over and picked up his magical mask. He never expected to see it again. Looking over at the slumbering guard, Harcourt got an idea.

CHAPTER 26

Dornell, dressed as a city guard but with the hood of a cloak pulled around his head, marched to the north district gate. Captain Flannis walked with him, shoving Na'Jala in front of them. The former gladiator's wrists were shackled. Dornell had spent hours in his room at the Crimson Crab Inn pacing back and forth, worried about his friend inside the castle having to deal with an extremely dangerous situation with only a Guild assassin to help him.

The former captain could not stand idly by and do nothing. He found Flannis and told him of a plan. Flannis readily agreed, as did Na'Jala who was risking much.

"Well, well, what do we have here?" asked one of the gate guards, looking towards the black-skinned prisoner.

"I caught one of the fugitives who had escaped the mines. The Chief Magistrate and the King will want to speak with this man personally. He carries important information," Captain Flannis replied.

"They are obviously busy this evening and will be unable to receive you," the guard stated.

"My orders were to deliver the prisoner no matter the day or the hour. And that I shall do," Flannis countered.

"Leave him with us then, we shall see him to the castle."

"So you can also take the glory? I think not," Flannis said, resting a gauntleted hand on the hilt of his sword. "We shall be delivering the prisoner ourselves. I caught him, the glory is mine."

Any man that worked the south district was not a man this guard wanted to cross, especially when he had the reputation that Captain Flannis had. He decided not to press the point.

Dornell breathed a sigh of relief when the guards opened the gate.

*   *   *   *

Chief Magistrate Krommel strolled into the crowded throne room and took in the scene around him. Filling the large room were Stonewood's wealthiest and most influential citizens. Important visitors from other cities also made up part of the crowd. Armored guards stood watch by several doors and lined the walls like statues. Staff members ran to and fro with trays of food and drink.

Krommel then spotted the King himself, flanked by his two personal guards, wearing a fake smile while he entertained conversation from a visiting ambassador. The High Priest knew the King was torn up inside over his missing son Denniz, but put on a brave face for the good of his people. *Do not worry, King*, Krommel thought to himself, *you will be with your youngest son soon enough.*

A gentle hand squeezed the Chief Magistrate on the

shoulder and he turned to face his loyal assistant.

"What took you so long?" Devi-Lynn asked. "I expected you here long ago."

"Something unexpected came up," he replied with an emotionless face. "Nothing I could not handle."

"Is it time then? The King will be sitting down soon for a toast and a meal. Shall I fetch the priestess?"

"Yes, the time draws near. Bring me the priestess."

"And your book? Will you require it?"

"No. I have memorized the passages to the ritual. I know them as well as I know my own name. Just bring the girl."

Devi left the throne room and could barely contain her excitement.

*　　*　　*　　*

Harcourt did his best to walk upright and provide the illusion that everything was fine. In reality, he was in pain, lots of pain. He wrapped the wound in his belly with strips from Jaspar's robes but oh how it hurt. And the blackened skin on his shoulder still stung.

He had thrown on the guard's tunic, with the crest of Stonewood, then stared at the man's face using the powers of the magical mask until he was sure that his own face resembled it as best he could. He had only passed two other guards but both had watched him walk by with only a nod.

The thief read the names on the second floor doors until he found the one he sought, the office of the Chief Magistrate. He glanced about making sure he was alone in the hall, then tried the door. It was locked. Out came a set of lockpicks and the master thief made short work of the lock. He drew his sword and entered the office, shutting the door behind him. He figured Feylane should have been able to find the office easily enough but found no sign of a struggle within the office itself. Now he wondered if something had happened to her before she could get here. It also appeared that Krommel was not here as well.

The thief could see down a short hall into what looked to be Krommel's bedchamber. That room was also devoid of any life. Harcourt silently cursed to himself. He had no idea where else to look in this massive castle to find Krestina.

He removed his mask and sat down at Krommel's desk, searching through the drawers for any possible clues. He found a black leather-bound tome and skimmed through the pages. A particular drawing caught his attention. On the page was a diagram of what could have been a demon, possibly Lucivenus, and a description of what five different hearts could do in breaking the demon's bonds. The one highlighted as the last and most important heart was a devoted heart. Harcourt immediately deduced that was how Krestina played into all of this. Her devotion to the temple would be her undoing if he could not find her in time.

Disgusted, he threw the book aside and pulled out a much larger and much thicker book. It seemed to be some sort of ledger written by Krommel himself. It detailed the firing and promoting of many individuals within the city. Krommel made notes such as, *he was beginning to ask too many questions*, or *she was catching on to us*.

Harcourt found something very odd about the journal. It dated back over fifty years and was all written with the same handwriting.

"How old are you?" the thief said to himself.

One name caught his eye from an entry made about fifty years ago. A note was made about the firing of Captain Kanalandiros, a hero in the defense of Stonewood from an invading army. It said the captain was instrumental in the final battle by leading troops through the sewers to emerge far behind enemy lines and catch them by surprise. The captain lost his leg in that battle but was later dismissed from the service.

"Old Kan," Harcourt whispered, referring to the one-legged beggar. "So you were telling the truth all these years."

A banging sound from what the thief had assumed was a closet caught his attention. Sword in hand, he cautiously approached. As he got closer, it sounded as if someone was kicking the door. He flung the door open and pointed his sword. Inside the closet he found Feylane, bound and gagged.

The thief sliced off the rope that bound her wrists and pulled down the gag. "What happened?" he asked.

"I followed Krommel in here," she replied, appearing somewhat groggy. "The man has powers beyond imagining. I failed."

The thief spun around and then grimaced in pain just as someone tried the handle to the office door. As a precaution, he had locked it behind him. When he heard someone fumbling with a key in the lock, he motioned for Feylane to remain silent and shut the closet door, then dove behind a nearby reading chair, doing his best to not even breath.

Devi-Lynn walked into the office and immediately

noticed the High Priest's tome on the floor. She shook her head and picked it up. Just because he did not need it any longer, did not mean he should just be casting things aside. Without the book, they could never have accomplished what they were about to achieve.

The priestess then stopped in front of a mirror that hung on a nearby wall and stared intently at her reflection, especially the lines that were forming under her eyes. She sighed, disappointed.

She walked over to the High Priest's liquor cabinet and picked up a particular clear flask with a sparkling golden liquid contained within. The priestess removed the stopper and took a sip. She placed the flask back where she had found it and went back over to the mirror. She smiled as the lines on her face were now gone, along with the few strands of silver hair that had just been previously visible. The priestess felt many years younger; the elixir had done its job. She needed to look her best for the High Priest. Once they summoned Lucivenus and took control of Stonewood, there would be no more pretending to be a simple assistant to the Chief Magistrate. She could then be known to all as Sister Devi, high priestess and lover to High Priest Sarvin.

Smiling with excitement again, she left the office to fetch the sacrificial priestess who would usher in a new era. As the door closed behind her, Harcourt jumped up and opened the liquor cabinet. He pulled out the curious flask that he had witnessed the raven-haired woman drink from. He poured a drop onto his tongue and felt a strange tingling sensation spread throughout his body. It felt invigorating. He tried another drop and then also walked to the mirror as the woman had done. He was now minus a few grey hairs. Very interesting, he thought as he wrapped the flask in a strip of clothing and tucked it away in a belt pouch.

He then opened the closet door and helped the beautiful assassin out.

"Can you walk? We have to follow her," he said.

*   *   *   *

"Ah, Chief Magistrate, there you are. You remember ambassador Ibra-Rahim and his lovely wife Myranda from the city Rashman-Haraj?" Magistrate Curtus said, motioning to the pair of visitors.

"No," was all Krommel said in response and walked away from the trio.

Magistrate Curtus politely excused himself and followed his co-worker. "Chief Magistrate, that was quite rude. Maybe you should…"

Krommel turned on the man. "Maybe you should shut your mouth and find someone else to bother."

Rendered speechless, Curtus quickly put distance between him and the much-larger and clearly angry man.

The time for niceties was over, Krommel thought. Soon none of this would matter and people had better show him the respect he deserved. He stared intently at the King, thinking Stonewood's monarch would be the first to bow his knee before his life was taken.

*   *   *   *

Dornell, Captain Flannis and their prisoner Na'Jala stood in a small, empty waiting room within the castle's east wing. Finally, they were joined by three others, two armored castle guards flanking a particularly creepy-looking, hook-nosed man with greasy skin. The man wore a wicked grin at the sight of the prisoner.

"So you have found one of the fugitives, good, good, good," replied the creepy man named Frogo. "The Chief Magistrate is much too busy this evening so I will take the man from here."

Captain Flannis spoke up. "My orders were to deliver him to the Chief Magistrate or the King, myself."

"I just told you that will not be possible. He will be fine in my care. He has much to tell us, this one does. And Lucivenus willing, he will part with all of it. Won't you?" Frogo asked, pulling out a cruelly-shaped knife and pointing it at Na'Jala. "I have never tortured one of your kind before," he said excitedly. "Tell me, does your blood run red like that of other men?"

"You will never know," Na'Jala answered.

With blinding speed, the former gladiator broke the chains that shackled his wrists, grabbed the spare sword that Flannis wore at his hip and removed Frogo's head.

After recovering from the shock at what they just witnessed, Frogo's two guards drew their weapons.

"Hold your ground,"Dornell shouted, his sword now in hand. "Who do you fight for?"

"What are you doing? Seize that prisoner! He has information vital to our cause. We must find his friends and bring them before the High Priest," one of the guards answered.

That was all Dornell had to hear. He had no wish to harm innocent guards but these were not innocent men. The former captain and his two companions advanced on the two men. It was important that they make short work of these guards and get to the throne room to warn the King of his impending danger.

* * * *

Evonne stood with her back against the throne room wall, scanning the crowd nervously. Something was in the air, she could just feel it and it made the hair on her neck stand on end. Vrawg felt it too; she knew by the way he shifted from foot to foot, not able to relax.

She spotted the Chief Magistrate but not his raven-haired assistant. The man was not very social, seemingly wanting no part of any conversations around him. He appeared to be waiting for something. There was an anxiousness about him.

For the tenth time, the petite bounty hunter second-guessed her decision to be here. Since when did they become heroes? This was a matter for Kings and royal guards, not for a former pirate turned bounty hunter with her half-ogre, outcast partner. She sighed and grabbed a glass of wine from a tray that was passing by her. She needed something to calm her nerves.

* * * *

Devi-Lynn walked through the secret sliding door that only members of their order knew of, and descending a short set of stairs, stood in a hallway lined with prison cells. She found the one she sought and smiled at the sight of the brown-haired priestess shackled to the wall of the cell.

"Do you have any idea the events you are about to set in motion, my dear?" Devi teased. "And where is your pathetic God now? Why has he not saved you?"

"Maybe because he knew I would," Harcourt said, slamming the hilt of his sword into the back of Devi's head.

The dark priestess went face first into the iron bars of the cell door, then slumped unconscious to the floor. The thief found the keys he needed after a quick search of her body and unlocked the cell. This time when he crouched next to Krestina and touched her hair, he knew it was really her.

"Krestina," he whispered. "Are you alright?"

The priestess looked up into his face while he began unlocking the shackles that held her to the wall. She was having another vision, she figured, or another dream. Again, Harcourt was here to rescue her only the man was dead. *Why do you tease me with these visions, God?* she wondered.

The pain in her wrists felt very real as the shackles fell to the floor. She did not usually feel things during her dreams. "Who are you?" she asked in a weak voice.

"It's me, Harcourt, do you remember?"

"Harcourt is dead."

"Yeah, I get that a lot. Long story, but it's really me. I am very much alive, I assure you. Now come on, let's see if you can stand," he said, gently helping her to her feet.

Krestina's legs were weak and she needed the thief's shoulder for support. She leaned on his wounded shoulder which pained him but he made not a sound, so happy he was that he actually managed to find Krestina. He was unacustomed to having plans work out.

Feylane who had been watching the entrance to the
secret door waited no longer and joined him at the cell.
"What are we going to do with this High Priestess of the
Cult? I should cut her throat," the assassin remarked.

As much as Harcourt would have liked that, he
decided against it. "Just chain her to the wall. I am sure the
King might like to speak with this one when all this is
done."

Feylane did not agree with the decision but dragged
the evil priestess into the cell anyway, making sure her
head hit the bars on the way in.

Harcourt helped Krestina into the hall and leaned her
against the wall while he searched the other cells looking
for the old wizard. Three cells down, he found Fezzdin,
similarly shackled to a wall, his mouth gagged. The
wizard's blue eyes shot open with surprise; he could not
believe what he saw. Harcourt unshackled him, ripped off
the gag and helped him up.

"You are indeed a man of many surprises, my young
friend," the wizard said with a giant smile as they joined
the two women in the hall.

"But how did they manage to capture you, Fezzdin?"
the thief asked curiously.

"I was deceived by the innocent look of a woman,"
the wizard answered.

"Well, you are not the first," Feylane said, striking a
provocative pose. "And you won't be the last either."

Harcourt managed a chuckle at that comment before
addressing the serious matter facing them. "Feylane, can I
ask that you get Krestina and Fezzdin safely out of here? I
need to get to that throne room and find Krommel."

"Like hell," she replied. "Krommel is mine!"

"Please, Feylane," the thief pleaded. "There is no more time for stealth here. If Krommel is in that throne room, he is most likely surrounded by many guards loyal to him. This is no longer your battleground. Please, see her to safety, I beg you."

That Feylane had to agree with. She was not equipped to battle armored guards and she did remember the power that Krommel possessed. "Be careful," she said to the thief. "Krommel is no ordinary man."

"No, he is not," Fezzdin added. "He is not to be underestimated. But he does need to be stopped. Firstly, I need a few things from my tower and I will join you shortly in the throne room."

"That will take too long," Harcourt said as the wizard vanished from sight with a puff of smoke.

"It really is you," Krestina then said, reaching out to touch the thief to confirm his existence.

He smiled. "Yes, it is really me. I promise I will explain everything to you when this is all over. Now go with Feylane, you will be safe with her."

"I don't want to leave you," the priestess said, tears running down her cheeks, wrapping the thief in a tight hug.

"I don't want to leave you either but you are in no shape to follow me where I am going. Now please, go with Feylane."

The sound of rattling chains drew Harcourt's attention to the last cell in the hallway. He sprinted down the hall, not wishing to leave anyone behind in this place, save for the evil priestess. What he saw stopped him in his tracks. The thief froze, standing like a statue as a wave of emotions and memories flooded through his mind.

If the man once looked like a skeleton wrapped with flesh, he was now a skeleton barely wrapped with skin. Andil opened his glazed eyes and a flash of recognition crossed his face.

Harcourt took a few moments to think things over before finally opening his mouth. "Feylane, I think there is one more person to join you."

* * * *

As their footsteps faded away, Devi-Lynn opened her eyes. She spoke a few words under her breath and the shackles on her wrists exploded into a thousand shards. She stood, then stumbled, feeling a little disoriented from the blow to her head.

She spoke the words to a second spell and her right hand began to glow a bright red. She grabbed the lock to her cell door and it melted from intense heat, the heat from the abyss itself. She kicked open the cell door and set off for the throne room. Their plans had been ruined and she meant to make someone pay dearly for it.

CHAPTER 27

"I see you made it," said a voice to Evonne's left side.

The bounty hunter turned to regard Harcourt who leaned against the wall next to her, a bloodied hand held against his stomach. The thief wore his own face, expecting that none here would readily recognize him. He no longer wore the guard's tunic, opting to use his medallion to get into the throne room as hired security.

"Did you find her?" Evonne asked.

"I did," Harcourt replied. "She is on her way out of the castle as we speak."

"What happens now?" she wondered.

"I know not. The Cult planned to use her heart in one last ritual to summon their demon lord. She is now beyond their grasp. But I am not letting Krommel escape," the thief said, finally spying the Chief Magistrate in the center of the crowded room.

"You will be arrested if you go anywhere near him. This is not the place for this. Don't be a fool. Let's all get out of here," Evonne urged.

"I am not letting him escape. Leave if you wish. Stay and I will compensate you handsomely."

Before Evonne could say another word, the thief began making his way through the crowd.

*   *   *   *

Dornell, Na'Jala and Flannis entered the throne room from the opposite side of the room from where Harcourt had stood. The guards at the door let the trio pass, seeing nothing out of the ordinary. Na'Jala now wore a guard's uniform and had his face covered with the hood of a cloak.

"What's the plan now?" Captain Flannis whispered in his friend's ear.

"Make for the King. You are known and respected. Tell him what we know. Na'Jala and I will find the Chief Magistrate," Dornell answered.

Flannis nodded and set off in the direction of the King.

*   *   *   *

Devi-Lynn marched into the throne room looking desperately for the High Priest. One of the clerks that worked with her stopped her and smiled, looking to chat. The Cult priestess roughly shoved the woman aside and continued her search.

Spotting Sarvin, she shoved many aside until she stood beside him.

An angry look crossed his face. "Where is the girl? We need to do this now. The time is upon us."

"There has been a problem. I was attacked. The prisoners, all of them, have escaped."

High Priest Sarvin's face turned a deep red, he clenched his hands in tight fists. He raged inside. "We have worked so hard for this, we need to do this tonight!"

"All is not lost. We can find another worthy heart within the week. Lucivenus will still be free, we just need to show patience," Devi said.

Patience? Patience, he thought? High Priest Sarvin had waited too long for this night to come. It was the perfect opportunity, all of his enemies were here right now, together in this one room. He growled in ultimate frustration and looked to his devoted assistant and sometime lover. Wait....*devoted* assistant. He knew of no other person who showed more devotion and loyalty to their cause.

Without a second thought, he drove his red-bladed dagger into the chest of Devi-Lynn. The priestess's mouth hung open in shock. She wanted to ask him why, but was unable to speak as she felt the blade pulse inside her and suck at her life-force.

"You are the most devoted," Sarvin said the moment before she died. "I can think of no other heart more worthy. You do me proud."

Suddenly a woman screamed in absolute horror, followed by a second, as the High Priest laid Devi's body on the floor and quickly began to remove her heart.

*　　*　　*　　*

The Cult sorceress Syrena hesitated as she watched the High Priest begin removing the heart of Sister Devi.

Syrena was disguised as a serving girl, doing her best to squeeze herself into the tight uniform, which garnered her much attention and many tips.

She was instructed to wait until this very moment, only she was not expecting Devi to be the victim. Well, she figured, she was not always privy to the reasoning behind the High Priest's decisions. With a shrug, she dropped her serving tray, letting glasses of wine shatter against the floor. Syrena chanted the words of a spell and then made the motion of blowing out a candle. Suddenly all of the torches and lanterns in the throne room were extinguished, casting the room into total darkness. Partiers shrieked in terror.

*   *   *   *

Harcourt was weaving his way through the crowd when two women began screaming and a moment later, the room went dark. Panic set in and people began stampeding towards the faint lights of the hallways. The thief was pushed and shoved until he lost track of where he had last seen Krommel.

"What madness is this?" shouted the King, whose voice could be heard above all others.

Guards began shouting for people to remain calm and stand still. Then Harcourt heard a distinct voice. Someone was chanting. It was not a language that he was familiar with and it was coming from somewhere in the center of the room. It had to be Krommel, he thought.

*   *   *   *

As soon as Syrena heard the High Priest begin chanting the words of the last ritual, she cast another spell. Suddenly his voice was not just coming from one place, it echoed around the room from every direction.

*   *   *   *

Dornell was nearly knocked to the ground as several people charged towards one of the doors. The room was thrown into total chaos. The former captain had been trying to reach the spot where the chanting originated when suddenly the voice came from everywhere all at once, making it impossible to pinpoint any one spot. He growled in frustration.

*   *   *   *

Evonne and Vrawg elected to keep their backs to the wall and avoid the chaos of the room. So far there did not seem to be any fighting breaking out, but someone, most likely Krommel, began some creepy chanting. The voice echoed all over the room.

Evonne pulled the crossbow off her back and held it ready out in front of her.

*   *   *   *

Fezzdin the Fantastic materialized in the throne room, closer to the King near the actual throne. The room was engulfed with darkness and people were panicking and running for the exits. *It has already begun,* he thought.

The wizard spoke the words of a spell which caused

all of the torches and lanterns to flare back to life, illuminating the chaos of the room.

Cursing, Syrena glanced around, curious to see who had reignited all the light sources. She spotted Fezzdin, standing near the throne, dressed in his blue robes with his blue conical hat, a wooden staff in hand. The sorceress had been told that the wizard would trouble them no longer. Something had gone wrong. She hoped the ritual was successful since she had no desire to match magical skills with the old man.

*　　*　　*　　*

High Priest Sarvin stood to his full height and held Devi's heart aloft. He was alone now in the center of the room. Everyone had put distance between themselves and the apparent madman. He finished the last few words of the ritual and the heart burst into flames. Smoke rose from Sarvin's hand and began to swirl about like a mini tornado. The tornado grew in size, then grew again.

Harcourt, Dornell, Na'Jala, Fezzdin, the King, everyone was frozen in place watching the spectacle before them, almost hypnotized by the swirling smoke which now took on a red tinge. There was a sudden *whooshing* sound, then an explosion of flames which sent the people closest cowering to the floor.

As the flames winked out, there was a collective gasp heard around the throne room at the sight of what now stood where the flames had been. Standing in the center of the room was an imposing figure. The Demon Lord Lucivenus himself stood there, eight feet tall with two horns protruding from the top of his head. His skin was a bright red and he wore a jet-black armored breastplate, with pants that matched. He wore a gold ring in his nose and as he looked about and smiled, he revealed razor-sharp teeth. Two giant bat-like wings were folded against his back.

"I am freeeeeeeeeeeeeeeeeeeeeeeeeeeeeeeeeeeeeeeeeeee," the demon lord bellowed in a deep voice that shook the furniture in the room.

Everyone was frozen in place, not believing their eyes. As badly as Harcourt wanted to get to Krommel, his legs were rooted in place while he stared in awe at the eight-foot monstrosity. The thief never truly believed there were such things as demons and certainly did not expect the Cult to actually succeed with their mad goal. How would one even fight a demon? he thought.

Lucivenus turned to Sarvin. "Who are you?" he said in his booming voice.

Sarvin stood in awe like everyone else. His chest then swelled with pride. "I am High Priest Sarvin, leader of our order. And I have freed you mighty lord. I have brought you back here, so that you may reclaim what you once had taken from you."

"Traitor!" screamed the King.

King Stonewood had refused to wear armor at his birthday party, but still wore his sword at the insistence of his eldest son. The King drew his sword, flanked by his personal guards, Edward and Hurshal, who were dressed in their gleaming platemail armor. Nearby, Prince Orval also drew his sword.

"Exercise caution, my King," Fezzdin suggested in a low voice.

The wizard was just as surprised as everyone else that

the demon lord now stood before them. Surely he knew of the existence of demons, he just did not believe that the man he knew as Krommel possessed the power or knowledge to free Lucivenus from his prison. He had been gravely mistaken.

"You are the current King?" asked Lucivenus.

"I am King Stonewood VII. I am the current King and plan to rule for much longer still. My ancestors had defeated you and imprisoned you. And so we shall again."

The demon lord laughed and his laughter shook the walls. "You do not keep company with the powerful beings that your ancestor did. I see none present here."

"We are mighty warriors and we are many. You cannot defeat us all!" the King shouted defiantly.

Lucivenus turned to Sarvin. "High Priest Sarvin, you will be greatly rewarded for freeing me and aiding me now, as will anyone else in here that aids in my retaking the throne. I will rule this city, choose your side wisely. I am not the forgiving type."

A gigantic flaming sword sprang to life in the demon lord's hand and he charged the King. Once again the room was thrown into utter chaos. Many guards present were loyal to Sarvin and turned on the other guards. Mass hysteria took over as nobody knew who exactly was friend or foe.

Captain Flannis witnessed a fellow guard impale another on the end of a spear. Flannis took the traitor by surprise and chopped off his right arm.

Dornell and Na'Jala found themselves surrounded by traitorous guards and the fighting became fierce.

Evonne was about to suggest to Vrawg that they leave when her giant partner sprang into action shattering a man's skull with his hammer who was aiming a crossbow at one of the King's personal guards. The blonde bounty hunter shot a bolt through the neck of a man who had turned to aim at the half-ogre. As she reloaded, she jogged over to stand next to Ruggard Bloodaxe who looked thoroughly confused.

"Do as the demon said and choose your side wisely. Krommel might have been paying us but he is one evil man. Look what he just unleashed on the world," shouted Evonne.

Ruggard would never have used the word hero to describe himself. He usually sold his axe to the one who paid the most gold. But he was not an evil man, he did have some morals. He would not work for a group of demon-worshippers. The red-bearded northman nodded to Evonne and planted his battle-axe into the chest of a cultist as the petite bounty hunter shot another.

Lucivenus brought his flaming sword chopping downwards to split the King's skull when Fezzdin aimed his staff and spoke a word. Sparks showered the area as the demon lord's sword met with an invisible shield right before making contact with the King's head. Another word and a beam of ice flew from the tip of his staff to strike Lucivenus on his right arm which was bare. The demon lord growled at the wizard then felt the sting of the King's sword strike his left thigh.

Lucivenus again swung his sword at the King and it was intercepted by Edward's sword. The move had saved the King but the sheer strength of the blow knocked Edward back several steps. With his free hand, the demon lord summoned a ball of fire and hurled it at the off-balance Edward. The fireball exploded against the man's armor melting a hole right through. He fell to the ground with a shriek.

Prince Orval roared with anger and took Edward's place by his father's side.

Harcourt positioned himself behind Sarvin and threw his boot-knife with all his strength. The blade should have buried itself in the back of the man's neck but bounced off harmlessly instead.

High Priest Sarvin turned to face the thief. "You?? You are supposed to be dead!"

"I have come back to haunt you," the thief said, drawing his sword and charging the evil priest despite the pain he still felt.

Sarvin smiled. His hand began to glow a bright red. Harcourt swung for his neck and Sarvin miraculously caught the sword blade in his hand. He squeezed the blade and it melted like butter. The priest raised his other hand and a now-familiar blast of wind sent the thief flying back several feet, crashing into a castle guard.

Na'Jala impaled the guard in front of him with his sword. He pulled it free and removed another's hand in the same movement. A third attacked from behind and the former gladiator side-stepped, then nearly decapitated the man. Dornell traded blows with another guard until Na'Jala pierced his ribs, then Dornell punctured his chest.

The former captain took note of Harcourt being blasted away from Sarvin and thought to take advantage of the priest's distraction. He charged Sarvin when suddenly a blast of colorful lights exploded in front of his face, momentarily blinding him.

Na'Jala noticed an olive-skinned, dark-haired serving girl who had been waving her fingers in Dornell's direction. The former gladiator quickly closed the distance and swung for the woman's head. The blade passed through nothing as the woman suddenly vanished. Syrena now stood behind Na'Jala and when he turned about, a blinding blast of colors found his face as well.

Lucivenus knocked Prince Orval's blade aside then felt the sting again from the King's sword. He raised his flaming sword above his head and rocked back as another blast of ice struck his chest.

Hurshal charged the demon lord then dropped to one knee as he was shot with a crossbow bolt in the back of one leg. Lucivenus lopped off the guard's head with ease. Another fireball formed in his free hand and Orval and his father dove away as it flew between them to explode against a wall.

Guards still fought fiercely with other guards as most of the partiers had now fled the throne room. Evonne kept her back to the wall and fired shots when a target presented itself. "Noooooo!" she shouted as she noticed her partner charging the giant demon lord.

Since leaving his homeland after being shunned by pure-blood ogres, Vrawg had never before faced an opponent larger than he was. The demon lord however, stood a foot taller. Lucivenus was about to skewer Prince Orval when the half-ogre's warhammer knocked him off-balance. The demon lord smiled and the two titans went to battle.

Vrawg blocked the flaming sword then countered, only to have his attack blocked in return. Each blow the giants blocked shook the floor around them. Evonne fired a bolt which skipped off the demon lord's skin, unable to penetrate. She quickly reloaded and tried again but met with the same result. She reluctantly dropped the crossbow and drew her curved sword. She had no desire to fight a demon but she would die to help her friend and partner.

Fezzdin rushed to the King as Prince Orval pulled his father to his feet. "We should consider leaving now, my King. Live to fight another day. Take advantage of the demon's distraction."

The King very much wanted to ask the wizard where he had been all this time but this was not the place. "I will not run like a coward and abandon my throne."

Fezzdin looked to the prince for support, a look of urgency in his eyes. Prince Orval was no coward but was no fool either. "Maybe the wizard is right, father. We need to regroup and gather our forces."

Captain Flannis who stood nearby after dropping another traitor pointed to the hallway nearest the throne. "Through there my King. The way is clear."

Flannis then made a choking sound as a crossbow bolt passed through his throat. He fell to his knees as another punctured his back, then a third found his heart.

Fezzdin hurled lightning at the two crosswbow men, killing one and injuring the other, who dropped his weapon.

A glob of greenish acid flew from Sarvin's hand towards Harcourt. The thief managed to grab a cultist and pull him in front. A scream of agony erupted as the acid splashed against the man's back and began to eat its way through.

Dornell could now see again and continued to charge the evil priest. A large mace made entirely of swirling black mist appeared in Sarvin's hand. He met Dornell's charge by parrying the former captain's blade then planted the head of the mace into Dornell's chest. Dornell had thought the priest unarmed and was not expecting the sudden attack. The head of the mace ate a hole through his armor and blackened his skin beneath, stinging with immense pain.

Na'Jala was there in seconds, drawing a line of blood across Sarvin's shoulder. The priest growled and swung his mace with amazing speed. The former gladiator stepped back out of reach and sliced the priest's arm. Na'Jala raised his sword for another attack when a crossbow bolt pierced his shoulder and he stumbled aside dropping his weapon.

Harcourt was on his way to aid his friends when he changed direction and threw a dagger into the chest of the man who just shot Na'Jala. This battle had gone from bad to worse. There was no winning here, the thief thought to himself. He needed to get his friends out of here.

He watched Dornell and Sarvin continue their battle though his friend was slowing, the wound in his chest taking a toll. "Fezzdin, a little help please!" Harcourt shouted.

A bolt of lightning rocked Sarvin back a few steps. It appeared to have done no damage but now the evil priest turned his attention to the wizard.

Lucivenus swatted Evonne aside with his free hand like a fly. The blonde bounty hunter flew several feet through the air before landing on her left elbow with a crunch.

Vrawg howled with rage and swung his hammer with fury but his anger made him sloppy. The demon lord saw his opening and slashed the half-orge across the chest with his flaming sword, splitting open his armor and burning his skin. The huge bounty hunter staggered back, clutching his chest.

At that sight, Ruggard had seen enough. He bolted down a hall, blending in with fleeing partiers after beheading another cultist.

Ignoring Fezzdin's advice, the King ran at Lucivenus with a roar. The demon lord gripped his flaming sword with both massive hands and swung with all his might. The King had no defense. His sword shattered, then his chest exploded with the impact. His body flew past Prince Orval to land on the floor, twisted and broken. The prince screamed and Lucivenus raised his arms in victory.

Fezzdin used a minor spell to amplify his voice for all to hear. "Friends of the King! Look around you now! Take note of your surroundings, it is time to leave." He then cast the same spell Syrena had used earlier and extinguished all light sources in the throne room.

Sarvin was just about to hurl a glob of acid at the wizard when everything went dark. Only the flames from Lucivenus's sword gave off any light, but only around the demon lord himself.

Syrena had thought to cast a burst of colorful lights but then did not wish to draw attention to herself. She could not undo Fezzdin's spell as he was a much more powerful wizard. So she crouched low to the floor and hoped their enemies were content with just fleeing.

Lucivenus bellowed with anger and began throwing fireballs around the room igniting pieces of furniture until most of the room was again illuminated. When the darkness receded, he saw that their enemies were gone, even the body of the King.

"They fled, the cowards," Sarvin growled, then turned to a group of loyal guards. "Track them, do not let them escape."

Lucivenus waved away the command. "It is no matter. The King is dead and the old wizard would be a fool to return. He is no member of the Circle of Three. Stonewood is mine again."

"It is indeed, my lord, and I am here to serve you. I have spent most of my life researching how to free you," Sarvin said, taking a knee and bowing before the demon lord.

"And you will be rewarded," Lucivenus replied. He walked over to the throne and took the seat. "Once the people have learned their King is dead, they will have no heart left to fight. There will be no resistance. I will then need an army. Whoever does not convert will be destroyed."

"My lord, you have an army. They now surround the city. Twenty-thousand wraggoth loyal to us," Sarvin said proudly.

"Where is Stonewood's army?" Lucivenus inquired.

"They have been sent far from the city and are led by my men."

The demon lord smiled, showing his many fangs. "You have done well, very well indeed. Now fill me in. What I have missed out on in the last few centuries?"

EPILOGUE

Krestina opened her eyes and then sat up straight, her heart pounding until she recognized her surroundings. She remembered that she was in a room at the Crimson Crab Inn. She smiled when she noticed Harcourt leaning back in a chair watching over her. They were in danger still, but at this moment she felt safe. God had returned her guardian-angel, and she knew Harcourt would look after her. Exhausted, she fell back asleep.

Harcourt watched the beautiful priestess lay back down and return to a deep sleep. They could not afford to stay here for too long but Krestina had been through a lot and needed some good rest. Harcourt too was in desperate need of rest but that had to wait. They were not out of trouble yet. Lucivenus and Sarvin had seized total control of the castle and their army of monsters had the city completely surrounded. A curfew was set and nobody was to walk the streets at night.

The thief knew they were being hunted but Stonewood was a very large city and, for the moment, this

Inn was a safe hiding spot.

Dornell and Na'Jala were in the room next door. Harcourt had not seen Evonne or Vrawg since the battle in the throne room and could only hope that they made it out safely. Harcourt planned to wait another day or so, then they would attempt to use Filbur's smuggling tunnel to see if they could slip past the wraggoth. After that, who knew. Harcourt was unsure if any help would be arriving to aid Stonewood.

He looked again to the sleeping Krestina. He owed her a lot of explaining. He figured when she woke, he would tell her everything; about the mask, about Weldrick. And he hoped she would forgive him his deceptions.

Harcourt's thoughts then turned to Andil. He had not seen the thief since releasing him from the cell. He had mixed emotions about that. Feylane must have brought him to one of the Guild's hideouts. Part of Harcourt wanted to speak with him again, the other part still wanted to strangle him. He thought it best to just leave it be and avoid his old *friend* altogether.

A quiet knocking at the door startled the thief from his thoughts. He drew a dagger and silently approached the door. He opened it just a crack. "What do you want?" he asked.

He spied a cloaked man whose face was completely hidden with his blue hood. "A moment of your time only," the man replied, revealing just enough of his face for the thief to recognize him.

"Fezzdin!" the thief said excitedly, then remembered to lower his voice. "Quick, come in."

He peeked down the hall to ensure nobody was about, then locked the door behind the wizard.

"I have been wanting to thank you. We probably would not have made it out of the castle without your help," the thief said.

"It is I who have been wanting to thank you. I was to be executed after their little party surprise. You saved my life," Fezzdin gave a warm smile.

"How did you know I was here?" Harcourt wondered.

"You remember my friend Lex? He has a knack for finding people for me. But I am curious, Harcourt, what are your plans now?"

"We plan to escape the city in a day or so. I am fairly sure that Krommel, or Sarvin, or whatever his name is, is not going to rest until he finds us and punishes us."

"You would flee this city of yours? Your home? And leave it in the hands of Lucivenus and Sarvin?"

"What else can we do, Fezzdin? We tried to fight them and look what happened. They are just too powerful for us."

"There is always a way. None of us was prepared for what took place in that throne room. But we can regroup, rally support and fight back," the wizard suggested.

"Rally support?" Harcourt said, shaking his head. "A demon just killed the King of Stonewood. The beloved King. People will despair. If Lucivenus can kill the King so easily, then what chance would anyone else have? The people will cower."

"What if the King didn't die? What if the King was going to fight back? For his people? For his city?" Fezzdin asked with a raised eyebrow.

"That is impossible. I saw what the demon did to the King. There is no way you can tell me that he survived that."

"No, he did not survive the battle, you are right," the wizard said sadly. "But nobody need know that truth. We can provide people with the hope that they need."

"How can you do that?"

"Not me, Harcourt, but you."

"Me? What do you mean, me?"

"Your mask. You can be the King. You can provide the illusion that the people will need to see."

"But what about Prince Orval? Surely he is King now. People can rally behind him."

"Prince Orval is young and untested in battle. The people of Stonewood will not readily see him as a savior, or believe him capable. But the King, the King himself can give them hope."

"Fezzdin, how can we fight the demon?"

"Fortunately for us, demons are notoriously lazy. Lucivenus will be content to sit on his throne and have others do the work for him. We deal with his minions while I find us a way to defeat him. It was done before, I am sure we can do it again with the proper research. Use your mask, Harcourt. Be the King of Stonewood and we can rescue our city and its people."

Harcourt thought long and hard. The idea of fleeing the city and leaving everyone to their peril did not sit well with him but he thought there was no other way. He hated to let Krommel win and would love to put an end to that miserable priest.

"I'll do it."

ABOUT THE AUTHOR

Jeremy was born in Scarborough, Ontario, Canada. He started creating his own characters and writing his own stories by the age of 9. He is a boxing fanatic, having been an amateur boxer and is now a professional boxing judge. In his spare time when not watching boxing, or reruns of Lost in Space and Rocket Robin Hood, Jeremy tries to find time to write some of the many stories floating around in his head.

www.ingramcontent.com/pod-product-compliance
Lightning Source LLC
Chambersburg PA
CBHW020248200626
46816CB00001BA/190